Three Weeks
with a Bull Rider

Three Weeks with a Bull Rider

An Oklahoma Nights Romance

CAT JOHNSON

ZEBRA BOOKS
KENSINGTON PUBLISHING CORP.
http://www.kensingtonbooks.com

ZEBRA BOOKS are published by

Kensington Publishing Corp.
119 West 40th Street
New York, NY 10018

All Kensington titles, imprints, and distributed lines are available at special quantity discounts for bulk purchases for sales promotion, premiums, fundraising, educational, or institutional use.

Special book excerpts or customized printings can also be created to fit specific needs. For details, write or phone the office of the Kensington Special Sales Manager: Attn. Special Sales Department. Kensington Publishing Corp., 119 West 40th Street, New York, NY 10018. Phone: 1-800-221-2647.

Zebra Books and the Z logo Reg. U.S. Pat. & TM Off.

First Brava Books Trade Paperback Printing: April 2014
First Zebra Books Mass-Market Paperback Printing:
December 2014
ISBN-13: 978-1-4201-3692-0
ISBN-10: 1-4201-3692-5

eISBN-13: 978-1-4201-3704-0
eISBN-10: 1-4201-3704-2

10 9 8 7 6 5 4 3 2 1

Printed in the United States of America

My thanks to everyone who has supported me and the Oklahoma Nights series since its inception, both from near and far, in big ways and in small. There are too many to mention—readers, bloggers, reviewers, friends—who were there for me daily, but I would be remiss in not mentioning just a few by name.

The owners, staff, and patrons of Joseph's Fine Foods in Drumright, Oklahoma. Together, we have changed the image of fried bologna sandwiches forever. I couldn't ask for better partners in our Keep Calm and Eat Bologna campaign. Bologna is sexy!

John Dollar for his input, support and promotion while, amazingly, he was deployed to Afghanistan and busy with far more important things.

The dedicated staff at Kensington who put their faith and support behind the Oklahoma Nights series.

Finally, my mother, who is my biggest supporter. If I can ever get over the idea of her reading the naughty scenes, I'll be even more appreciative.

Chapter One

"You're really not gonna come with me?" Eyes wide, Jace Mills stared across the driveway at the man who was supposed to be his best friend.

"It's not that I don't want to." Leaning back against his truck, Tucker Jenkins drew in a deep breath and let it out in a huff. "Don't you understand? I can't."

Jace ran his hand across his forehead beneath the band of his cowboy hat. "Because why again?"

"I told you already."

"Tell me one more time, just so I can be sure I heard you right the first time." Jace waited for the response. He already knew the answer but he needed to hear Tuck admit the foolishness out loud again. Maybe this time he'd realize how stupid he sounded.

Tuck sighed. "I have plans to go out with Becca and Logan and Emma."

"And this *double date* of yours is to where, exactly?" Jace made sure he stressed the most ridiculous part—the cozy couples outing that somehow took precedence over Tuck riding in a competition.

Another sigh proceeded Tuck's answer. "A winery in Drumright."

"Yes, indeed. A winery." Jace nodded, lips pursed. "You hate wine. Always have. You do remember that small detail, don't you? Or did marriage give you brain damage or amnesia or something?"

He'd seen it before when a man got pussy on the brain, but Tuck was married to Becca now. That stage should be over.

"Listen, Jace. When you get married, you'll see. A man has to choose his battles."

And there it was—that annoying defense that all married men loved to throw in the face of smart, unmarried men like Jace. *When you get married, you'll see . . .*

"Fine, Tuck. Pick your battles, but I'm telling you right about now would be a damn good time to stand your ground and fight. There's fifteen-hundred added money. How can you pass that up? We don't even have to travel far for it. It's an hour away. Right off the damn highway in Shawnee."

"I know, but apparently it's this vineyard's big annual festival and harvest event or some shit like that. They only have it once a year. Look, I'm not happy about it either, but I gotta do it."

It was small consolation to Jace, but Tuck's expression did say he'd rather be riding in Shawnee than sipping wine, any day. Jace figured it all came down to the path of least misery. Becca could make Tuck's life harder than Jace could, so she won this battle.

"Look, Jace. Just go to Shawnee on your own, win the purse, and be happy I'm not there as competition so I can't take it away from you."

"Oh, you're not my competition." Jace shook his

head, not willing to concede to Tuck's boasting, just because Tuck had won a couple championship buckles way back when. "Maybe you used to be, before you got soft, but not anymore. Besides, you know how I feel. When I'm on the back of a bull, it's me against him. I could care less who rode before or who's fixin' to ride."

"Fine. I've gone soft. Whatever." Tuck dismissed the insult with a wave of his hand, which didn't give Jace as much satisfaction as it would have if he'd gotten a rise out of his friend. "I still can't ride tonight and there's nothing I—or you—can do about it."

"I don't see why Becca and Emma can't go alone. They can drive themselves to Drumright. Hell, it's like twenty minutes away and she knows the way. You guys are always going there for that smoked bologna you love so much. What the hell's the name of that restaurant again?"

"Joseph's."

"Yeah, Joseph's. The point is, Becca can drive to Drumright without you. This wine tasting crap is a chick thing anyway. Or, hell, you know what? Logan can take the girls. He probably likes wine." Jace felt far less camaraderie toward Logan since he'd stolen Becca's sister Emma away.

"I already suggested that."

"Really?" That was interesting. Maybe Tuck hadn't handed his balls over to Becca at the wedding after all. Jace settled back against his own truck, parked next to Tuck's in the driveway. "And?"

"It went over like a fart in church." Tuck blew out a breath filled with frustration. "It's crazy to go to a wine tasting this year anyway. Emma can't even drink—"

The moment Tuck uttered that statement, he got

an *oh shit* look on his face. His expression, as much as his words, brought Jace's attention around.

"Why can't Emma drink?" Jace leaned forward, anticipating the answer.

Tuck swallowed hard. "No reason. She just doesn't want to right now."

It was becoming very apparent why the woman Jace had asked to be his date to Tuck and Becca's wedding in June had up and gotten hitched to Logan in August, just two months after the first time they'd met. Jace hadn't even known they'd been seeing each other, but they'd obviously been doing something together. "Tuck, is Emma knocked up?"

"Crap." Tuck ran a hand over his face, giving Jace his answer.

Emma and Logan had tied the knot not two weeks ago. If this were a honeymoon baby, which Jace doubted, would Emma know for sure this soon? Now that he thought about it, Emma's clothes had looked a whole lot more filled out in the bust area recently. Why hadn't he noticed that before? He was usually a boob man.

He supposed a person didn't tend to see the things he didn't want to and shook his head. "Damn, I can't believe I didn't figure this out sooner."

"Jace, please. For everyone's sake, don't say anything to anyone." Tuck pinned him with a glare. "Let Emma and Logan announce things in their own time and their own way."

"Of course, I won't say anything. Shit, Tuck." Jace scowled that his friend would think he wouldn't keep his confidence. "Who do you think you're talking to? I can keep my doggone mouth shut."

"Yeah, I know you can." Tuck let out a snort of a

laugh. "It's your ability to keep your pants zipped that's the problem."

"Oh, real nice. Thanks a lot." Jace drew his brows low in a frown. "And what the hell's that supposed to mean, anyway?"

Tuck was the one who'd gone on a streak of whoring after his divorce from his first wife, before he'd met Becca and settled down. Logan was the one who'd gotten Emma pregnant and had the shotgun wedding, yet Tuck was giving Jace shit. Hell, Jace's sex life had been in such a slump, he wouldn't be able to identify a pussy in a lineup.

"Exactly what it sounds like, Jace. You ditched your date at my reception to go screw around with your ex-girlfriend. How do you think Emma ended up with Logan to begin with?"

"I didn't."

"Uh, yeah, you did. There's video of the first dance to prove it. The whole wedding party was there except you. I saw my sister Tara, and my brother Tyler on that DVD, and I saw Logan and Emma, but you know what? You were nowhere around." Tuck's brows rose, disappearing from view beneath the brim of his cowboy hat. "Didn't ditch Emma, my sweet ass—"

"I *meant* Jacqueline and I didn't screw around that night." Jace cut short Tuck's rant. Sure, Jacqueline and he'd had sex since they'd broken up—wild, crazy, frantic sex—quite a few times, but not on the night of the wedding. "All we did was talk. She was upset."

"Upset about what?" Tuck's frustration was evident in the raised volume of his voice.

"That I was going to your reception as Emma's date." Jace lifted one shoulder in a half shrug.

"Jace." Tuck's eyes opened wide. "You and Jacqueline are broken up. You have been for a long time."

"We were together for a long time, too." Jace met Tuck's icy stare. "Just shy of seven years."

"I know how long it was. I was there when you met her. I was also there for the drinking after she threw you and all your stuff out and you were homeless. Let's remember that, shall we? She broke up with you. And now she expects to control who you date?"

"Nah, I don't think she wants to do that. She just said it was hard to see me with another woman even though we're broken up."

The conversation had taken a severe left turn and Jace didn't like it. It was supposed to be about Tuck bailing on tonight's event, not about Jace's relationship with his ex-girlfriend.

Tuck couldn't understand how complicated things were between Jace and Jacqueline. How could he? The break-up of his first marriage had been a no-brainer. After Tuck had found out his ex-wife was screwing another guy while he was deployed, he'd filed for divorce and never looked back. And now, Tuck was walking around in the haze of marital bliss, happy as a clam with his new wife Becca.

What right did he have to criticize Jace's decision to show some compassion toward Jacqueline when she was upset? But that was what Tuck was doing—judging him.

"I can't believe it." Tuck's eyes widened. "You're still in love with her. I can see it in your face. She dumped you over a year ago and you're still hoping to get back together."

"No, I'm not." Jace dismissed that idea with the flick of a hand.

"Then why haven't you dated anyone else in all that time? Hell, why aren't you even getting laid? I mean, yeah, you talk a good game, and carry around a box of condoms in your gear bag, but I never see you go home with anybody."

"I *tried* to date Emma and your friend Logan stole her away from me. Besides, you don't know that I'm not getting laid." Okay, maybe Jace hadn't gotten sweaty with anyone besides his ex lately, but he could if he wanted to.

"Don't I? Who have you been with? Since Jacqueline, name one woman." Tuck pushed himself off the tailgate and rose to his full height. He stared down at Jace, making him feel shorter than his five-foot-nine inches.

"You want a name? Fine. Emma. I hooked up with her after the rodeo the night you first met Becca."

"First of all, that was a year ago. And hooked up? That's a pretty broad term you're using there, Jace. Did you two have sex or not?"

"I'm not telling you what happened between me and your new sister-in-law." Jace crossed his arms over his chest.

Leaning back against the tailgate again, Tuck mirrored Jace and crossed his own arms, but he accompanied it with a smug smile. "That's because nothing happened."

As much as it pissed Jace off to admit it, Tuck was right. Jace remembered why nothing had happened. Jacqueline had texted him that she had a flat tire and he'd left Emma's hotel room when they'd been about to tumble into bed, to go and help Jacqueline.

Jace had just opened his mouth to form some sort of protest that didn't involve that truth when Tuck barreled right over him. "Don't bother trying to lie, Jace. If you had done anything more than kiss Emma good night, you would have been in her hotel room when I called you the next morning. Instead, you were at home, bright eyed and bushy tailed as if you'd had a full night's sleep in your own bed."

"Fine." There was no lying to Tuck. They'd known each other too long. "No, I didn't have sex with Emma. I'd think you'd be happy about that, since she's married to your friend and having his baby."

"Oh, I am. Believe me. If I'm going to be an uncle, it's a relief that it's Logan who's the father."

"Real nice. Way to cut a man down. Thanks a lot, Tuck." The conversation was going downhill fast. If that was how his best friend talked to him, Jace should start hanging out with strangers.

"Sorry." Tuck sighed. "It's nothing against you, Jace. It's just Logan's ready to be a father. He's older. He has a steady job, health benefits, and a good retirement plan through the army."

Jace frowned. "Hey. I make a damn good living. I can hardly keep up with all the work."

Things had never been busier for Jace's landscaping company. Between cutting lawns all summer, and then snow and tree removal in the winter months, he was sitting pretty. As for his rodeo career, Jace had been riding great, placing in the money damn near every competition this season. And he had health coverage—he paid for catastrophe insurance. That would cover hospital stays and surgery. The other kind of insurance that paid every damn time a person got a snotty nose and ran to the doctor was just a money-making racket, anyway. He didn't need that.

So what if he didn't have a guaranteed paycheck and an army pension like Logan and Tuck? Jace could still support a baby should it happen, not that he was looking for that anytime soon. Hell, no.

Still, Tuck should know he'd take care of what he was responsible for, just as well as Logan could. The fact Tuck didn't think so, hurt, and had Jace pretty pissed off.

"Jace, look. All the other shit aside, you seriously need to get over Jacqueline and get on with your life. Do I have to quote your own saying back to you?" One of Tuck's dark brows cocked up.

"No."

"Then say it."

"Don't want to." Jace had a bad feeling he might have actually pouted. He didn't much like having his own philosophy thrown in his face.

"Come on." Tuck grinned, obviously enjoying this torture.

Jace sighed. "The best way to get over one woman is to get under another one."

"There you go." Tuck smiled. "Now go to Shawnee, find yourself a buckle bunny, and start getting over Jacqueline."

The one kink in that plan was that Jace wasn't in the mood for a quick, mindless tumble with a stranger. After being in a committed relationship for seven years, he was afraid he might never have a taste for buckle bunny again—though he'd rather take a hoof to the gut than admit that to Tuck.

"A'ight. I'll go to Shawnee by myself." Going alone would be better than getting a lecture the whole way there and back from Tuck, anyway.

"And . . . while you're there?" Tuck waited.

"I'll see if there's anybody interesting hanging around." Jace tried to sound enthusiastic. He was pretty sure he failed.

It wasn't lost on him that back in the day when he and Tuck were just out of high school and trying to make a living on the rodeo circuit, *interesting* wasn't a qualifying factor for which women they bedded. *Willing. Drunk. Easy.* One or all three were the usual traits they sought out. On occasion, if there happened to be one particular girl they both had their eye on, they'd take turns with her if she was into it. That's what traveling partners did. They shared things. Traveling expenses. Hotel rooms. Women. Whatever.

Then Tuck got serious and got married to Brenda. He'd joined the army, and left the circuit, and then Jace had met Jacqueline. The rest was history. Seven years together and a year broken up, and Jace was still texting, if not talking to Jacqueline daily. He was more than aware that history tended to repeat itself. What if they did get back together? Then what? Another seven years of screaming fights followed by a night of makeup sex until one of them broke it off again?

"I think you're right, Tuck." The admission tasted bitter on Jace's tongue, but he was man enough to speak the truth. "It's time I made a clean break from the past. Moved on." *Moved on to where? To whom?* He didn't have those answers.

Tuck tipped his head in a single nod. "It's good to hear you say that."

Too bad saying it and doing it were two very different things.

Chapter Two

"There's no way it could be broken. I just bought it." Tara Jenkins threw her hands in the air.

From beneath the hood, the old cowboy she'd roped into looking at her new car—make that newly purchased, but very old, used car—glanced at her.

"Not a surprise that whoever owned it before you wanted to get rid of it." He straightened up, wiping his hands on a rag. "It's a piece of shit, pardon my language. Looks like it needs a new radiator. Good chance the block is cracked."

"Is all that expensive to fix?" Tara was afraid she wasn't going to like his answer.

He let out a snort. "There ain't no fixing a cracked engine block. You'd have to replace it and in my opinion, this car ain't worth that. Did you take anybody there with you when you bought it?"

"No."

"You shoulda. Folks are gonna take advantage of a pretty young thing like yourself. Next time, take a man with you." He cocked his graying head to one side and delivered that annoying, chauvinistic but true advice a week too late.

Tara tangled her hands in her hair and swallowed a scream. Shoulda, coulda, woulda. It was too late now.

Maybe she had gone a little crazy after she'd found out Logan was getting married to that interloper Emma from New York. The pain of that news had made her desperate to get out of town. She had to get away from him and the hurt, and get on with her life.

In hindsight, going back to school, and signing up for an internship that required she own transportation had been foolish. Tara had emptied out her bank account and bought this thing. The whole time, she'd been so proud of doing it all on her own with no help from her parents or her brothers.

That's what she got for being independent.

"There's a salvage yard not too far from here. I bet they'd give you a decent bit of cash for the scrap metal." He shrugged. "Cut your losses and take what you can get. It's better than walking away with nothing."

Nothing was exactly what she had. Nothing left in her bank account. Nothing to drive. And if she couldn't complete her internship, no sports medicine degree at the end of the upcoming semester and nothing to show for all those years in college.

Thank goodness this stock contractor happened to be parked nearby when she'd pulled the smoking and sputtering car into the arena parking lot. Tara wouldn't have known what to do on her own. She would have called a tow truck or a garage, and they would have charged her an arm and a leg to tell her what this guy had told her for free.

She drew in a breath. "All right. Thanks for looking at it for me."

"My pleasure, little lady." He nodded, tipping his hat. "You have someone to call for a ride?"

"Yeah, my brother lives in Stillwater. He'll come get me if I give him a call. If he's not already here riding tonight." Tara glanced at the trucks parked in the lot. There was a good chance Tuck's was around somewhere.

He'd no doubt give her a nice long lecture about her stupidity for buying the car alone. Maybe a free ride wasn't worth that after all.

It didn't matter. Neither a lecture nor admitting her mistake would solve her problem for the near future. How was she going to finish the three weeks of her internship requirement if she couldn't get to the competitions and work with the sports medicine team? The Central States Bull Riding Association ran competitions a few days a week all around Oklahoma and Texas, a different town for every event. Tara needed to be mobile.

"I hate to leave you here like this, but I got a truck full of stock to unload." He closed the hood with a slam and stepped back.

"No, of course. You go. Sorry I kept you so long. I'll be fine." She hoped that last statement were true. She'd be fine or she'd be stranded there. One or the other. She needed to call Tuck to find out which.

After the man tipped his hat and took his leave, Tara pulled her cell phone out of her jeans pocket and dialed Tuck's number. Tapping her foot, she waited through the ringing, and then through the voicemail prompt until finally it was her turn to talk. "Tuck, I'm in Shawnee at the arena and my car broke down. I was hoping you were here riding . . . anyway, call me back. I'm stuck and I need a ride. Bye."

Damn. She disconnected the call and shoved the phone back into her pocket. She'd have to go inside and check the day sheet to see if Tuck was entered. If not, he'd better answer his damn phone so he could come get her.

With a huff, Tara spun on the heel of her cowboy boot, bound for the building. She stepped from behind her car and into the path of a truck going way too fast for a parking lot. It skidded in the gravel and rocked to a stop as she leaped back. After a second, the maniac behind the wheel swung the vehicle into the empty spot next to her car.

The driver's side door opened and Tara recognized the truck and the man who'd almost flattened her.

Jace Mills. That figured. Chief idiot and number one annoyance from among her brother's roster of friends, and he'd nearly run her over. "Jesus, Jace. You coulda killed me. Slow the fuck down."

"You kiss your momma with that dirty mouth, Tara?" Jace raised one sandy brow high above his hazel eyes. "And you stepped right out in front of me. Look where you're going from now on."

Tara clenched her jaw and tried to control the string of obscenities she'd love to let loose on him.

"I was distracted, but you should still be more careful. There are families walking around here with kids and stuff." She frowned at the empty cab of Jace's truck. "Tuck's not with you."

"That is an excellent observation, Tara. I always knew you were smarter than you look."

Couldn't this man cut her even one little break? Every tiny piece of information she got out of him was a struggle. "Why isn't Tuck with you?"

"That is a very good question."

She rolled her eyes in frustration. "Do you have an answer?"

"I do, and it's a doozy." Jace waggled his brows. "Wanna hear?"

"Dammit. Yes, Jace, I wanna hear." Tara would need dental work from gritting her teeth if she continued this painful conversation with this obnoxious, frustrating, annoying man who made her want to scream.

A wide grin stretched across Jace's lips. "He's at a wine tasting with Becca, and Emma, and his BFF Logan."

Tara's gut twisted at hearing Logan's name. Having Jace mention it in the same breath as Logan's new wife made it even worse. She'd loved Logan for as long as she could remember, and Becca's sister Emma had swooped in and stolen him from her. Tara swallowed away the bitter taste in the back of her throat, nauseated all over again by the memories of her last conversation with Logan. It had been on the day of his wedding. He'd told her he'd never loved her and never would. That he loved Emma.

Needing to focus on the situation at hand, and not her broken heart, Tuck's sudden interest in wine over rodeo left Tara stuck without a ride. "Crap. I need Tuck to be here tonight."

"We're going to have to talk about that potty mouth of yours, young lady." Jace folded his arms across his chest and leaned against the truck. "But before we do, why do you need Tuck here? And come to think of it, why are you here?"

"Not that it's any of your business, but I'm working with the sports medicine team to fulfill my internship requirement for graduation."

"Sports medicine? That's what you're going to

school for?" Jace frowned. "Hmm. I thought it was veterinary studies."

"You're so observant." Tara rolled her eyes.

Jace's only response was to lift one shoulder in a shrug.

Unfortunately, as much of an idiot as he was, it looked like he was also her only hope of a ride. Her parents' house and school were too far away to go there, but if Jace would drive her to Stillwater, she could crash for the night at Tuck and Becca's place.

"Can you tow a car with that thing?" Tara eyed the monster behind him. A man with a truck that large must be severely lacking in other areas.

He hooked a thumb at his vehicle. "This thing? Tow a car? Uh, yeah. I could tow a tractor trailer if I had to. Why?"

"My car is dead." She tilted her head in the direction of the piece of crap behind her. "One of the stock contractors took a look at it for me and suggested I tow it to the local scrap yard and junk it."

Jace eyed the vehicle and let out a long slow whistle. "That bad, huh?"

"Apparently. And then, I also kind of need a ride to Tuck's place." She'd play on her brother's sympathies when she got to Stillwater. Maybe she could convince Tuck to loan her his truck for the next few weeks.

It's not like he needed it. He and Becca both worked at the same damn place. They should carpool. Save the environment. Reduce their carbon footprint, and all that good stuff.

A smug smirk appeared on Jace's face. "So what you're saying is, you need my help."

"Forget about it. I'll find another ride." Tara let

out a huff. She'd just keep calling Tuck until he answered.

"I didn't say no. Stop pouting. God almighty,
you're such a child."

Gasping at the worst insult he could have thrown
at her, Tara had no words except to deny it. "I am
not a child. You're a—"

"Tara, stop. If you'd shut up one doggone minute
and listen, you'd hear I'm saying okay. I'll help you.
I'll take a look at your car and if it doesn't look fix-
able, I'll tow it to the scrap yard and drive you back
to Stillwater."

The man was so infuriating. She'd love to plant
the toe of her cowboy boot right where the sun
didn't shine, but he was willing to help, so she'd
have to play nice.

"And what would I have to give you in exchange?
I'm warning you. I've got hardly any cash on me.
Not even enough to help pay to fill that monster of
yours with gas. Seriously, like next to none. I emptied my account for that piece of shit car."

"What's with the Jenkins family that y'all always assume I'm destitute?" Jace scowled. "I don't need
your money. I have plenty of my own to pay for gas,
thanks."

That comment confused her. She honestly didn't
think or care about Jace's finances, but she still
didn't trust him as far as she could throw him. He
wouldn't do her a favor for nothing. He must have
some ulterior motive. "Then what do you want?"

"Hmm, let's see. What do I want?" Jace stared up
at the sky and tapped one forefinger on his chin. "I
know. You have to be nice to me. No name calling.
No smart-ass comments. None of your usual bullshit.
Think you can do that?"

Not likely. "I don't know. For how long?"

"Until we get to Stillwater. Starting now."

"How about starting the moment we get inside the arena until we get in your truck for the drive to Stillwater?"

"You're unbelievable." Laughing, Jace shook his head. "All right. It's a deal."

Jace extended one big, rough hand and though she'd never willingly touched him before, Tara shook it to seal the deal on this unholy alliance.

One day, far in the future, when Tara had a successful career and a happy marriage, she'd look back at this time in her life. At how she'd had her heart broken by Logan, the only man she'd ever loved, and survived to be a stronger woman because of it. How, stranded in Shawnee during week one of her internship, she'd hitched a ride with the devil. And how, being the mature person she knew herself to be, she'd even been nice to him for one whole night . . . Lord have mercy.

"Hey, Jace. Good to see you, man."

Jace swallowed the swig of water he'd just taken and glanced up to see Dillon McMahan striding toward him. "Hey, Dillon. Good to see you, too. Since you weren't already here when I walked in, I figured you were laying out again this week."

"Yeah, I left the house late. The baby's sick and the wife is stressed out." The younger man dropped his gear bag on the ground and took out his bull rope. "Thank God I got the go-ahead for tonight. I was about going crazy being kept out of competition. Frigging doctor wouldn't let me ride last week. Concussion."

Jace let out a short laugh at Dillon's scowl over the doctor's diagnosis. "Figured you would have been here anyway, trying to convince the doc otherwise."

"I would have been, but I know what's good for me. The wife says stay home, I stay home." Dillon shot Jace a sideways glance. "At least I do if I ever want to have sex with her again."

Jace really laughed at that. "Oh, man. Married life. You and Tuck can keep that shit for yourselves."

"Where is Tuck?"

"One guess why Tuck's not here tonight, and I'll give you a hint—it has nothing to do with a concussion."

"The new wife?" Dillon glanced up, brows raised.

"Yup." Jace did his friend a huge favor by not telling where Becca had made Tuck go rather than letting him ride. Tuck should thank him for that. "When you up?"

Dillon started to prep his rope, running a stiff brush over it to knock off any dirt. "Second. Figures, right? The one day I'm late. You?"

"If things don't change, it looks like I'm up next to last." Jace had a long while to wait.

He'd already cleaned and rosined his own bull rope when he'd first arrived. He wouldn't strap on his chaps and spurs until later, right before he climbed into the chute. To avoid boredom, he had been occupying his time watching Tara scamper around the arena like a puppy following after the doctor in charge of the sports medicine crew.

Dillon put on his riding glove and yanked it down the length of the bull rope he'd tied on the rail, warming the rosin and working it into the fibers. "So who's the new hottie?"

"Hottie? Where?" Jace glanced around. He'd like to meet her. He could tell Tuck about it and get the man off his back.

"The one you keep staring at over there by the exit. Jeans. White shirt. Long dark hair, braided. Nice little body on her."

"You mean Tara?" Jace glanced once again to where the sports medicine team was standing, with Tara right in the middle. He guessed Dillon's description was accurate, except for the hottie part. "Tara's not a hottie. She's Tuck's sister. She's got some sort of internship thing with the sports medicine team . . . for her schooling."

"Ah, okay. Gotcha." Dillon nodded. "Cowboy code. No sisters. You have to stay away from her whether she's smoking hot or not."

"What?" Jace laughed. "No, that's not it at all. She hates my guts, and I enjoy pissing her off as often as possible. That's the extent of it."

Tara was young and annoying, but definitely not *smoking hot* as this kid had put it. Dillon and Jace definitely did not cross paths when it came to taste in women.

Jace caught a glimpse of Tara again, walking away from him toward the back area with one of the docs. Her jeans were a little tight. Belted, and with the button-down white shirt tucked inside, it did give the appearance that she had more curves than her usual straight as a board, boyish shape. That must have been what caught Dillon's eye—that illusion of a small, nipped-in waist above rounded hips that swayed a bit when she walked in the cowboy boots.

But a hottie? Tara? Nope.

Dillon would reevaluate his opinion fast enough once she opened her smart mouth and the insults started to fly. Though not tonight. Jace remembered their deal—one whole night with no running commentary from her, no matter what he said or did. He intended to thoroughly enjoy it, smiling just thinking about it.

Glancing up, he found Dillon watching him with brows raised.

"What?" Jace asked.

"You sure there's nothing going on between you and her?" Dillon tipped a head in the direction Tara had gone.

Jace frowned. "Are you nuts? Of course, I'm sure."

"I won't tell Tuck if there is. I swear, man. My wife's brothers used to hate me. She and I had to sneak around for years, so I get it." Dillon's sincerity was heartwarming, and completely ridiculous and unnecessary.

"Dillon, seriously. No. If Tara ran me over in the street, she'd only stop long enough to back up and do it again."

Lucky for Jace, she was without a car. He should have stuck to his guns and made her be nice to him for the drive back to Stillwater, too. That was going to be a hell of a painful ride if she was in a pissy mood. Knowing Tara, it was very possible.

"All right. Whatever you say, Jace."

Jace ignored the doubt in Dillon's tone as Tara made her way toward them. He watched her progress, and the attention it got from the bull riders along her path. Apparently all these guys shared Dillon's taste in girls. Every cowboy hat in the vicinity swiveled as the man wearing it turned to watch her walk by.

Tara was eating it up. She treated one guy to a smile, another got a nod. By the time she arrived, her cheeks were pink and her eyes bright. She loved the attention—and that would make it extra fun for Jace to ruin her good time.

"Hey, darlin'." When she was close enough, he reached out, wrapped one arm around her shoulders and reeled her in, holding her tight against him.

An expression of horror settled on Tara's face. Her blue eyes popped open wide as they moved from his fingers wrapped around her shoulder, to his face smiling down at her. "What the hell are you doing?"

"Just being friendly."

"Well, stop it," she hissed and glanced around them.

"Now, now, Tara. Remember our deal. Better be nice to me. It's a long walk to Stillwater." Her scowl had Jace laughing. "So what can I do for you? Or did you come over just to visit with me and wish me luck?"

Tara clenched her jaw. "I know what I wish—"

Jace's slow clucking and the sway of his head had her cutting off her comment.

"I came to tell you—I mean *ask* you—if it would be all right for me to stay after the end for about fifteen minutes to take care of some paperwork for the internship."

He smiled at how she'd gone from demanding to asking if he'd wait for her to finish her business. "Of course, darlin'. I stick around to sign autographs anyway, so it's fine."

"Thank you." Judging by her sour expression, her thanks had left a bad taste in her mouth.

Meanwhile, every cowboy nearby had seen Jace with his arm around her, even Dillon, who could barely contain his grin as he bent to strap on his spurs. The nearest group of riders had shifted their attention away from Tara, and over to a couple of girls who were hanging over the rail and showing a good amount of cleavage.

Yup. The other guys thought Tara was with Jace because his arm had been around her. Not a one of them would dare to even look at her, forget about touch her. Jace was certain she'd hate him even more.

This was fun. Maybe he'd drag his feet and stretch the night out longer, because once they were in that truck, the deal expired. All hell was sure to break loose. Truth be told, he was looking forward to it. Nothing like a little verbal sparring to make the hour-long drive more interesting.

"I have to get back to work." Tara leaned away from him.

"Do I get a good luck kiss before you go?" Jace tapped one finger to his cheek.

A deep frown creased Tara's forehead. "No."

He laughed. "Oh, all right. Knock 'em dead back in the medical room, darlin'."

She raised one dark brow. "Thanks. Hope I don't see you back there."

"Aw, that's the sweetest thing you've ever said to me. You don't want me to get hurt."

"More like I don't want to have to take care of you when you do."

"No worries. I'm good. I don't get hurt too often. Though I did have that groin pull last year. You got a special treatment for that?" Jace grinned.

With a sigh of disgust, Tara pulled away. "See you later. Don't leave without me."

"I wouldn't dream of it." Jace watched her walk away, then turned back.

Dillon was laughing. "Yeah, there's nothing between you two at all."

"Whatever." Jace rolled his eyes. "Which bull did you draw?" Time to get back to business and get his head in the game.

Bull riding was as much mental as physical. Luckily for Jace, he was good at clearing his mind of everything except the bull beneath him. Tara would probably comment that was because his head was empty.

Something between him and Tara? Jace snorted. Dillon couldn't be more off base about that if he tried.

The amplified voice of the announcer echoed off the walls of the arena. Jace felt the excitement start to build inside him just from the sound. There'd be the presentation of the colors, an opening prayer, and then show time. His body knew what was coming. The adrenaline started to flow, flooding his bloodstream and making it hard to stand still. Every sensation surrounding him—the smell of the bulls, the pounding of the music, the heat building from the crowd—got him primed and ready.

He'd channel it all for that eight-second battle between him and the bull. And any residual that was left? Well, he could use that for his battle with Tara later.

Jace grinned and turned toward the arena. Bring it on.

Chapter Three

"Hmm."

Tara swiveled her head toward Jace where he sat behind the wheel. "*Hmm*, what?"

Across the cab of the truck he lifted one shoulder in a half-hearted shrug. "I thought you'd be a ranting chatterbox during the drive to Stillwater, is all."

She shot him a look she hoped would say that she was too tired to bother fighting with him, that at the end of a long night topped off by a long drive with her archenemy, all she wanted to do was go to bed. That reminded her, she had to call Tuck and arrange for a bed. Or at least a sofa and a blanket.

"I'm tired, is all." Digging through her bag, she searched blindly for her cell phone. She'd tossed it in there during the team meeting after the event.

"Oh, poor baby. Are you tired from a little work? No surprise, really. Was it your first time? You know, actually working?" He smirked.

"Shut up, Jace. You're an idiot." It had been a tough night, and Tara imagined it was typical of what she could expect at every event.

One guy got hung up, had his leg stepped on, and his femur broken. He'd been sent to the hospital in an ambulance. Another guy got thrown off into the rail and was hurting, but nothing was broken. In between were any number of other near emergencies, not to mention all the guys who came injured to the event and rode anyway. They needed ice and bandaging up. Torn ACLs. Bad shoulders. Broken hands. Cracked ribs. Sprained ankles. Those guys rode with it all. They'd grin and bear it for the eight-second ride, then limp back to Tara and the rest of the medical team to be patched up. It was nuts.

The only saving grace was that Jace hadn't passed through the door of the medical room. Maybe he was as good a rider as he pretended to be. Whatever. At least she hadn't had to see him during the event, since she'd agreed to be nice to him. But now that deal had expired, she could say exactly what she felt.

"I'm the idiot who's towing your piece of crap car sixty miles from Shawnee to Stillwater, so you'd better be nice to me."

He was throwing the favor he was doing for her in her face again. Was it her fault the stupid scrap yard closed early so they had to take her car back to Stillwater with them?

"I have to call Tuck and tell him I'm coming." Changing the subject, she scrolled through the numbers on her phone.

"You didn't do that already? Good God almighty, Tara. You should have taken care of that earlier. He's probably sleeping by now. What the hell did you do all night long?"

"I worked! I told you I was busy." Jaw clenched, Tara listened to the ringing on the phone line. "It's ten o'clock on a Saturday night. Why would he be sleeping?"

"Because he's a pussy-whipped old married man now, that's why."

Tara scowled at Jace's use of that nasty term in relation to her brother and at the ridiculous notion that Tuck could be in bed at ten on a weekend.

"Hello?" Finally, Tuck answered, his voice gruffer than usual.

Tara had to admit, he didn't sound very awake. "Why didn't you call me back? I left a message for you hours and hours ago that my car broke down in Shawnee."

"I didn't see any message."

Nice. Good thing she hadn't been stranded on the side of the road. Or kidnapped, tossed in the trunk, and using her one and only chance to call for help before the bad guys found her phone. "How could you not see it? I left it when I got here. Before the event started."

"Tara. Shh. Stop yelling at me. Becca got me drunk at that tasting thing and I have a headache. Frigging wine. Never drinking that shit again."

Good. Tara was glad he had a headache since he'd totally let her down. "Whatever. I'm on my way there. Lucky for you, I got a ride with Jace or you'd be here picking me up."

Hung over and all, Tuck managed to laugh at that. "No, *you're* lucky you got a ride with Jace. No way I could have driven anywhere tonight, forget about Shawnee, to get you. Emma had to drive us all home from the winery in Drumright."

Emma. The woman who'd married Logan. It would be too soon if Tara had to ever hear her name again, much less ask her for a favor. Unfortunately, Emma was Becca's sister, so for better or worse, their paths were bound to cross. Maybe Tara should move out of state after school.

Somewhere in the back of her consciousness she was aware of Jace's phone vibrating on the dashboard, and him reaching to answer it. He should be using two hands to drive this monster vehicle of his before he killed them both. She'd have to yell at him about that later. At the moment, she had to deal with her brother.

"Anyway, Jace is taking me to your place. I need to crash there tonight."

"All right. I'll leave the door unlocked for you." There was a rustling on the line, most likely Tuck getting out of bed to go unlock the door. Jeez. Jace was right. Tuck was an old married man, asleep before ten on a Saturday night.

"You're not even going to be awake when I get there? I wanted to talk to you." How was she going to ask him to borrow his truck for the next three weeks if he was asleep?

"I doubt I'm gonna make it 'til you get here. Just let yourself in. We'll talk in the morning."

"Fine. I'll be there in an hour."

" 'Kay. Night."

Unbelievable. Tara disconnected the call and was about to rant to Jace when she noticed he was still on his phone. A closer inspection revealed he wasn't acting like his normal cocky-ass self, either. He pressed the cell close and was talking in such a soft voice, she could barely hear him over the radio. Resisting the urge to reach over and turn the volume down so she could eavesdrop better, Tara went very still and listened.

"It's nothing. I'm just doing her a favor. She's nobody to me." Jace let out a huff of breath. "Jacqueline, I swear to you I'm telling the truth."

Tara got the distinct impression the *nobody* Jace had referred to was herself, although she was more intrigued than insulted by that. Jace's ex-girlfriend was seriously jealous? And of her and Jace? What a joke. The woman was crazy.

"Stop. Please." Jace shot Tara a glance. "Look, I'm driving. I gotta go. . . . No, not so I can concentrate on her. So I don't crash my freaking truck. I'll call you back when I get to Stillwater."

There was no good-bye, just Jace glancing down at the display and hitting END CALL before he put the phone back in the console. Had the former little Miss Rodeo Queen Jacqueline hung up on him or had he hung up on her?

Wow. Hell of a temper as well as a jealous streak on that one.

Tara bit her lip as she waited for Jace to say something about what had just happened. The silence in the car stretched between them for a couple of highway miles. Finally, Jace glanced at her across the dark cab. "Go on. I know you want to."

Tara chose to play dumb. "Want to what?" Oh, yeah. She totally should have been an actress.

"Spout whatever smart-ass comments you're dying to make about that phone call."

"Honestly, Jace, I've got nothing to say." Tara shrugged.

"You? Don't have anything to say? Sure." Jace snorted.

"I don't. I feel bad for you."

"Bad for me? Why?"

Why did she? Tara had to think on that for a second. "I guess because if she's jealous of me of all people when you're broken up, I can imagine how bad it was during all the years you two were dating."

A muscle jumped in his cheek as his jaw clenched. Tara got the feeling she'd hit the nail right on the head.

"I think I'd have rather had your insults." Jace reached out and spun the volume on the radio up.

Tara wondered exactly how bad it had been.

The hour drive felt more like ten hours as the darkened scenery passed by the window. He didn't talk to her again. The only sound in the cab was the radio. She hated to admit it, but bickering with Jace would have made the trip feel shorter. It definitely would have been less awkward.

Of all the many times in the past she'd insulted him, calling him everything from a pervert to a drunk to an idiot, now he got upset? When all she'd done was show him some compassion?

Finally, they pulled in front of Becca and Tuck's place. Tuck had left the light on, and Tara hoped the door was unlocked as he'd promised. If it wasn't, she'd just bang the door down knocking until he woke up, but she sure wasn't going to ask Jace to wait to see if she got inside safely. Not in his mood.

Silent and stone-faced, Jace parked alongside the curb. He got out and went directly to the back of the truck and unhooked her car from the trailer hitch. Tara stood by and watched. She sure as hell didn't know how to help, and in his mood, she was afraid to offer.

That done, he knocked off the dirt from his hands against his jeans and adjusted his hat. "Well, that's it. Good night."

"Good night, and thank you."

He nodded and started toward the driver's door.

"Wait. Jace?" When he stopped and turned back, Tara said, "I'm sorry if I said anything out of line. I didn't mean to."

Jace shook his head "It's not about you, Tara. But do me a favor. Next time I see you, can you please go back to treating me like shit? I prefer it to your pity."

"All right." Tara watched him get in the truck before she turned toward the house.

She made her way to the front door, passing her dead car parked along the curb where it would stay until Tuck helped her dispose of it. Tomorrow, she'd worry about the car, and how she was going to finish her internship, and what was up with Jace's strange behavior. Right now, she couldn't think much past a bed for the night.

Jace drove to the next block, and then pulled to the side. Letting the truck idle, he picked up his cell phone and dialed Jacqueline. He was tired. Bone deep exhaustion began in his heart and had nothing to do with the competition tonight.

Jacqueline answered on the second ring. "It's after eleven o'clock."

"I told you I'd call when I got to Stillwater so I'm calling."

"It doesn't take that long to drive from Shawnee. What did you do? Pull over and fuck her?"

"Yeah, Jacqueline. I fucked her nine ways 'til Sunday, right here in the truck. Then I dumped her off with her brother—my best friend—and told him what a great lay she was." Jace's heart pounded as

hard when he fought with Jacqueline as it did when
his hand was strapped to the back of a ton of bucking bull. That kind of stress couldn't be healthy.

"Then why did fifty miles take you over an hour?
I know how fast you like to drive."

"It's closer to sixty miles and I was towing her car
behind the truck. I had to drive slow. Then I had to
take the time to unhitch it when I got to Tuck's
place." Jace gripped the phone tight and tried to
maintain calm.

Maybe she'd believe he was telling the truth.
Maybe not. That was always up in the air when it
came to Jacqueline. He heard the sniffle and the
shaky intake of breath.

"There's nothing to cry over." He was safe, back in
Stillwater and alone. What the hell more could he
offer her? Still, the tears always did him in. It seemed
more so now that they were broken up. "Hey, you
know what else? I came in second. And even better,
I didn't get hurt."

Jacqueline let out a snort. "Too bad."

Jace smiled at that. She'd stopped with the accu-
sations about other women and resorted to insulting
him. He knew they were on the upward slope of the
fight. "This should make you happy. A young kid riding injured beat me out of first."

"That's because you're old."

"Pfft. Those young guys don't know shit. You
know that. Now me, I'm old enough to know where
everything is and how to use it." Jace's voice dipped
down, low and suggestive.

"Do you have to work early in the morning?"
Jacqueline's tone had softened.

"No." He never scheduled jobs for the morning
after he rode. There were times he needed the re-

covery time, or a visit to the hospital. Either way, he didn't want to leave a customer expecting him and then not show up.

"Can you come over?"

His cock heard the invitation in her voice and immediately rose to the occasion. The damn thing was like his parents' dog when he was growing up. Buster could be at the other end of the house, hear the can opener and come running, thinking it was time to eat. Like a reflex reaction, Jace's dick heard Jacqueline's voice and figured it was time for some lovin'. Truth be told, he hadn't taken it out for a spin since the last time he'd been with her.

He drew in a shaky breath. "All right. I'll be there in five minutes."

Jace had taken his time on the drive from Shawnee to Stillwater, but he didn't on the way over to Jacqueline's apartment. He risked a ticket and sped down the dark, deserted streets as the clock on the dash told him it was getting closer to midnight. He wouldn't stay the night. It would be too painful. How could he hold Jacqueline all night, wake up next to her in the morning in the home they used to share, and then get up and leave to go back to his empty apartment?

This was self-destructive behavior, and yet he was pulling his truck into her driveway, throwing it in park, and heading for the door . . . and her bed. They needed to talk. He needed to stop this. She needed to stop inviting him over. They both had to get on with their lives.

But not tonight. He'd come over tomorrow in the light of day when he wasn't so tired and needy. They'd talk like adults and agree to be friends.

Jace felt satisfied with his plan as she opened the

front door. He was good with it right up until she grabbed his shirt and pulled him inside and her mouth crashed into his. Then all rational thought was lost. He thrust his hands beneath the silky fall of platinum blond waves that hung nearly to her ass. She'd been the local rodeo queen the year he'd met her, and he had no doubt she'd still be able to take the title all these years later.

Yanking her head back, Jace took possession of her mouth. Without breaking the kiss, he backed her inside, kicking the door closed behind him.

Jacqueline wiggled both hands between their bodies. Blindly, she unhooked the buckle on his belt. After seven years of being together and a year of having sex while broken up, it was no surprise she could maneuver his belt as well as he could. She went to work on the fly of his jeans as he anticipated what would be next—her hands on him. Them on the bed. Him inside her.

He tugged the bottom of the tank top out of her pajama bottoms. Sliding his hands beneath the elastic waistband, he felt the bare skin of her ass. He loved how she slept commando. No underwear. Nothing beneath those PJs but his warm, smooth woman . . . except that she wasn't his. Not anymore.

But for tonight—for the next hour or two—she'd be his.

Jace hoisted her up and she wrapped her legs around his back as he carried her to the bedroom. As he cleared the doorway of the room so familiar to him, he noticed she'd gotten a new lamp and painted the walls. The changes were physical reminders, like a fist to the gut, that they weren't together. He tossed her onto the bed where she landed with a bounce on the mattress. He followed her down and knew with certainty they shouldn't be doing this.

Yanking his T-shirt off over his head, Jace tossed it to the floor, realizing it wouldn't remain there long. He'd put it on after they were done and drive home. In the morning, he'd wake up alone in his own bed. Tomorrow, he'd go back to wondering when the next phone call or text would come from her. When she'd ask him to come over again. And he'd do it, knowing it would hurt like hell afterward.

He didn't want to live like that anymore.

The knowledge tickled the back of his mind, but the words never made it out of his mouth. Maybe because his mouth was too busy biting her neck, marking her. She raked her nails down his back, likely leaving marks of her own.

Their sex always had been intense. Rough. Passionate. Almost violent, just like their relationship. The worse the fight, the harder the makeup sex. Today's argument had been nothing compared to their usual, but Jace was too needy, too deprived for too frigging long to not take her hard and fast.

Two fingers thrust inside her told him she was wet and ready. The damn woman always had gotten off from arguing with him. Jacqueline threw her head back, eyes slammed shut from the feel of his invasion. He could bring her to orgasm fast enough. Just a thumb or his mouth on her would do it. He knew her so well, it would take no effort at all, but he was mad and he needed to be inside her. Needed to pound away the emotions.

Jace reached for the drawer next to the bed.

"There aren't any more in there. You used the only one left last time you were here."

There'd been plenty of times he had gone without protection with Jacqueline throughout the years, but not now that they were broken up. Especially not after Tuck's revelation about Emma and Logan's unplanned surprise. He sat up. "I have some in my gear bag. Be right back."

"You what? You carry condoms in your gear bag?" Her eyes opened wide.

Crap. He realized his mistake too late. Jace knew that tone, knew that look. He sighed. "Yes, I have a box of condoms in the truck."

"Why? Who are you fucking at the arena, Jace? Her? The one I heard on the phone tonight?"

"I'm not having sex with anyone besides you, Jacqueline."

He should lie and tell her he'd picked up a new box because he'd remembered they'd used the stash he always kept in her drawer, but she'd see the box wasn't new. Some were missing.

He could tell the truth, that he'd started carrying that box around with him shortly after they'd broken up. Since he hadn't been with anyone else, he'd never used even one. The strip missing were the ones he'd given to Tuck the night he met Becca. But there was no winning a fight with Jacqueline when she got jealous and irrational.

"You're a pig! You fuck your little tramp and then come here to my bed?" Jacqueline reinforced her accusation by grabbing the phone next to the bed and throwing it at him.

Only his quick reflexes blocked it from hitting him in the face. It bounced off his forearms as he held them in front of him. She threw a pillow next, which was fine. That couldn't hurt, but when she reached for the lamp—the new wrought iron lamp he'd noticed when he'd walked in—he took a step back.

He couldn't count how many times he'd walked away from a fight with Jacqueline, scratched and bruised. Being a bull rider, he was always hurt, so no one questioned or even noticed a few more injuries. The physical stuff healed. The hurt inside . . . not so much.

Yanking the plug from the wall, she hoisted the lamp over her head and his anger broke through. Jace had never once laid a hand on her. Even when she'd broken his nose, he'd done nothing but try to protect himself from the blows.

No more. He grabbed her forearm and held tight, hard enough to leave bruises from his fingers. The way he teetered on the edge of losing his temper and his control, if she hit him with that lamp, one or both of them would end up in the hospital.

"No, Jacqueline. No more."

"Don't you dare tell me what to—"

"No. No more berating me, or jealousy, or hitting me. No more sex. No more phone calls. Nothing. I have never once cheated on you. Never given you cause to feel or act the way you do. I can't do this anymore. Don't call me. Don't text. Don't come by my house or my work. I'm sorry, but we can't even be friends. We sure as hell are no good at it." He managed to keep his voice calm even as his heart thundered.

The hand that held her shook, but still he held tight. He stayed strong. He couldn't do this anymore. Live in limbo. Hang on to a small thread of a relationship that he knew deep down was toxic to them both. She'd begun to act crazy months after they'd started dating, but he'd lived in hope she'd get over it, that she'd realize he wanted to be with her and only her. Obviously, that wasn't going to happen.

Jace released his hold on her and remained braced to block a blow, but it didn't come. She stood before him, wide-eyed and shaking, looking small and vulnerable and making him want to do the one thing he couldn't let himself—wrap his arms around her and comfort her.

This woman drove him nuts. He'd survived two of the rankest bulls on the circuit tonight, but he'd be lucky to get out of her apartment without a concussion or a few broken bones from a hundred and twenty pound woman wielding a bedside lamp.

In the midst of it all, he felt sorry for her. How crazy was that?

Jacqueline was his drug, his addiction, his kryptonite, and because of that, the only thing to do was go cold turkey. Walk out that front door, drive away, and never look back. No matter how much it hurt both of them.

"Good-bye, Jacqueline." He turned and headed for the bedroom door. Flinching at the sound of the lamp hitting the floor, he kept walking.

"Jace." The sound of her footsteps followed him down the hallway. "Please, wait."

He put one hand on the doorknob and turned it, ignoring her plea and the sob that followed it.

Outside, the cool night air hit his face as he strode for the truck.

"Fine. Never come back!" Her front door slammed behind him, hard and loud, the sound cutting through the quiet of the night. With the truck doors locked and the key in the ignition, he let himself glance back, half expecting to see her running at him with the lamp, or the baseball bat he knew all too well was in the hall closet. But the front door didn't open again. He pulled away from the curb. Only then, did Jace let himself breathe freely again.

The first text came before he'd left her block.

I'm sorry. Please come back.

In the past, this would have been where he'd make a U-turn. Spin the truck around, go back, and bury the anger with makeup sex. Things would be fine until the next fight began. He couldn't do it anymore. Drawing in a bracing breath, he stayed on course for his own apartment.

The second text followed before he'd driven five more miles.

Where are you? Going over to fuck her? Have fun!

Jace shook his head and swiped a palm over the moisture in his eyes.

This Jacqueline—the angry, irrational one—was a hell of a lot easier to resist than the soft, tear-filled one. He hit the button to power down his phone. He knew her. The texts and phone calls wouldn't stop all night. In fact, there was a good chance she'd drive over, if not tonight, then by tomorrow at sunrise, and bang on his door until he let her in to prove he didn't have a girl inside. In fact, given the mood she was in, it was almost a certainty.

He couldn't go home. The battle would just continue there. Knowing that, he swung a sharp left and headed away from his apartment, toward the practice arena used by the Oklahoma State rodeo team he sometimes helped Tuck coach.

He'd slept in his truck before, and chances were he'd do it again. It was part of life on the rodeo circuit. Sometimes it was easier to pull over and sleep for a few hours rather than get a hotel room for the night. It was sure as hell cheaper. There'd been other times he'd spent the night in the truck in a parking lot, sleeping off a drunk. He didn't drink and drive, but that didn't mean he always took a taxi home. The truck was good enough for him for one night at times such as those, and it was good enough now.

Eventually, he'd have to turn on his phone again and go home. He'd figure out what to do about that later, after some sleep and distance. Jace cut the engine and stared out into the night. Peace and quiet. Nothing but the stars and the empty practice arena.

Easing the seat back as far as it would go, he tilted his hat lower, slumped down and closed his eyes. Tomorrow would be a better day. True or not, he had to believe it.

Chapter Four

Tara was startled awake by something she couldn't identify in her current state of exhaustion. She was lucky she remembered where she was, she was so tired. Slowly, the surroundings began to make sense, and so did the noise that had awoken her.

No way. That could not possibly be Tuck and Becca having sex in the next room. They wouldn't do that knowing Tara had slept in the guest room just one thin wall away. Would they?

As the sound of moaning filtering through the wall grew louder, Tara decided that yes, they would.

Pale morning light was just beginning to filter through the window blinds when she forced herself all the way awake. Figuring that getting up and heading for the kitchen, even at the insanely early hour, was better than staying in bed and being subjected to the horror of listening to her brother have sex, she swung her legs over the edge of the bed.

Last night, Tara had had just enough energy to take off the clothes tinged with arena dirt and had slept in her oversized white T-shirt. It was good enough to sleep in; it would have to be good enough to make tea in. The hem reached down to mid-thigh. She was covered enough to stumble out of the spare room, down the hallway, and into the kitchen. If her sex-maniac brother came out to the kitchen and found her in her shirt and no pants, too bad. She might be up, but she wasn't awake enough to get dressed.

She was so not ready to be awake yet, but at least she was on the other side of the condo and out of hearing range.

Padding around the kitchen barefoot, Tara decided, sex sounds aside, it wasn't such a bad place. Tuck had good taste for a man and he always kept his stuff impeccable. That must be the army training. Now that he was married to Becca, she'd added a few more feminine touches, such as the teakettle and the assortment of flavored teas. It had to be Becca. Tuck would sooner drink out of a puddle along the side of the road than drink hot chamomile or vanilla chai tea.

Tara perused the assortment, smelling a few, reading the boxes of a few others. Finally she settled on one. She grabbed a cinnamon teabag and dropped it into one of the mugs she found in the cabinet above the stove. While she waited for the water to boil, she glanced around her.

Nope, the place wasn't too bad at all.

The condo was nice and big. The town of Stillwater was centrally located. It had lots of places to eat and plenty of men Tara's age with OSU right there. It might be the perfect place to come back to and crash between travels to the competitions in the next three weeks. If Tuck loaned her his truck as she expected him to, it would work out perfectly. He'd have his precious vehicle back when she wasn't using it.

She glanced at the stove and made a face at how long the hot water was taking. It was true—a watched pot didn't boil. She wandered over to the refrigerator. Might as well get out the milk she'd need for her tea. As she reached for the handle, a brightly colored orange magnet caught her eye. She squinted at the magnet's text, promoting the place in Drumright that had catered Tuck and Becca's wedding, and the restaurant's famous fried bologna sandwich.

Tara shook her head and laughed. Tuck and his fried bologna. Her brother was nuts about the stuff.

About to yank the door open, Tara noticed what was held under that fridge magnet. She froze with her hand on the handle and her stomach in knots. Staring back at her, eye level, were the smiling faces of Logan and Emma in their wedding photo.

Becca's newly married sister now lived just a few miles away with the man Tara had loved since she could walk. Emma had stolen Logan from her and married him just weeks ago.

Tara flashed back to the last time she'd spoken to him. She remembered standing in his parents' kitchen on the day of his wedding, professing her love to him and begging him not to get married. Logan had said he'd never love Tara that way then left her there alone and went to get married.

In a nutshell, that was why she couldn't live at Tuck and Becca's during her internship. In spite of all the things in the plus column for Tara staying with them between events for the next three weeks, there was one big—huge—reason why she couldn't and it was staring her right in the face from beneath the Joseph's Fine Foods magnet.

"Shit."

"Why are you cussing at my fridge?" Tuck's gruff morning voice came from behind Tara.

She grabbed the milk, swung the door closed, and turned toward her brother. She wasn't about to tell him it was because his wife's sister had stolen the love of her life, but she had a question of her own for him. "Why are you and Becca having such noisy sex so early in the morning when you have a house guest?"

"Our *house guest* was uninvited." He got a little red-faced and then scowled, but it was hard to look tough with bed head and the creases from the pillow still visible on his cheek. "The way I see it, I can do whatever I want. It's my house and my wife."

"And my ears and my lifelong trauma that will require therapy." Annoyed, Tara poured the hot water, boiling or not, into her mug and dunked the teabag.

Tuck wandered to the counter and frowned at the empty glass coffee carafe. "You didn't make coffee?"

"No. Why should I? I hate coffee. Remember?" She took her mug to the island and perched on a stool.

"I forgot." He let out a breath and reached for the bag of ground coffee on the counter next to the coffee maker. "Shit, my head hurts."

"I guess you shouldn't have drunk all that wine then." That was another thing Tara hated—wine.

The *sisters fabulous*—Becca and Emma—loved nothing more. Thanks to them, even her beer-loving brother had caved and drank it. Tara sighed. There'd been far too many changes lately, and it had all started with the invasion of the Hart sisters from New York.

"You shouldn't be picking on me the morning after I was nice enough to let you sleep here." Tuck shot a glance at Tara over his shoulder. It might have been meant to be intimidating, but a barefooted Tuck in boxer shorts and a T-shirt wasn't going to scare her.

"Where's Becca?" Tara knew he was always on better behavior when the little woman was around.

"Shower."

Tara cringed at Tuck's answer when she remembered what she'd heard and how Becca probably needed a shower after all that noisy sex.

Ick. Too much information. Tara decided to push that image away and move on before she got ill. "So I wanted to talk to you about something."

"About what?" He sprinkled one heaping teaspoon of ground coffee into the filter, then, frowning, dumped a bunch more in without measuring. Thank goodness Tara didn't drink coffee. She could imagine what that pot was going to taste like.

"I signed up for an internship. It's one of the last things I need to complete the program and get my bachelor's degree."

"Good. About time."

She rolled her eyes and bit her tongue. It was not the time to fight with Tuck. She knew what he thought, but she'd needed that semester off before starting college to decide what she wanted to do with her life. It wasn't as if she'd been a bum, lying around the house watching reality TV all day. She'd worked odd jobs here and there.

"Anyway, I'm working with the sports medicine team that follows the Central State circuit."

"Hmm, that'll be good for you. Maybe you'll be a little more understanding of me and Jace when we drive home from a competition all torn up from a run-in with a bull."

"That's what I wanted to talk to you about, driving to the competitions. My car broke down—"

A noise on the counter interrupted Tara. She glanced over to see Tuck's phone attached to the wall charger, light up and vibrate its way across the tile.

"Hang on. Someone's texting me." Tuck reached for the phone and frowned. "It's Jace. He wants to know if I'm awake so he can come over."

They'd gotten home late. She sure as hell wouldn't be up if she hadn't heard her brother and his wife. It was too horrifying to think more about that so she pushed it out of her mind and said, "This early? Why?"

"With Jace there ain't no telling." Tuck shrugged. He punched something into his cell, set it down on the counter, and then glanced at her. "When did you get yourself a car?"

"Never mind that." She dismissed the question with a wave of a hand. Tuck's looming lecture about her foolishness for buying a car on her own, and the disastrous results of her actions, would overshadow what she really needed to focus on—borrowing his truck. "The point is, I have to get to every one of the organization's competitions for the next three weeks to fulfill my internship requirement and now I have no car. So I was wondering if I could use your truck. You and Becca could carpool to work."

"Nope. You're not touching my truck. Sorry." He said the last over his shoulder as he strode to the front door, flipped the deadbolt open, and then came back to the kitchen.

"Then can I borrow Becca's—"

"Oh, hell no." Tuck shook his head while heading for the coffee machine.

"Why not?"

"Because you're the worst driver on earth. I've been living with the dents and scratches you've left in every vehicle I've owned since the day you got your learner's permit and first got behind the wheel."

"But I have to get to the competitions or I won't get my degree. How am I supposed to do that? Bus? Or maybe hitchhike? Yeah, that's real safe. Momma and Daddy will love that plan."

Sometime during Tara's rant, Jace had let himself in the front door. He stopped in the doorway of the kitchen but she didn't bother saying hello. She was too busy being shocked at her brother's lack of common sense in seeing how logical it was for him to lend her his truck.

Tuck shook his head. "Sorry, Tara, but you should have thought of this before you signed up for the internship."

"I did!" She threw her hands in the air. "That's why I bought the car."

"And what's wrong with this new car of yours, anyway?"

"It's broken."

"What did you do to it?"

Of course Tuck would assume it was her fault.

"I didn't do anything—"

"I'll drive her." Until that declaration, Jace had stood silently in the doorway, watching the battle between her and Tuck as if it was a tennis match. Now, he came all the way into the kitchen and eyed the dark liquid filling the glass carafe. "Coffee ready?"

"Uh, yeah. Should be." Tuck took down another mug from the cabinet and turned to Jace as he filled it. "What do you mean, you'll drive her?"

Taking the coffee Tuck handed him, Jace shrugged, glancing at Tara before looking back to his friend. "Just that. I'm driving to the events to ride anyway. She can ride along with me."

"Um, wow. Thanks." Of all the people Tara had hoped would help her out in this situation, Jace was the dead last one she'd expect to volunteer.

"No problem." Leaning against the counter, he raised his mug and sucked in a big swallow of steaming liquid.

Tara noticed the arena dirt staining the knees of his jeans where he'd hit the ground after making his eight-second ride last night. In fact, he was in the same exact clothes he'd been wearing yesterday, right down to the dusty logo-covered shirt. Now that she looked closer, dark circles shaded beneath his eyes, as if he hadn't slept.

Normally, she would have joked that he'd been up indulging in buckle bunnies all night, but since he'd dropped her off so late and driven off alone, she knew that wasn't the case.

"What the hell did you do last night? You look like shit." Tuck said what Tara had been thinking. For once, her brother was proving useful.

"Thanks a lot, Tuck. Is that the gratitude I get for towing your sister's car all the way here from Shawnee?" Jace swung the subject back to her piece of crap car, the exact thing Tara didn't want to talk about. "By the way, I took a quick look at it in the parking lot. I think it'll cost her way more to fix it than it's worth, but you can take a look yourself before towing it to the scrap yard."

Tuck's gaze swung to her. "What the hell is that about, Tara? You get a car and before you've had it—how long?—it's ready to be junked!"

"Uh, I gotta get dressed." Tara hopped down off the stool at the island and headed out of the room before her brother could yell at her. She didn't go far. She wanted to hear what Jace was going to tell Tuck about her ill-advised car purchase so she'd know how bad the lecture would be when it came.

She hovered in the hall, out of sight but within earshot.

"It could be a cracked block. Might need a radiator," Jace said.

"What the hell? Was she driving with no oil or coolant in it? Wouldn't surprise me if she was." The judgment was clear in Tuck's tone.

"Don't know. Maybe there was a leak. I didn't look that close. Sorry." At least Jace wasn't throwing her under the bus and jumping on the *Tara is too stupid to own a car* bandwagon with Tuck. Jace's support was shocking, but nice.

"Don't apologize. Not your fault. And thanks for bringing her and the car home last night. I couldn't have driven to Shawnee even if I had seen her message."

"Too much wine?" There was a smile in Jace's tone.

Tara heard Tuck laugh. "Yeah. That shit sneaks up on you. So, what are you doing up and out this early on a Sunday?"

"I'm just . . ." Jace released a loud breath of air. "Hell, I was gonna make something up, but I'm too damn tired. I'm here 'cause I can't go home."

"Why the hell can't you go home?"

"Jacqueline and I had it out again last night. It got

pretty bad. Now she's stalking me. I slept in my truck in the parking lot of the practice arena, but when I drove past my apartment just now, she was sitting outside in her car so I turned around and came here."

Tara's eyes opened wider. The fight she'd heard last night between Jace and his ex-girlfriend on the phone must have continued live and in person. Feeling guilty for invading his privacy, she still inched closer so she could hear better.

"Good Lord, Jace. This is insane. You have to cut ties."

"I know. I told her that last night, but she won't leave me alone. Look at my phone. There are a dozen texts from her and almost as many voicemails." The frustration was clear in Jace's voice.

"I'm sorry, man. When I introduced you to her at that event all those years ago, I never imagined she'd turn out to be some sort of crazed stalker."

"Not your fault, Tuck. Hell, her parents are friends with your parents. It was inevitable we'd meet at some event or another. You sure as hell didn't tell me to move her to Stillwater with me three years ago, or to live with her. With her still living in our old place and my apartment being so close . . ."

"You can't get away from her, even in your own home."

Jace let out a snort. "Pitiful, huh?"

"You know you can hang here if you need to. We have a spare room."

Tara screwed up her face. That figured. Tuck was giving Jace the room she was hoping to stay in if she needed a place to crash between competitions and didn't want to drive all the way to her parents' house, not that she had anything to drive. Didn't being family count for anything?

"I thought about that, asking you if I could crash here for a bit. But besides you and Becca being newlyweds who sure as hell don't need me as a roommate, hiding out here's not gonna help. Jacqueline knows where you live. I figure I'm on borrowed time drinking this coffee. It's likely she'll be doing a drive-by any time now. Thanks for the offer, though."

"So what are you gonna do?" Tuck asked.

"See if the kid who works with me can handle my weekly lawn-cutting customers for a little while, push the bigger jobs off until next month, and follow the Central States circuit. Life on the road. Cheap hotels and greasy take-out food for the next three weeks. It'll be just like the old days when you and I did it, except it'll be me and your sister. Traveling partners." Jace laughed. "Imagine that?"

Tuck echoed Jace's laugh. "Ah, no, I can't imagine that. That's a hell of a plan you got there, Jace. Now I know you're desperate."

"Desperate times, Tuck. Desperate times. I figure by the time Tara's done with her internship and I come home, Jacqueline will have cooled down enough to at least talk rationally. I hope, anyway."

"That's if you and Tara don't kill each other before then. You and my sister. On the road. Twenty-four seven. I wish you good luck with that, 'cause you're gonna need it."

"You ain't kidding."

Feeling a little insulted, Tara shook her head at both men and their comments, although her mother always had said nothing good came of listening in on others' private conversations.

It didn't matter. Tara had a ride for the duration of her internship, and she hadn't even had to grovel to Tuck about borrowing his truck to get it. Problem solved. Sure, it meant putting up with Jace for the next three weeks, but for a free ride, she could put up with a lot.

With newfound energy, she headed for her room to get dressed. There was a competition in Bixby tonight. It looked as if she and her new traveling partner would be driving there together, and the sooner they left the better. Apparently, they had to evade Jace's stalker ex-girlfriend.

Tara's weekend may have started out crappy, but things were sure looking up.

Chapter Five

Hands on the steering wheel and eyes on the road, Jace began to plan out the next few weeks. "Read me the schedule."

"Please."

He shot Tara a look that he hoped showed her how he felt about her treating him like child. "Listen here, girl. We're traveling partners. That means, like it or not, we're going to be spending a lot of time together in close confines, in good moods and bad, healthy and hurt."

"Sounds like wedding vows."

"Traveling partners are closer than married people. At least Tuck and Becca are apart while they're at work. We're even gonna be together then. Get used to it. Little things like *please* and *thank you* tend to fall by the wayside. Got it?"

"Still, I don't see why—" Tara glanced in his direction and cut herself off. She folded her arms and looked out the side window. "Fine."

Jace waited, and then finally cleared his throat. "Tara? The schedule."

"Oh. Right." She dug into her purse, nearly as big

as his gear bag, and emerged with a fist full of papers. "Tomorrow is a travel day. Then Tuesday and Wednesday nights are in Broken Arrow. Thursday is a travel day. Norman is on Friday and Saturday. Sunday—"

"Okay, gotcha." When Tara glanced up at his interruption, Jace explained. "It's pretty much the same as it used to be when I was riding full-time with Tuck. Ride a couple of days and then drive to the next venue."

"Do you miss it? Riding full-time?"

"Oh, hell no. What I'm doing now is perfect. Ride on weekends, work during the week."

"Yet, you're riding every event now." Tara's unspoken question hung in the air. If she were fishing for information as to why he was riding full-time again, she'd be disappointed because he wasn't biting.

"Yup." Jace left it at that.

She didn't come back with a follow-up question.

Thank God for small favors. It seemed Tara would let the subject drop. The truck's cab remained quiet save for the DJ on the radio babbling about something Jace had no interest in.

Nice and peaceful . . . until the cell phone in the console vibrated.

He didn't need to check to know who it was, but he did. A glutton for punishment, he picked it up and glanced at the readout. Jacqueline. Drawing in a breath, he slid the phone, unanswered, back to where it had been. There it continued to vibrate, doing a little dance within the confines of the console beneath the dashboard.

Tara looked sideways at Jace. "Not gonna answer that?"

"Nope."

"All right." She turned to stare out the window and the peace and quiet returned.

Maybe this drive wouldn't be so horrible, after all. He'd been prepared to lay down the law with Tara. Tell her that if he was going to drive her all over the state of Oklahoma, and cover the cost of the gas himself, there were going to be some rules. No nasty comments. No personal questions. But maybe the lecture wasn't necessary.

He was too tired to give it right now, anyway.

Jace leaned back farther in his seat, set the truck on cruise control, and let his mind go on autopilot. He was just starting to relax and get into that Zen state a long drive always put him in, when his phone started to do its thing once again. He set his jaw and reached for it, far less calm this time.

No surprise, it was Jacqueline calling again. He should have known to expect that, which made him madder at himself for not doing what he should have before they left Stillwater.

Jace swung to look toward Tara. "You have your phone on you?"

Her dark brows rose. "Yeah."

"Is it turned on so Tuck can get a hold of you if he needs to?"

"Yes." She nodded, still looking at him strangely over his questioning.

"Okay." Glancing down at his phone, Jace hit IG-NORE and then powered the cell totally off.

That was one way to handle things with Jacqueline. Not a long-term solution by any means—Jacqueline got even more crazed when he didn't answer her calls—but if it got him to Bixby in peace, it would do for now. He braced himself for Tara's onslaught of questions, but they didn't come. He waited another mile and when she still didn't start her interrogations, he let himself breathe easier.

He leaned back in the seat again, letting the miles of road stretched before him soothe his nerves. Nothing like a road trip to get a man's mind off things. He wouldn't let himself admit what this really was—running away. He'd face his problems and Jacqueline . . . eventually.

With the phone off, the miles passed quickly. Even after taking the time to stop for take-out, they pulled into town way early for the competition, which left them plenty of time to find a hotel. Bixby wasn't a terrible drive from Stillwater. Jace could have driven out and back in one night in a pinch. He'd done it in the past to keep Jacqueline happy. Every time he slept away from home after a competition, she assumed it was because he had another woman in his bed.

Tonight, he'd be getting a room. Partly because he was so tired he didn't trust himself to stay awake for the drive home. Mostly because he knew what would be waiting for him in Stillwater.

Jace steered the truck into the parking lot of a hotel not too far from the arena. He'd stayed there years ago when he rode full-time. Back then, it had been clean, cheap, and convenient—the three things he looked for when on the road. He'd done without one or two of those qualifications in moments of desperation, such as when he was too drunk or too hurt to look for a better place.

He turned to Tara in the passenger seat. "Here we are. Home, sweet home for the night."

She glanced at the sign announcing there were vacancies, free Wi-Fi, and HBO. "Is it expensive?"

Jace glanced at the building, which looked as if it hadn't been renovated since the nineteen-fifties, right down to the hole in the ground with a cover over it—a pool that had never been operational for as long as he'd been staying there. It wasn't the Ritz, but still, hotels cost money. "Not so bad. Why?"

"I'm on kind of a tight budget. Internships don't pay anything, and most of my savings went to buying that car."

The car that was on its way to the junkyard. "This internship is three weeks long?" he asked.

"Yeah."

"How you planning on getting by with no income and no cash? Traveling with the circuit takes money, darlin'."

"I'll just have to get by as cheaply as possible."

"You ask your parents?"

"No. I don't want to. They already pay for my college tuition and give me spending money for expenses. It's my own fault I blew it on the car." Tara shook her head. "I'll be fine. You driving and paying for gas is helping a lot. I guess I'll just have to figure out how to afford someplace to sleep . . . and eat."

Tara's financial situation explained why she'd been so quiet on the drive. Jace was far happier she was being nice to him because she was desperate for the ride he was providing than because she pitied him over whatever she knew about his personal situation.

Even with as much as they'd fought in the past, he'd been where she was now—broke and needing to travel anyway. Sleeping in the truck because he needed the money to pay his entrance fee to compete. Eating as cheap as he could. Carpooling to split the travel costs. It brought him right back to the old days—the pre-Jacqueline days, which was a good thing.

"All right. I'm gonna offer up a suggestion and you see what you think about it."

"Okay." She sounded wary, but open.

Jace figured that was as good as he could expect from her, given their history together. "Back when Tuck and I used to ride full-time, money was tight." Wasn't that an understatement. "There were nights we'd cram four, sometimes five or six guys into one hotel room to save money. Now, I can pay for the room, but being away from my business in Stillwater, I'm going to be hitting up my own savings. I can't be paying for two rooms a night. If you're agreeable, we could get a room with two beds—"

"You'd really pay for the room and let me sleep there?"

She looked so excited about the prospect, Jace felt he had to clarify. "Not your own room. One room with two beds, and I'll be sleeping there, too."

"Oh my God, Jace. That would be so great."

He frowned.

"What?" Tara asked, frowning herself.

"I was expecting some sort of comment. Like how you'd rather sleep with a snake. Or how you're not gonna share a room with me and my buckle bunny du jour."

Tara broke into a smile. "That would have been a good one. Too bad I didn't think of it. Nope. No comments. Beggars can't be choosers. I'd always heard that saying but now, I know what it feels like."

"And you're gonna be okay with sharing a room with me?"

"I grew up with two brothers. I've shared rooms

and a tent . . . even a bed with them a few times when I was little."

"They were your brothers. I'm not." The last thing Jace needed was Tara freaking out when he came out of the shower shirtless or something. Better to make everything clear now, rather than have her crying for her own room in the middle of the night after he was broken up and exhausted from riding.

She rolled her eyes. "Jace, jeez. It's like we're brother and sister. We fight as if we're related. And I have no interest in you physically whatsoever. Do you have an interest in me?"

He drew back at that question. "No. Of course not."

"Then there you go. We're traveling partners and roommates. Just like you and Tuck used to be." She laughed. "Me and you attracted to each other? What a joke."

"Yup. Funny," Jace agreed, while thinking she didn't have to put her total and absolute lack of interest in him quite so vehemently.

Good God, he'd better still be attractive to other women or he had no hope of getting over the last one. He'd been with Jacqueline for so long, maybe he'd lost his mojo. On that depressing thought, he reached for the door handle.

"Come on. Let's go check in." He waited for Tara to climb down from the truck, and then headed for the office to book a room for him and his platonic female roommate who'd laughed at the thought of being attracted to him—the one he'd be sharing a room with every night for the next three weeks. Even if he did miraculously get his taste back for buckle bunny, he had nowhere to indulge it.

He drew in a deep breath and let it out slowly.

How in the world had his life gotten so pitiful? He wished he knew.

"Thanks for the hotdog, Jace." What was it about arena food that made it taste twice as good? Tara hadn't eaten a hotdog at home at her parents' house since she was like twelve, but at an arena she loved them.

"No problem." He devoured the last bit of his dog and bun and wiped his mouth with the napkin. They'd stopped for lunch on the road not too long ago, but he had eaten his frank as if he was a starving man. Then again, most men ate like that.

Tara still had half of her own to eat, but she wanted to set something straight before taking another mouthful. "I want you to know I do have some money. You don't have to worry you have to feed me or I'll starve."

He leveled his gaze with hers. "Tara, it's a hotdog. Just eat it and stop worrying."

"Okay. And thanks again."

She hated that Jace was being nice to her because she'd told him she was too poor to afford a hotel room. Things seemed easier when they could insult each other and then go on their way. He was right though, with them together day and night for the next three weeks, they'd better keep the peace. Hopefully that's why he was acting like a human instead of a walking dickhead—the whole traveling partner code of ethics she'd never thought about before.

"Thanks again for paying for the room, too."

"You're welcome. Again." A smile tugged at the corners of his mouth.

Okay, maybe she was being overly grateful. She'd listened at check-in and the room had been pretty cheap, and he did have to pay for one for himself anyway, so having her in it too didn't cost him any extra. Still, it was more generous than she'd ever given Jace credit for. The whole situation threw her opinion of him on its ear. Tara didn't like change in general. Even changes for the better were hard to get used to.

"You sure you're okay with that? The room situation?" he asked, watching her.

"Yes. I told you I was. I have brothers. I'm used to all the burping and farting that men do, if that's what you're worried about."

He smiled. "That wasn't my concern, but good to know."

"Then what's wrong?" Tara frowned until realization dawned. "Oh, you're worried about that other thing."

Jace's brows drew down beneath the brim of his hat. "I'm a little afraid to ask, but what other thing?"

"You know. What happens to men in the morning. Down there." She glanced at the crotch of his jeans.

Jace looked torn between laughing and blushing. He bit his lip and nodded. "Now that you mention it, that could be a concern."

She waved one hand. "Don't worry about it. I know it's like a reflex or something. I won't take it personal. It's not like it's because of me or anything."

"All righty." He nodded and hissed a breath in through his teeth. "Sure glad that's cleared up."

"Oh sure. No problem. I'm fine with all of it."

"Good to know." He stood and reached down to pick up his gear bag. "I'm gonna go prep my rope."

With that, she figured their strange alliance was signed, sealed, and delivered. "Okay. I have to go find my boss, anyway. See you later."

"See ya."

"Ride good," she said as he turned away.

"I'll sure try. Doctor good," he said back.

"Will do."

With a crooked grin, Jace turned on one boot heel and headed for the chutes.

Tara finished her frank and, fueled up and ready for action, headed back to the medical room. Killing time with this new version of Jace had been relaxing, but it was time for her to catch up with the doctor and the two other technicians on the team as they prepped for the night ahead. She knew things would get more hectic once the event started.

It was kind of like working on an ambulance and at a physical rehabilitation facility at the same time. The crew had to switch on a second's notice. Tara had learned that just from her few hours working with the team in Shawnee the night before. One moment she'd be strapping an ice bag to a guy's shoulder with an Ace bandage, the next there would be a rider laid out and unconscious in the middle of the arena . . . with the bull still in it with him. It was as insane as it was exhilarating, and she was pretty sure she loved it.

"Hey, Tara. You're here nice and early."

"Yeah, we pulled into town early so we figured we might as well come on over."

"We?" Doctor Chandler raised a brow.

"I'm traveling with Jace Mills."

"Really. I didn't realize you two were together."

"Oh, oh no. No, no. We're not. He's one of my brother Tuck's best friends and since my car crapped—I mean broke down, I didn't have a way to travel, so Jace offered. We're definitely not together." She shook her head a few more times to make sure that was totally understood.

"All right. It doesn't matter either way to me. Just asking."

"Well, no. It's not like that." Tara drew in a deep breath. "So, yeah. Anyway, need me to do anything?"

"Today's event will go pretty much the same way yesterday's did. You feel good about last night?"

"Yeah. Nothing I couldn't handle."

"Good. Good to hear. I do want to keep an eye on that kid who got hung up in his rope last night. Make sure he's okay to ride and not hiding something. I noticed him favoring his riding arm. That's one thing you need to learn about bull riders. You can't listen to them when they tell you they're okay. Not only do they seem to have a higher threshold of pain than most people, but they're so used to hurting, they ignore it. More than that, they'll outright lie. Say they're not hurt just so I'll clear them to ride. You gotta use your own judgment and watch for signs."

"Okay. I'll remember that." Tara flashed back to when she was much younger.

Tuck would sometimes come home from a competition barely able to get out of the truck. He'd hobble into the house until she'd comment on it. Then he'd straighten up and walk normally, like nothing had happened.

Well, almost normally, but not quite. There was still something off about his gait. And a set to his jaw that told her he was hiding the pain. She was definitely well equipped for this job after growing up in a house with a bull rider. Rooming with one during the internship would give her even more experience. She would keep a close eye on Jace. It would be good training.

She glanced in his direction and found him surrounded by bull riders—hot young guys all seemingly riveted to his every word. What the devil was going on there?

"Just your brother's friend, huh?"

"Pardon?" Tara turned toward the doctor and found him smirking.

"You're staring."

"Oh, sorry. I was just wondering what's going on over there. It looks like he's holding some kind of class."

"Could be. Jace is always teaching the rookies something or other. When you've been around the sport as long as he has, you pick up a lot of tricks. It's nice he's sharing them with the younger guys. Some riders wouldn't be that generous with their time. They don't want to be bothered with the rookies."

"Really? Hmm." Tara had never thought of Jace as generous with his time or his money, and he'd surprised her twice in one day.

"Yup. Jace is always helping wherever he can. Your brother, too. He's just not around as much as he used to be since he got himself a girl."

"She's his wife, now."

"That's right. I'd heard he'd gotten married. Anyway, I'm going to check on the staff in the medical room."

"Okay." Tara continued to watch Jace, still amazed how the young guys looked at him like he was serving up the secrets of the universe.

"Tara?"

"Yeah?"

"You wanna come with me? There's guys who need wrapping before they ride."

"Oh, Lord, of course. I'm sorry. I'm still getting used to the job."

He shot Jace a parting glance before he smiled at Tara and turned away.

That's all she needed, to lose the internship because she was acting like a ditz, because she was so busy watching Jace's little impromptu bull riding lecture for the rookies.

Tara jogged to catch up with Dr. Chandler. She didn't have time to watch and wonder about Jace. In fact, she hadn't even gotten a chance to watch his or any of the rides the night before because she'd been so busy. She expected tonight would be the same.

For the rest of the night, one hundred percent of her attention would be on the doctor, her job, and any injuries.

Chapter Six

Dirty, tired and exhilarated, all at the same time, Jace made his way back to the medical room.

Another event was done. He'd ridden in both the long round and the short go, and he'd come out of it healthy. That he hadn't been to visit medical out of necessity, but was going to retrieve Tara to drive her to the hotel, was pretty amazing. In fact, he hadn't been hurt, not even a little bit, during the two competitions that she had been with him. He was beginning to believe she might be his good luck charm—strange as that seemed.

Superstition was nothing new in sports, particularly in rodeo. Not that he was into that kind of stuff. He wasn't about to attribute tonight's third place, or yesterday's second, to the new three-pack of underwear he'd picked up at the store last week. Although, maybe he would save that third new pair to wear at the next competition, and just wear an old pair tomorrow for the travel day.

It would be interesting to see if he finished in the money while wearing them. If he did—well, he might have to reconsider how he thought about things . . . and which boxer briefs he put on before riding.

There was a good chance Jace had stayed healthy for two nights straight because deep down he didn't want Tara tending to him. Sure, she looked capable enough. He'd watched her working with the doc for two competitions and she'd seemed nothing but professional with the guys who'd been hurting. He knew if he got really injured, she'd do her job and fix him up alongside Doc Chandler just fine. He just didn't want to deal with it or her.

Chances were high he'd have to pay a visit to the medical room and face her in that capacity at some point over the next three weeks. Major wrecks happened to all of them. In bull riding, it wasn't a question of *if* a rider got hurt, just *when* and *how badly*. Jace had tangled with the wrong side of a bull more times than he could count. He'd depended on dumb luck, fate, and the bullfighters to get him out of deadly situations.

Still, the reality was that Jace was far more likely to do something small to injure himself, like pull a groin muscle. That's when the cocky comments would come from his little traveling partner. Something snappy like what a shame his lower half was out of commission and how all the buckle bunnies would be crying over the loss.

At least Tara was always consistent in her insults. It was amusing as hell, some of the stuff she came up with. He smiled at the memory of some of her zingers just as she came into view. "Hey, Tara. You almost ready to head out?"

"Is it late? You're done with autographs already?"

"Yup."

"Can you give me five minutes? I've got one more guy to check on before I can leave." Looking flustered, she glanced at the doorway of the medical room.

"Sure." Jace dipped his head. "No rush."

"Thanks so much. I'll be quick as I can." She took off down the hall, as Jace ambled at a slower pace behind her.

It had been a busy night for sports medicine. He may have placed third, but statistically, the bulls had won the night in sheer number of buck offs and injured riders.

He wandered into the room Tara had disappeared into to find Justin Mays laid out on a table. Jace tipped his head to the kid. "Hey, man. How you feeling?"

"Well, I'm seeing two of you instead of one, but other than that, not so bad."

Jace shook his head. "You should wear a helmet, kid."

"You don't."

"I didn't learn with one. I'm not used to it. You, on the other hand, did learn to ride in a helmet. I know damn well you rode on your high school team and schools require helmets, so stop being a stubborn idiot and wear your doggone helmet. Got it?"

Justin's pout made him look even younger than his twenty-one years. "Yes, sir."

"Good. I better see it on you next event . . . whenever that will be after you get cleared from what I bet is a nice concussion." Jace noticed Tara hanging off to the side. "Sorry. I'm in your way."

"No, not at all. You're fine." She moved in closer to her patient, but not before shooting Jace a sideways glance. "I agree with Jace. I'm not a bull rider but I've studied enough about head injuries and I've gotten quite the introduction to them over the past two days. A helmet would have prevented yours tonight. You should start wearing it. We wouldn't want to see that handsome face of yours get messed up, now would we?"

"All right. I'll go back to wearing it." Justin half smiled while looking dazed, whether from the injury or Tara's flirting Jace couldn't be sure.

"Glad to hear it." Tara nodded as she whipped out a penlight to shine into the kid's eyes.

Justin was probably seeing two Taras instead of just one smiling down at him, so he was doubly smitten.

Jace grinned at how the rookie, blushing at Tara's attention, had caved so easily. It would be a good profession for her. She could get the riders to do whatever she wanted by sweet-talking them.

Tara turned to get something and caught his grin. "What's so funny?"

He shrugged. "Nothing. Just watching you work your magic."

One dark brow cocked up high. "Not magic, just medicine."

The kid on the table watched Tara's every move. Jace could see he had to stare extra hard to focus through the haze of the concussion. "Nah, I think it's a little bit of both."

"What's that mean?"

"Nothing." Jace shook his head. "Don't mind me."

"Easier said than done." Tara pulled a face, before turning back to the patient. "Doc Chandler is gonna want you to see your regular doctor first thing tomorrow for a follow-up. Okay?"

"Okay." Justin's gaze dropped away from Tara's. He was lying.

Jace knew what the kid was thinking. He'd been on that table himself more than a few times. There was no way Justin would go to the doctor for a bump on the head. Heath insurance was a luxury in this business, so most guys did without visits to the doctor.

As for himself, if Jace wasn't coughing up blood or didn't see shards of broken bone poking out through his skin, he wasn't going to any hospital or the doctor. For little things like cracked ribs, or sprained ankles, or dislocated shoulders, or concussions, what was the point? The doc couldn't make things heal any faster than nature could on its own.

A doctor would hand this kid a big bill for the pleasure of hearing he should take it easy and not ride for a while. Jace would lay down good money that Justin would be back on a bull by the weekend event, if not sooner.

"You shouldn't drive. Do you have a ride home?" Tara asked him.

"Yeah. My parents were here watching tonight. They'll take me home. They're waiting just outside."

Poor kid. The wreck of the night and it was in front of his family. Oh, well. At least his momma would take care of him. That's more than Jace had had when he'd started out riding pro with no daddy and his mother living in Florida.

"All right, then. You can go. You need me to help you walk?"

Justin's eyes opened a bit wider at Tara's offer as he held up one hand. "No, I can do it."

No guy wanted a girl he thought was cute to help him walk. Pride wouldn't allow it. Jace stopped himself from offering and watched and waited, on alert to jump in and save the kid from a fall.

Justin slid off the table and braced himself for a few seconds before taking a tentative step. When it looked as if he wasn't going to fall flat on his face, he took another step and reached for the doorway. His perception was definitely off, judging by how he missed the doorframe with his hand by a good two inches the first time. The second time he made it, turning his whole body back to look at Tara, rather than just his head. "Thanks . . . for everything."

"You're welcome." Tara sent him a smile that lit her entire face. "Feel better."

"I'll try." The kid was obviously hurting, but he managed a smile in return before he left.

Jace shook his head. "That kid has it bad."

Moving around the room putting supplies away in plastic bins, Tara nodded. "Yeah, he'll feel it even more tomorrow."

"I didn't mean the injury." While Jace watched her work, he leaned his ass against the edge of the examining table. This wasn't such a bad place to hang out, *if* you were healthy. Quiet. Lots of places to sit and relax. Being in there while he was hurting—now that was quite another story. "I meant he has a serious crush on you."

"What? No, he doesn't." Tara frowned at Jace, then glanced at the doorway. "You think?"

"I don't think. I know." Jace laughed.

"Hmm." She looked as if she was considering that concept. "Doesn't matter, anyway. He's a patient. It would be unethical for me to think of him as anything other than that."

Jace raised a brow. "If that's your standard, then you've just wiped out your entire dating pool at this job because every one of us will be your patient at one time or another." Even him, like it or not. "You know very well, in bull riding—"

"It's not a question of if you'll get hurt. It's when and how bad. I know. I've heard it a million times from Tuck."

"I'm sure you have. And I hope you listened. Tara, didn't you ever notice how the bucking chutes are the same size and shape as a grave?"

"That's not why they made them that way." She scowled.

"No, it's not. But it's pretty symbolic, don't you think? Kind of prophetic how it worked out that way. Six feet down, three feet wide, and nothing but you and the bull inside those metal rails. Something to think about."

Tara was quiet, and actually looked as if she was listening. Jace even thought she might have been impressed with him, which would have been a first, but then she rolled her eyes and let out a snort. "Quite the redneck philosopher, aren't we? Come on. Let's go. I'm done. I can leave."

At least things seemed to have returned to normal. She was back to being insulting and demanding. Jace liked it when everything was status quo. It was comfortable that way.

"Don't get snippy, girl. I was the one waiting on you." He pushed off the edge of the table. He was dirty, hungry, and tired. He was something else too—riding always got him revved up for sex—but that sure as hell wasn't happening tonight. Not with Tara as his roommate.

That was fine. A quick pass through the drive-thru, a hot shower, and a hotel bed would fix him up right. Since it seemed he was incapable of being with anyone besides Jacqueline, he was better off not satisfying his other need.

Bed would feel real good. But now that he'd be sharing a room with Tara, Jace wished he'd packed a pair of gym shorts or something to sleep in. Something that offered more coverage than his underwear in light of their surreal morning hard-on discussion earlier. That had been real fun.

Oh well. Too late now.

"You sure you're okay with this?" Jace asked from across the hotel room.

Tara pulled sweatpants and a T-shirt out of her duffle bag and turned to see Jace watching her. "Yeah, why wouldn't I be?"

"Well, for starters, I'm about to take a shower, and since I don't own pajamas, when I get out, I'm going to put on a clean pair of boxer briefs, then I'm going to get under those covers. I'm not sleeping in my jeans in my own room that I paid for." Jace took a pull on the take-out cup's straw and looked smug, as usual.

"Jace, seriously, it's not as if you've got anything I haven't seen before." Tara did have two brothers. And she was in the medical field. One body was just like another to her. Okay, so she wasn't an actual doctor, but she almost had her bachelor's degree in sports medicine. That counted.

"Yup. Females always say that, right before they start blushing and acting all weird after getting a good look at the exact part they say they've seen before." One sandy colored brow rose high. "Don't say I didn't give you fair warning."

Tara rolled her eyes. "Fine. Whatever. I'll try to

control my weak female self around your extreme masculinity."

Jace grinned the smile that had won him the hearts, and other body parts, of countless buckle bunnies over the years . . . when he wasn't sharing a room with his best friend's little sister, of course.

The sleeping arrangements were definitely going to put a cramp in his style, which was why Tara had been so surprised he'd offered to bunk with her. She'd been grateful, yes, but shocked nonetheless. Who knew Jace had any restraint when it came to buckle bunnies? That was as surprising as discovering he had such generosity hidden away inside him. Not just about the money he was laying out for the room, either. He was selflessly giving up his privacy to help her out of a jam.

Then again, he could always go to the place of whatever bunny he picked up. That's probably what his plan had been all along.

Fine with Tara. She'd get a free room, and have it all to herself. She could take advantage of the privacy if he did ditch her. A nice, quiet night with a long, hot shower followed by snuggling under the covers with the trashy romance novel she'd packed—that all sounded pretty good to her.

"When you're done, I'm heading in there for a shower, so don't dillydally."

"Men don't *dillydally*, as you put it, but please be my guest. You go first."

"No, I can't do that. You're paying for the room. You should be able to get first dibs on the shower."

"If I wanted first dibs, I would have taken it. Go on. That way I get to finish my shake before it gets all melty."

He mocked her for saying *dillydally* but he could say *melty*?

Grinning, Jace plopped his butt into the chair by the desk and kicked his legs out in front of him. He picked up his cup and sucked in a loud slurp of milk shake.

"Fine. I'll go first." With her sleep clothes in one hand and her toiletry bag in the other, Tara headed for the bathroom.

The arena was a dirty place. Even if she wasn't competing in the events herself, the dirt and dust seemed to get everywhere. Ground deep into the knees of her jeans from kneeling to check on a fallen rider. In her hair and on her skin, making her feel gritty. Even her teeth had felt kind of sandy at one point during the night.

They'd have to find a Laundromat soon. She'd be out of clean clothes to wear to work before the weekend. Jace might be able to get away with riding in jeans with dirty knees, but Tara sure couldn't work on the medical team like that.

Rid of the remnants of a few hours spent up close and personal with arena dirt, Tara emerged from the bathroom wearing her comfy sweats and a T-shirt and feeling a million percent cleaner.

"Can we look for a place to do laundry in the next town?" She scrubbed her head hard with the rough hotel room towel to get as much water out of her hair as she could. It could take forever to dry, even with the blow dryer in the bathroom.

It wasn't until she put the towel down and it no longer obscured her vision that she realized why

Jace had never answered her question about the Laundromat. He was flat on his back across the mattress sideways, fully clothed right down to his boots, which were propped one ankle on top of the other on the floor.

His eyes were closed and his slow, even breaths were deep enough to raise and lower the hands he held clasped across his belly. He was good and truly asleep.

Not sure what to do—leave him be or wake him up so he could sleep properly—Tara stood still and quiet, deciding. He wasn't drunk, but in the past, he had probably passed out plenty of times in the exact position—dirty, dressed, and sideways. It wouldn't hurt him to stay like that until he woke up on his own. Besides, she wasn't the man's momma, or even his girlfriend. It wasn't Tara's place to tuck him into bed.

Decision made, she tiptoed to her side of the room and slipped beneath the covers of her own bed. She'd woken early this morning and the day had been long. It was no wonder Jace had fallen asleep waiting for her to get out of the shower.

When even the cheap hotel linens seemed comfortable, Tara knew she'd soon follow his example. She'd be out like a light in no time. With that thought in mind she considered what to do about the lights. She settled on turning off the room lamp, but got out of bed and turned on the bathroom light, closing the door almost all the way so just a sliver showed through the crack in case he woke up in the middle of the night and didn't remember where he was or needed to find the bathroom.

Feeling like a good and responsible roommate for thinking of that, she crawled back beneath the covers and rolled onto her side. Facing away from Jace and the sound of his steady breathing, she closed her eyes and felt herself begin to drift away.

A loud buzzing infiltrated her slumber. In a state between waking and sleeping, Tara knew the sound was annoying but didn't know what it was, or what to do about it.

Movement from the other side of the room confused her until, slowly crawling toward full consciousness, she woke enough to remember Jace in the other bed.

"Hello?" His sleepy voice confirmed it, as well as what the noise had been—his cell phone vibrating.

At least it didn't require any action on her part. Tara could stay right where she was, comfortable and warm, though she did wonder what time it was and how long she'd slept. Finding out would require rolling over to look at the clock between the beds and that seemed like far too much effort. She wasn't that interested in knowing, and maybe if she closed her eyes and willed it, she'd go back to sleep.

"Jacqueline? *Shit.*" Jace hissed the last word so quietly Tara barely heard it. That was enough to pique her interest, and keep her from falling back to sleep.

"I'm on the road competing," he continued softly, but Tara could still hear the annoyance in his voice.

She couldn't decipher words, but she could hear the woman's screeching through the cell across the room in Jace's hand.

"No, I'm not. And I told you, I'm not doing this anymore." Jace disconnected the call without a good-bye and slammed the phone down on the nightstand.

Tara was more than intrigued. So much so, she wasn't even pissed about being woken up.

Okay, so she was being nosy, but it wasn't as if she had a love life of her own to worry about. She rolled over to face Jace and reached for the light between the beds. "You okay?"

"Yeah. Sorry for waking you up, Tara."

"Not your fault."

"Yeah, it is." There were dark circles beneath his usually bright hazel eyes, and even his voice sounded weary. "Last night when we got in, I turned my phone on to check if the guy helping me out with the lawns had left a message. I must have forgotten to turn it off again."

Because he'd passed out cold, that's why. Tara remembered the odd conversation in the truck, his comment about keeping her phone on in case Tuck called, so he could turn his off. He was dodging Jacqueline's calls. After being privy to one side of just a couple of them, Tara could see why.

She got a look at the clock. It was after midnight. No one called that late unless it was an emergency— or they were a crazy ex-girlfriend. No use pretending nothing was going on. "Everything all right back home?"

"Yeah, it's fine. Go back to sleep." He reached out and switched the light off.

She heard him get up and the bathroom door click shut. The sound of water pounding against the tile told Tara that Jace was finally getting the shower she'd hijacked from him earlier. Tomorrow, she'd let him go first so he wouldn't fall asleep in his clothes again. She had a feeling he might not get much sleep. Not after that phone call.

Chapter Seven

Through the haze of early morning consciousness, Jace heard soft footsteps padding across the carpet, and then the bathroom door close. A few moments later, the door opened again, followed by a thud and, "Ow."

Tara's annoyed and pain-filled whisper had Jace smiling, even as tired as he was.

"You don't have to creep around in the dark. I'm awake." He reached over and turned on the lamp before she broke a toe, if she hadn't already.

"Sorry I woke you." Tara cringed. "I was trying to be quiet, but I had to pee. Then I stubbed my toe on the corner of the dresser."

"It's fine, Tara. I was already awake." One side effect of the middle of the night conversation with Jacqueline had been a crappy night's sleep. "You okay?"

"Yeah." Tara kicked her foot up on the edge of the mattress and inspected her big toe. She shrugged and put her foot down on the floor again. "Might lose the toenail that's starting to turn blue, but I'll live."

Jace had forgotten what it was like to be around a tough female. Tara, having grown up with boys, was more tomboy than he was used to. Had Jacqueline stubbed her toe that hard, he'd be driving her to the nearest ER, or at the very least to a nail salon to have her pedicure repaired?

Tara's stomach let out a loud rumble. Eyes opening wide, she pressed her palm against her abdomen. "Jeez, I guess I'm hungry."

He had also forgotten what it was like to be around a woman who wasn't afraid to eat. He'd thought twice before buying Tara that hotdog yesterday because Jacqueline would have rather died than eat something so fattening, and in public where someone might see her. The former rodeo queen was obsessed with not gaining weight. Tara didn't have an ounce of spare flesh on her, and she could use some, but she put away food as fast as any bull rider.

He was thinking far too much about Jacqueline. The point of this trip was to stop doing that by getting away from her. Hard to do when she called and texted incessantly, but that was easily enough remedied. He'd make certain not to leave his phone on again. In fact, maybe he'd call the guy cutting the lawns for him and give him Tara's number. Say his phone had broken and until he got a new one, any texts or calls would have to go to her number.

Of course, he'd have to tell Tara before doing that. Maybe he should accidentally drop his cell in the parking lot and run it over with the truck. It was the coward's way out, but hell, a man had to do what was needed to survive.

Jace threw back the covers and swung his legs so

he was sitting on the edge of the bed. That left his boxer briefs, and what they contained, exposed and facing Tara, so he flipped the corner of the sheet back over his lap. He needed to stop at a store and pick up a pair of shorts or something because in the rush to get the hell out of Dodge, he hadn't packed any.

When he'd snuck back into his apartment after hiding at Tuck's and threw some things in a bag for the trip, the dead last thing he'd imagined was being roommates with Tara for three weeks. Then again, he never would have guessed that they wouldn't have killed each other by now, either.

He glanced at the clock. "We can go out and find somewhere to eat if you want. It's seven. Someplace should be open."

"You sure you don't want to sleep a little more?"

She looked wide awake, so the offer, made in her gentle doctor to patient voice, was for his benefit. It was another thing that was totally unexpected—Tara being nice to him. It wasn't her. She was coddling him because she pitied him. The close proximity of their sharing a room meant she'd been privy to private conversations between him and Jacqueline that he'd never intended anyone to hear. Particularly not Tara.

"Stop worrying about me, okay?" He hated her pity, and that made his statement come out sounding harsher than he'd meant it to.

A frown creased her brow. "Fine. Forgive me for trying to make things easier for you."

He was too tired from the constant battling with Jacqueline and his lack of sleep to be dealing with Tara. "Well, I don't need you to make things easier for me, Tara. I need you to be your normal, bitchy self."

"Bitchy. Real nice. Thanks." She shook her head and turned away toward the suitcase.

Jace breathed out a sigh. "I'm sorry."

"I don't want you to be sorry. I want you to stop being a dick."

He laughed. This was more like it. "All right. I'll work on it."

She shot him a look over her shoulder as she pulled clothes out of her bag. "Good. See that you do. And we need to find a Laundromat or a store where I can pick up another white shirt because I can't go to work in a dirty one."

"We can find both."

"Thank you." She bit out the two words, but Jace knew they were sincere.

"You're welcome."

It couldn't be easy for her to have to be totally dependent upon him. For her transportation everywhere, as well as the bed she slept in. Tara was nothing if not independent. It must be killing her to accept help from him, of all people. They weren't exactly friends. More like frenemies who put up with each other for Tuck's sake.

They'd made a deal and they both had to live with it. Jace scrubbed both hands over his face. Time to wake the hell up and get moving. It was a day off from competition, but also the day they needed to drive to the next venue and do everything that needed doing, like shopping and laundry.

Tara glanced in his direction again. "I never knew you had all that ink." She stared pointedly at one particular tattoo on the left side of his chest.

It was a heart, located just above his own heart.

The black script letters across the red ink spelled out *Jacqueline.*

In hindsight, that one had been a bad idea. He'd never regret the one beneath it—a cross with the name of a friend who'd died. Nor would he regret the bull's horns, or the barbed wire on his bicep, or even the skull and crossbones, his first one when he wasn't even old enough to get it. But that heart . . . yeah. That one had to go.

"It's time I go get another one."

Not a new one, but a cover-up of an old one. Tattoo parlors made a good living doing cover-up tats for people with regrets. Permanently marking his body with her name hadn't convinced Jacqueline he loved only her, or was faithful to her. He'd hoped it would, but it hadn't. Nothing could convince her. It was something inside her he couldn't fix, much as he'd tried.

"What would you get?" Tara asked.

"Not sure. Any ideas?" Absently, Jace rubbed the tattoo.

Tara's gaze followed the motion. "It'll have to be something big and kinda round."

Crap. The damn girl was more observant than he'd given her credit for. She knew he was thinking about a cover-up for Jacqueline's name.

She continued. "A championship belt buckle, maybe? That would be cool."

He laughed. It was a damn good idea, except for one detail. "I've won my share of events, but I don't have a real impressive championship buckle to immortalize in ink."

It had been Tuck who had won the state championship so long ago, not Jace.

"Then you better win yourself one." One dark

brow rose high as she bundled a bunch of clothes in her arms. "I'm going to get dressed. You need the bathroom or can I go change in there?"

Boy, she didn't beat around the bush or pull any punches, now did she? "No, you can go on in."

With a nod, she headed into the other room, leaving Jace surprised yet again. Tara was proving easier to room with than Tuck. With Tuck, there would have been questions and judgment and advice about Jacqueline, whether Jace had asked for it or not. Not so with Tara. Whether it was because she just didn't give a shit, or that she was giving him his privacy, he didn't know. Either way, it was working for him so far.

He flopped back against the pillow and flung one forearm over his eyes. Good thing he wasn't riding tonight. He was bone deep tired. The kind of tired that came from mental exhaustion, more than physical.

The sound of the bathroom door opening again pulled Jace out of the zone he'd fallen into—that place between asleep and awake. Another thing he had to get used to—a woman who got ready as quick as he did. Jacqueline used to want an hour's notice to run to the store. It required full makeup and hairspray and the proper outfit.

He opened his eyes to find Tara scowling at him. "I knew you were still tired. You fell back to sleep."

"Did not. I was just checking my eyelids for cracks." His answer brought a smile to her face, even as she shook her head at him.

Lying down had been a bad idea. Jace rallied his energy and sat up, glancing at his phone on the nightstand. He needed to check it to see if the guy working with him had any problems or questions.

He risked looking at Tara and found she was sitting on her bed, busy going over some papers. It looked like the schedule of events they'd be attending. Perfect. She was distracted so she hadn't noticed him hesitate before he turned on his phone.

Drawing in a deep breath, Jace hit the ON button. It took the phone a few seconds, then it booted up . . . and went crazy in his hand, vibrating as the texts and voicemails loaded.

Eleven texts and six voicemails, and he was going to have to go through every one just in case any were from Mike, even though he was sure most, if not all, were from Jacqueline.

"Shit." The cuss escaped him before he could stop it. Jace glanced up again and wasn't so lucky this time—Tara was watching him. He needed privacy so he stood. "I'm taking a quick shower. Then we can go eat and get a move on."

"Jace."

He'd just turned toward the bathroom, the phone he'd come to hate in his hand, when Tara's voice stopped him. He glanced back at her. "Yeah?"

"I know we're not friends or anything, but we are stuck together for the next few weeks, so I wanted you to know . . . we can talk, if you want."

There was that look of pity again. He was going to have to give her some explanation, eventually. Just not right now. "Ain't nothing to talk about."

He strode to the bathroom and closed and locked the door behind him.

"So, I feel like I owe you some sort of explanation." Jace kept his eyes on the road and both hands tight on the steering wheel.

About damn time. Tara bit back that comment and played dumb. "Explanation for what?"

He looked about as uncomfortable as a man could. As if he was about to face a firing squad—or the tampon aisle in the drugstore. "For all the phone calls."

"Okay." Tara nodded. If he had thought she was going to say no and tell him that she didn't need an explanation, he was going to be disappointed.

"Jacqueline and I . . ." Jace glanced at Tara, then back to the highway in front of them. He let out a sigh. "I don't know. It's complicated."

Tara waited for what seemed like a long time in the silence of the truck, though it was probably about thirty seconds or so. He didn't continue, so she decided to prod him into it. "I thought you two were broken up. For like a year now."

"We are." He let out a short laugh. "That's the complicated part."

She stayed quiet, mostly because she wasn't sure what to say, but kept an eye on him while the truck remained silent. Nothing but the noise of the road beneath the tires.

"Things were great in the beginning." Jace stared ahead, almost as if he was talking to himself. "About four months in, I was on the road, following the circuit and competing full-time, just like now. I got banged up pretty bad one night. Couple of cracked ribs. Nothing critical, but I hurt like hell. There wasn't anything the doc could do about it, so I did a few shots of whiskey to numb the pain and passed out to sleep through it. I forgot to call her that night, and I forgot to plug in my phone so it went dead. When I woke up in the morning, it was to a dozen messages from her flipping out."

"Didn't you tell her what had happened?"

"Yeah. She didn't believe me. Said I didn't call because I must have brought a girl home with me. I finally put some of the guys on the phone to confirm I was hurt and had gone to the hotel alone."

"Did she believe you then?"

"She said she did, but I don't know. She put me through hell when I got home. I did everything I could to make her believe I hadn't and I wasn't going to cheat on her. But she'd throw that one night in my face every chance she got. Every fight we had. Every time I spent a night on the road. I ended up driving home between competitions in the middle of the night rather than getting a hotel room, just to keep the fights down. And if she felt I'd taken too long getting home, she assumed it was because I was screwing someone at the arena before I left."

"Wow." Tara hadn't meant to breathe a word to interrupt him, but the exclamation slipped out.

Jace dragged in a breath and let it out. "That's the way it was from then on. For the next six years or so, until last year when I came home one night and found all my stuff out on the front lawn."

Tara's eyes widened and she made a tiny noise of shock.

Jace glanced at her and snorted. "Oh, don't be so surprised. That wasn't the first time it had happened. She'd throw my shit outside at least a few times a year. She'd break up with me every time we had a fight. It just never stuck because I'd work on her until she let me back in. Except for that last time. I don't know why but that time I didn't stand outside the door and talk until she let me back in. I put all my shit in the back of the truck and drove to Tuck's. That really pissed her off. That's when I went and rented my own place."

Tara started to get a clearer picture of the break-up, as well as the relationship. Jacqueline had broken up with him because that's what she always did, but he'd essentially ended it by not groveling until she'd taken him back. "Can I ask you something?"

"Sure. Why not." His enthusiasm was less than overwhelming.

"Did you ever cheat on her? Were her suspicions justified?"

"No." The single word was delivered in a low, firm voice.

Tara remembered when she was younger—about nine, she guessed. Tuck and Jace would roll in from a weekend of riding, reeking of booze and talking about all the girls they'd been with. They never knew she could hear every word they said through the wall of her bedroom. Of course, that had been before Tuck had started dating his first wife Brenda, and before Jace had met Jacqueline.

"Jace, you can tell me the truth." Tara tried to keep her tone from sounding like she was accusing him or she and Jace would end up in a fight of their own.

"I am! I swear to God, Tara. I'm not saying I was an angel before I met her, because I wasn't. But I never touched another woman after she and I started dating. I might forget to call. Or forget to charge my phone or hell, I even forgot to pack my charger sometimes, but I wasn't running around on her." He took his eyes off the road to glare at her for so long, Tara began to fear for their safety.

"Okay, Jace. I believe you."

He let out a snort. "No, you don't."

All right, he'd caught her there. "What I'm having

trouble with is why you stuck it out for so long if things were so bad." An innocent man would have told Jacqueline to take her suspicions and shove them, and then left.

"It wasn't because I was feeling guilty, if that's your point." There was an angry set to Jace's jaw.

"Then why? You said you owe me an explanation, so explain. Help me understand." Inexplicably, Tara found she was interested in knowing—cared about, even—Jace's motivation.

"Because it wasn't always bad. Sometimes it was really good. When we weren't fighting. When she was in a good mood." He let out a breath. "And because I love her."

"Love. Present tense?" Another interesting revelation, and one Tara was pretty sure he'd let slip accidentally.

"No. Loved. Past tense." He drew in a breath and let it out slowly. "I don't know. I guess a part of me will always love her. Or hell, maybe I'm just remembering the good times. It's confusing when I see her now."

"*See her* meaning what? When you run into her like at Tuck's wedding? Or are you *seeing* seeing her?" Tara stressed the word twice, so he'd get her meaning.

Jace looked as if he'd rather do anything than talk about it more. "I go over to her place sometimes."

Realization dawned. "Are you still having sex with her?" That would explain a lot, such as the midnight phone calls, the jealousy . . .

"Yeah." He didn't make eye contact at all. He concentrated on the road through the windshield as if his life depended on it.

"But you're avoiding her phone calls." It was like

pulling teeth. One tiny revelation at a time, and Tara had to dig for every one.

"Because I can't do it anymore. Tuck was right. He told me I'd never move on until I cut ties with her completely."

"I don't often agree with my brother, but in this case, I think he's right." Not that Tara was any relationship expert, but even she could see the one between Jace and Jacqueline was a bad idea.

"I know. That's why my phone is turned off."

"I'm not sure that avoiding the issue is going to solve it."

"I know that too, but it's the best I can do right now. Okay?" His tone grew sharp.

Sometimes running away was the easiest path to take. "I understand."

"Do you really?" His sandy-colored brows rose.

"Yup." Tara had done a bit of running herself lately. She glanced at Jace and found him looking in her direction. "What? You don't believe me? Jace, I totally do understand."

"No, I do believe you." He smiled, a small, sad lifting of one corner of his mouth. "You're right. We're not friends, so why would you bother lying to me?"

"Exactly." She nodded. "Same reason why you wouldn't bother lying to me about what's going on with your ex."

This strange collaboration of theirs might just work out after all. It seemed they were both running away from something. Jace from Jacqueline. Tara from seeing Logan with his new wife.

"We'll be in the next town by afternoon, then we'll look for a hotel and see about doing laundry." Jace was obviously changing the subject.

That was fine with her. "All right."

Now that they had their mutual understanding settled, they could move on to other things. Perfect.

"Oh, I gave your cell phone number to the guy handling my lawn jobs while I'm gone, in case he needs to get in touch with me."

Tara raised a brow but decided, in the interest of keeping the peace and in deference to all Jace had done for her lately, she wouldn't comment on his making that assumption without asking her first. "Fine."

"Thanks."

It was short, but at least it had been something. Tara responded just as short. "No problem."

And so the truce continued.

Chapter Eight

"Today was a good day." Tara smiled and looked as if she meant it.

"Was it?" Jace asked, surprised.

"Sure. We did all our laundry so we have clean clothes again. We went shopping. You got shorts so you can stop flashing me your panties. Now, we're going out—"

"First of all, men don't wear *panties*." Jace frowned as he interrupted her. "Second, I warned you when we agreed to share a room you might end up seeing things you wouldn't like, such as me in my drawers."

She grinned wide. "I know. I'm just cutting up with you."

He wasn't finished quite yet. "And third, are you even old enough to be going in here?"

Jace paused with his hand on the door of the bar they'd spotted when they'd first pulled into town. It was close enough they could walk back to their hotel if they had to, not that he was planning on getting drunk.

They were just going to kill some time so they

didn't have to be cooped up in the hotel room all night with nothing to do, but if Tara wasn't over twenty-one they'd be turning around and looking for somewhere appropriate for the underage sister of his best friend—such as that fast food chain with the game room for the kids.

"Yes, I'm old enough, you idiot." Scowling so deeply he had to laugh, Tara reached past him and yanked the door open herself. She strutted inside and headed directly to the bartender.

For lack of anything else to do, he followed her in. Jace arrived at the bar in time to hear her ask, "Anything on special?"

Wiping the wooden surface with a white rag, the bartender nodded. "Dollar bottles of domestic beer tonight."

"Then I'll have one of those." While reaching into her pocket, Tara glanced over her shoulder at Jace. "You want one?" She pulled out a folded bill and laid it on the newly cleaned surface.

"Yeah, but let me get it." Jace reached for his own wallet.

"No. You paid for the room and for the burgers. The least I can do is buy you a dollar beer."

"All right. Thank you." Knowing her financial situation, he wouldn't let her pay for much, but this he'd let her do. It was kind of nice having a woman offer to pay for a change, even if it was just a beer.

She turned back around and slid the money toward the server. "Make that two, please."

Jace glanced around the place as the bartender got her change. "Looks like some of the guys are already here."

Two bottles in her hands, Tara followed his stare

toward the table of young bull riders in the back corner. "We can go over and say hello to them if you
want to. It's fine with me."

"Nah, I don't—"

"Jace!" Dillon had spotted them from his place at
the table and was waving him over.

In his role as surrogate big brother, Jace had been
planning on keeping Tara away from these guys. If
not at the arena, where she'd have to be in contact
with them for her job, then at least at the bar he'd
been dumb enough to take her to. Now, no such
luck.

Jace waved to Dillon and glanced down at Tara,
taking the bottle she handed him. "Okay, but just for
a minute."

She shrugged. "Whatever you want. They're your
friends."

Dillon was, maybe. He was okay, married and
faithful. But the other guys? Jace wasn't so sure
about them. Justin was back there, concussion and
all. He'd already almost fallen off the examining
table in the medical room from being under Tara's
spell, so they shouldn't be hanging out with him.

Then there was this new kid on the circuit, Klint
Daily. Jace didn't know enough about him to form
an opinion based on facts. Until he knew for sure
what Klint's deal was, Jace would like to keep Tara
away from him, too.

All he did know for certain was that some of the
riders were real players. A different girl at every
event. Love 'em and leave 'em. Never sticking around
long enough to worry about the consequences. Tara
was not getting involved with any one of them. Not
on his watch.

As they made their way to the back of the room,

the irony wasn't lost on him. There'd been a time the love 'em and leave 'em game had been the one he'd played. That had been before Jacqueline. It felt as if that was a lifetime ago. It might as well have been.

"Guys." That was all the greeting Jace had for the young guns who seemed far too interested in the girl he'd put himself in charge of for the next few weeks. He sure as hell wasn't going to introduce her and hand her over to them on a silver platter. Sure it was rude, but they'd get over it.

"Pull up a chair." Dillon made the offer, but it was Klint who jumped up from his seat.

He eyeballed Tara. "Here, take mine. I'm tired of sitting, anyway."

"Um, okay. Thanks." Tara moved to sit in the chair he held out. He even pushed it in for her. The guy was working it hard.

Jace narrowed his gaze at the cocky newcomer. He grabbed an empty chair from a nearby table for himself and sat, leaning closer to Dillon. "Hey. What's his deal?"

"Klint? No deal that I know of. Why?"

"Nothing." Jace leaned back and sipped from his bottle, but his attention never left Klint and the brilliant smile that seemed only for Tara.

"I thought you said nothing was going on with you and the new doctor chick." Dillon cocked a brow.

"Tara?" Why did Dillon keep asking that? "Nothing is going on. I already told you that last time you asked."

"All right. Just checking."

"And why were you checking? You're happily married with a baby and a damn gorgeous wife. How you landed her, I don't know, but still—"

"Hey, now. No need to get insulting. Just looking out for your best interest, man."

"My best interest? Really. How's that?"

"When you guys were up at the bar, Klint was asking about Tara's status."

Jace shot Klint a look. "Next time he asks, you can tell him her status is *off limits*."

That's how Tuck would want it. Hell, that's how Jace wanted it, too. No woman in her right mind would hook up with a full-time bull rider. He should know, having been one of them.

While Jace wrestled with his thoughts, Tara was smiling big time at Klint, who was buying shots for her from the girl walking around with a tray full of them.

Crap. "Uh, Tara. I don't think you should be drinking anything stronger than beer." And not too many of those either, if Jace had anything to do with it.

She frowned at him. "Why not?"

"Because I think that right there is a bad idea." Jace tipped his head at the blue-colored shot poised in her hand.

"Then you don't have to have any. Doesn't mean I can't."

Jace reached across and gripped her forearm before she raised the alcohol to her lips. "Tara, I mean it."

Klint watched the exchange before he leaned down toward Tara. "Are you with him?"

"If you mean is he my boyfriend or something, the answer is no. He's nobody to me. He drove me here, which definitely does not give him permission to tell me what I can or can't do." Tara's answer was as much for Jace as it was for Klint.

The *nobody* comment hurt Jace. It shouldn't, but after all he'd done to be nice, to have her say that was a slap in the face. He pushed it aside. If nothing else, he knew Tara's sharp tongue well and how she hated being told what to do. He had never let it get to him in the past and she'd called him far worse than that. He shouldn't let it get to him now.

He shook his head. "You're right, Tara. I'm nobody. Go for it. Try that fluorescent green shot next. That looks like nothing but fun in a glass right there."

When Tara started puking later, which she would after a few more of those things, she'd better not look to him for sympathy. She'd also better not toss her cookies in his truck or in their room. She'd be cleaning it up herself if she did.

"Jace, you're worse than Tucker. You seriously need to lighten up and have a little fun. Here." Tara bounced out of her seat and came at him, a frightening-looking shot in her hand.

He would—and had—downed his share of tequila shots, but this sweet, colored shit the young kids liked to drink nowadays turned his stomach.

"No. I don't want it." He shook his head while she tried to follow his mouth with the shot and press it to his lips.

"Come on. Stop being a party pooper." She ended up straddling his lap as he held her back, his hands on her hips.

"I said no. Tara, stop." More than not wanting the shot, Jace couldn't have her in his lap. Bouncing against his groin. Waking up parts of his anatomy that had been neglected and were happy for any attention.

She was relentless in her pursuit. Damn, he'd

paid strippers for lap dances that hadn't gotten as intimate as this. "Tara, I mean it."

"Fine." Tara gave in. She let out a breath of frustration, which caused her body to sag heavier in his lap, pressing her crotch against his.

He realized his hands remained wrapped around her waist. He'd been trying to hold her still. Now it seemed he was just holding her.

Jace dropped his grasp. "A'ight then. You can take that shit that looks like window cleaner and go back to your own seat now."

Tara didn't get up. She downed the shot while sitting right there in his lap, and then licked her lips, slow and thorough, drawing one hundred percent of his attention to her tongue and how it rimmed her mouth. "Doesn't taste like window cleaner."

Finally she stood, and Jace could breathe again. As she made her way around the table to the chair she'd left vacant, he dared to glance at the group of guys. The eyes of every one of the three younger riders were on him.

Clearing his throat, he stood. "Uh, anybody need a beer?"

Jace managed to get Tara out of there after only one more round and before she got too drunk. Though, judging by the look she shot him across the cab of the truck, she wasn't happy. Maybe he was acting like the party pooper she had accused him of being, but what choice did he have? He couldn't sit by and watch Tuck's little sister get shitfaced at a bar he'd taken her to.

"All right, what's wrong?" he asked after he could no longer ignore her glaring at him.

"You need to lighten up and let loose and let me do the same."

"So we can both feel like shit all day tomorrow because of those shots you like so much?"

"I can handle two beers and two shots." She stared out the side window at the passing scenery while he navigated the short distance to the hotel.

"Three shots, that I saw." Who knows what those guys had bought for her when he'd left her alone with them and went to take a piss.

"Whatever. You know, I always thought you were a wild man. Jeez, was I wrong." She mumbled something more that sounded like *old man* as Jace pulled into an open parking spot in front of their room and cut the engine.

He wasn't sure what to do about her accusation. Defending himself by telling her he could drink any one of those kids under the table didn't seem the best solution. Nor did telling her that back in the day there were nights he and Tuck didn't even think about hitting their beds until the morning sun had risen. And often, it was to tumble into those beds with whatever women they'd scooped up at the bar before closing time.

"Come on. This old man needs to get some rest so he can ride tomorrow." Jace wasn't that tired. He'd gotten his second wind and could have lasted much longer, if he hadn't felt he was starting to lose control over the girl currently in his charge.

Walking from the truck to the door, Tara stumbled on the curb and tripped head on into him. He caught her by the shoulders and realized he'd made the right choice to get them out of the bar. Whatever that sweet shit in those crazy looking shots was could get a person messed up and fast.

"You okay?"

"I'm fine." Tara pushed back from him. "And I'm not drunk if that's what you're thinking. I just didn't see the curb."

"Mmm, hmm. That's what I figured." He faced the door to hide his smile as he slid the key into the lock.

She followed him into the room and flung herself, fully clothed, backward onto one of the beds. "You know, when Logan got married to that woman—"

"Emma?"

"Yeah, her. Anyway, when Tyler drove me back up to school and we were talking, he told me Logan is too old for me."

"Tyler is right. Logan is too old for you."

"You don't get to have an opinion. You're not my brother."

"You're right. I'm not." That left Jace wondering why she was telling him all this to begin with, if she didn't want his opinion.

"The point is, tonight I was trying to hang out with guys my age, and you made me leave early."

"You shouldn't be hanging out with those guys. You don't want a bull rider, Tara."

"Why not? They seemed nice enough. Dillon showed me a picture of his wife and his daughter."

"Yeah, what he didn't tell you is that the daughter came before the wife. And yes, he's a good enough guy that he married her after he knocked her up. Not every guy would have done that. So, no, you're not getting serious with any of those guys. Not while I'm driving you around."

"Jeez, Jace. I don't want to marry one. I just want to have some fun." Still flat on her back and looking sleepy, she managed to turn her head so she could stare at him from her bed.

"Yeah, I got it, and you're not doing that either." Shaking his head and grumbling under his breath, Jace grabbed the white plastic bag from the store with his new shorts in it. "One unplanned pregnancy per family at a time."

"What?" Tara rose from the bed like the dead resurrected. "Oh, my God. Is Becca pregnant?"

"Crap. You don't know."

Of course she didn't know. Tuck had only told Jace because it had slipped out. It seemed the secret was a slippery sucker since it had just slid out of Jace's mouth like it had out of Tuck's. Now he had to deal with the consequences.

"No, it's not Becca."

Tara's eyes grew wide and she drew in a gasp. "Tyler got somebody pregnant? Oh, my God. My parents are going to flip—"

"No, not Tyler. Stop guessing and let them tell you when they're ready." Jace swore he could see the pieces of the puzzle assembling in her brain.

"They. Plural. Like a couple." She frowned as if she was thinking hard. Then the color drained from her face. "Logan?" Tara spoke the word softly as she raised her gaze and watched Jace for confirmation.

Shit.

"Yeah." Jace nodded. Nothing else he could do. He'd already screwed up royally.

There were times in the past when he would have enjoyed bursting Tara's bubble. Taken joy in teasing her. There was no joy now.

The pain showed on her face as she stood and swiped at her glassy eyes. "I, uh, gotta get out of here."

He took a step after her. "Wait. Where are you going?"

"For a walk." She didn't look back when she answered, but he heard the tears in her voice. The door slammed behind her before he had a chance to ask if she had her copy of the key.

Tara had a huge crush on Logan. Jace knew it had nearly killed her when he'd married Emma out of the blue. He'd have to give her time to cry in private and absorb what she'd learned, what he'd told her, even if it was by accident. *Crap*. Logan and Emma needed to get off their asses and tell people. It's not like they could hide it forever, and Tara was family for God's sake.

Jace drew in a breath and walked to the bedside table where he'd left his phone plugged in but turned off. Not knowing if she even had her phone on her, he powered his on, just in case. The expected texts and voicemails loaded, making the phone vibrate across the wooden surface. He'd have to sort through all of those, and then leave the phone on in case Tara called. It was the least he could do after his screwup.

Tara pushed through the door of the bar and spotted the guys still at the back table. She hadn't planned on going back there, but it's where her feet had led her. Now that she was there, she wished she didn't have red eyes from crying over a man she'd thought she'd shed her last tear for the day he told her he'd never love her.

She drew in a bracing breath and made a beeline for the three bull riders. "Hey, guys."

"Hey! Look who's back. And without her bodyguard, too." Justin grinned wide and spun an empty chair toward her. "Have a seat. I thought you were heading to bed."

"Yeah, well, you know. I put the old guy to bed and came back out." She made the joke to cover the truth.

Dillon cocked a brow. "Jace know you came back?"

"No. You gonna tell him?"

"Not if he doesn't ask me. If he does, then I'm not gonna lie."

"He's not my boss or my brother, but you do what you got to do." *Damn Boy Scout.* Hard to believe Dillon hadn't been prepared and had gotten his girlfriend pregnant like Jace said.

"What you drinking, sweetheart?" Klint's chair scraped across the floor as he stood.

"I don't know. What are you guys drinking?"

Justin held up his cup and laughed. "I don't think you want this. It's vodka and Red Bull."

"Sounds good. That's exactly what I want."

Klint raised a brow. "All right. You got it."

Once Klint had left the table to get her drink, Dillon leaned forward and braced his forearms on the table. "So how's Tuck doing? Is it strange, his being married and all?"

Tara let out a snort. "I don't want to talk about my brother right now. And I really don't want to talk about his wife or her sister."

Dillon leaned back again. "All righty. Gotcha."

Justin's eyes opened a tad wider as he watched the exchange and Tara realized she'd been a little bit harsher in her answer to poor Dillon than she should have been.

When Klint appeared next to her bearing her

drink, Tara was happy for the distraction. "Thank you."

"You're very welcome."

She took the cup and drew in a long, cold sip, letting the liquid infused with alcohol numb her mouth even as she hoped it would numb her pain. She didn't know why Justin hadn't thought she'd like it. It tasted pretty good. Refreshing. She took another sip.

Klint swung his chair around the table, closer to hers. "So you going to be at all the events now that you work with the doc's team?"

"It's an unpaid internship for a few weeks to fulfill a school requirement for my degree."

"But then you should totally get a job with him. You're great at it." Justin sounded so enthusiastic, she believed him.

She couldn't help the smile that crossed her lips. "Thanks for saying that. I really do enjoy the job."

"Well, I haven't been hurt since you started, but I think I might have to make it my business to be soon, just so you can tend to me." Klint winked.

Tara laughed, making him grin wider.

He leaned closer. "So tell me, beautiful. What do you like to do for fun?"

She took another sip of her drink and realized she had somehow reached the bottom. "Well, I enjoy hanging out with the young stars of the pro bull-riding tour, such as yourselves."

Justin tipped his glass to her in salute. "You ever ride one yourself?"

"A bull? No, I could never. I've seen my brothers Tuck and Tyler get too broken up from doing it. I could handle a cowboy though." Smiling, she emptied the cup. Flirting was easy with these guys. Judging by Justin and Klint's smiles, she was really good at it, too.

Dillon's phone sounded from its place on the table. He glanced at the readout. "Crap. Wife calling. I'm gonna take this outside."

"Sure." Klint dismissed Dillon with a wave of one hand, but his eyes never left Tara.

That was exactly what she needed to forget about Logan. Compliments from two sweet, single guys who made her feel as if she were the only girl in the room. Jace didn't know what he was talking about.

"Hey, you know what I read the other day?" Justin leaned his elbows on the table.

"When do you read?" Klint frowned at his friend.

"I read stuff on my cell phone. Anyway, somebody posted this article on their timeline saying that all the kids' games we used to play in middle school are coming back, but for full-grown adults. Things like a strip version of Twister. Or Spin the Bottle and Seven Minutes in Heaven."

"Really? Well, now, those are some games I wouldn't mind playing." Klint looked to Tara. "How about you?"

Her gaze dropped to his mouth. She'd been kissed. She'd even been fondled a bit when the guy had slid his hand under her clothes, but that was it. Her entire life she'd saved herself for Logan, but that had backfired. She might as well be in middle school as far as her sexual experience was concerned. Meanwhile, Emma, older and from New York City where women had no morals, had thrown herself at him. Had sex with him the weekend they'd met.

Tara would have given everything to Logan, but why would he want some inexperienced virgin who didn't know what she was doing? Not with Emma and her tons of experience with men—the 'ho.

No more playing good girl.

"Sure." Tara nodded. "I think that sounds like a hell of a lot of fun."

Grinning, Justin grabbed Jace's empty beer bottle, still sitting right where he'd left it. Turning it on its side, he laid it on the table. "Go ahead, Tara. Give it a good spin and see which lucky one of us gets to kiss you first."

"Aren't there supposed to be more people for this game?" Her brain seemed to be moving a little slowly but it was still very obvious that she was the only girl. Unless these guys were going to kiss each other, which she very much doubted, every kiss was going to be with her.

"Hell no. Then we'd have less of a shot. I like these odds. Fifty-fifty." Klint's hand covered hers. "Spin the bottle, sweetheart."

"Yeah, then I can see if there's someplace we can slip away to be alone for my Seven Minutes in Heaven with you," Justin added.

"Or *my* seven minutes with her," Klint corrected. "I already know the place. There's a broom closet right next to the men's room."

Alone with these guys. Letting them do whatever they wanted. Touch whatever they wanted. Tara's stomach twisted, but she wasn't sure if it was with yearning or fear. Probably a bit of both. She was drunk enough not to care.

She sent the bottle into a wild spin she couldn't quite follow with her eyes. It didn't matter. The guys would tell her which one she was supposed to kiss—or do more than that with.

The twisting low in her gut radiated all the way to

between her thighs. An itch that needed to be scratched. A sneeze you felt coming but couldn't quite get out.

When she was able to focus her eyes again, she saw the bottle had stopped spinning and Klint was grinning wide. He reached for her hand and pulled her out of her seat.

"Come on, sweetheart." He glanced at Justin. "You'd better time us, because I'll be too busy."

Justin pouted. "Yeah, fine."

Klint pulled her to the back of the bar where it was darker except for the illuminated exit sign and the thin slice of light coming from beneath the men's and the ladies' room doors. He reached for the knob of the door that wasn't marked and smiled. "You ready?"

Tara swallowed away her nerves. "Yeah."

The room was impossibly dark but that didn't matter. They didn't need to see. Once Klint pushed the door shut, he pressed her against it. She felt the smooth hard steel behind her and his body in front. Every sense seemed heightened in the dark. His breath was warm against her lips as he hovered close before pressing his mouth against hers. His tongue breached her lips and she could taste his drink and something else. Chewing tobacco, maybe.

The stubble on his face stung the skin around her lips as he worked her mouth like he was trying to devour her. Her face was going to be scraped and red by the time she left the closet.

His buckle cut into her stomach, he pressed so hard against her as he wedged his thigh between hers. Still it wasn't enough. Not enough to block the pain of not being good enough—woman enough— for Logan. Not enough to ease the ache deep inside her. Tara craved something more, but she wasn't sure what she sought. What would cure the hurt and the ache.

Whatever it was, she had a feeling she wasn't going to find it in seven minutes in the closet with Klint. Would being with Justin help? What would be enough?

Maybe there was no cure for how she felt. Or maybe the combination of guzzling the drink and the taste of tobacco in Klint's mouth was going to make her vomit.

Tara wasn't sure of anything.

Chapter Nine

Jace emerged from the bathroom showered and freshly shaved, but to an empty room. Tara was still gone. Where could she have gone for so long? He went to the nightstand and picked up his phone. No missed calls. A miracle in itself, but he'd been hoping for a text or something from her.

"Crap." He needed to go find her. He pulled off his shorts and pulled on his jeans again, not taking the time to bother with underwear.

Socks, boots, and a shirt, and he was ready to go. He shoved his room key and phone in his pocket, his hat on his head, and headed for the door, grabbing his truck keys along the way.

Where the hell was he going to look for her? She couldn't have gone too far on foot. He'd have to drive around and troll the streets like he was looking for a damn runaway dog.

He headed out of the lot and turned toward the bar, figuring she'd walk in the direction they'd driven before, a way she was familiar with. How long had she been gone? Not incredibly long, but he didn't see her on the main road and he'd already driven a mile. He was about to spin the truck around and head in the other direction when he saw Dillon's truck still parked in the bar's lot.

Maybe she'd stopped in there. He could ask Dillon if he'd seen her. It was worth a shot, anyway. Jace pulled the truck into the lot for the second time that night, parked, and got out. He was surprised to see Dillon standing outside the front door.

"Hey, Dillon." Jace strode toward him. "Strange question, but have you seen Tara?"

"Hang on, baby." Dillon lowered the cell Jace hadn't seen and hooked a thumb toward the door. "Yeah, she's inside with Justin and Klint."

Smothering a curse, Jace grumbled something close to thanks and pushed through the door. He shouldn't be surprised. She was nothing if not contrary. Doing the opposite of what he wanted was a perfect fit for her character. But leaving in tears, not saying where she was going and making him worry—that was unacceptable.

He went to the table where Justin sat alone. "Where is she?"

"Jace. Uh, hey. I thought you'd gone to bed."

"Is that what she told you? Forget it. I'm here. Where is she?"

Justin swallowed hard and pointed toward the back.

"The bathroom?" Jace asked. These weren't difficult questions, so why was Justin having such a problem answering?

"No. Um, not the bathroom."

"Justin, what the hell? Just tell me. Where is she?"

"She's in the closet with Klint."

"In the closet? Why?"

"You know . . . for that game. Seven Minutes in Heaven?"

Frowning, Jace pawed through his memories until he came up with what game Justin was referring to. When he finally put the pieces together, his blood pressure rose so high his scalp began to tingle.

"She's alone with Klint in the closet?"

Tara could be making out, or worse. Hell, she could be having sex with Klint. It wasn't out of the question. A young kid like that wouldn't even take the full seven minutes before he shot off.

"She said you weren't together." Wide-eyed and pale, Justin looked as afraid as Klint should be. "Jace, I swear to you we didn't know—"

He didn't wait to hear Justin out. Jace was already on his way back to tear every door off its hinges until he yanked Tara out of whatever situation she'd stupidly gotten herself into.

The choices were limited, which saved the bar the expense of replacing many broken hinges. He bypassed the two bathrooms and moved to the door between. Gripping the knob, he found it wasn't locked. He turned it with a hand that shook with barely contained rage and yanked.

Tara spilled out backward, with Klint glued to her.

Jace caught her beneath the arms as she crashed into him.

Klint was on his own. For all Jace cared, Klint could fall flat on his face—the face that had just been sucking on Tara's.

"Come on. We're going."

"Stop telling me what to do." She pouted with lips swollen from kissing.

"Tara, don't push me." Jace rarely lost his temper. He felt close to losing it now.

"Let go of me."

When she said that, he realized he held her by the back of the neck like a momma cat gripping her kitten. Too bad. It was this or throw her over his shoulder in a fireman's carry. He steered her toward the front of the bar as she tried to wiggle out of his grasp and swatted at him.

Klint followed behind. "I think you should let go of her. If she doesn't want to leave with you—"

Jace spun to face the kid who dared to get in the middle of his private business with Tara. The expression on his face was enough to dissuade Klint from interfering. He stood silent and watched Jace, hand still on Tara, turn toward the front of the bar.

As they neared the exit, the door opened and Dillon walked through. "Jace, what's—"

"Not now, Dillon." Jace pushed past his friend and out the door into the parking lot. Still holding Tara by the back of the neck, he steered her to his truck's passenger door, tugged it open, and waited for her to climb up. If she didn't, he'd pick her up and toss her in himself.

Lucky for both of them, she got in under her own steam, though she did shoot him a dagger-filled look as she reached for the grab bar and hoisted herself inside.

Once she was firmly closed inside the cab of the truck and he was pretty sure she wasn't going to bolt, Jace made his way around to the driver's side and got in. She didn't look at him again, or say a word, but her silence was the loudest thing he'd heard in a while.

Jacqueline had never been one for the silent treatment. She'd been a yeller. She'd shout at him long after he'd slammed the front door, then call his phone and scream at him some more on his voicemail.

This—Tara's stony silence—was almost harder to handle. He glanced at her. "You gonna say something?"

Nothing. She crossed her arms and stared straight ahead.

Wonderful. How long would this shit last? He'd feel better if she did yell at him a little. The angry silence punctuated by the occasional deadly glare would make for a lovely drive to the next venue. Real cozy roommate conditions, too.

Oh well. It wasn't the first time Jace had pissed off a woman, and he was certain it wouldn't be the last. It didn't change the fact he'd been totally in the right. Seven Minutes in Heaven with a guy she'd known for what? An hour? What the hell had Tara been thinking? She hadn't been, obviously.

How much had she drunk, anyway? She hadn't even been gone that long, but her eyes were glassy and unfocused—when she looked at him long enough for him to see them. Jace refused to believe it was the effect of Klint's kisses, so he was going to attribute it to whatever alcohol those guys had given her.

Thinking of that kid with his hands on her had Jace clenching his jaw. More than his hands were on her. Jace didn't miss how the bastard had scraped the skin around her mouth raw. How the hell rough had he kissed her? Jace's anger built.

"You have to be more careful, Tara." He tried to keep his voice even and calm. He failed.

They reached the hotel lot. He hadn't even

shifted into park yet when she flung the door open and jumped out of the truck. She was going to be the death of him, if she didn't get herself killed first.

"Dammit, Tara." Jace got out, slammed his door, and strode after her.

Tara had taken her key. By the time Jace reached her, she was glaring at him from inside their room. Right before she slammed the door in his face.

Gritting his teeth, he dug in his pocket and took out his copy of the key. If she chained the door, he didn't know what he'd do. Probably kick it in, given his current mood.

Thank goodness, she hadn't. When he turned the handle and shoved, the door swung open. He drew in a bracing breath and went inside.

He found her standing by her bed, pawing through her suitcase. "Going somewhere?"

"The bathroom. Is that okay with you? Do I need your permission to do that, too?" Jaw set, she stood, holding the oversized T-shirt and sweats that functioned as her pajamas. The same items that made her look like a little kid swimming in someone else's clothes, which Jace found in direct contrast to her razor sharp personality.

At least she'd talked to him, though she might not after he'd had his say. "No, you don't need my permission. But that's because there aren't a couple of bull riders intent on getting into your pants in our bathroom."

"Maybe I want them in my pants! Ever think of that?" She slammed the bathroom door hard, as if shouting hadn't already gotten her point across.

"Nice. Real nice," he yelled through the laughably thin door. "That's not happening on my watch, so you can just forget about it."

He heard the sound of the lock being turned. Hell of a lot of good that lock would do her. If Jace wanted in that room, he'd be in that room. Lucky for her, he didn't see the need to break in there. With no window in the bathroom, there was nowhere for her to go. Tara could sleep in there for all he cared. At least he'd know where she was.

This felt familiar. He was back on level footing. He'd had plenty of experience with screaming and door slamming. Fighting was as natural as breathing to him after all his time with the master— Jacqueline. Tara had no idea who she was dealing with.

Jace reached for the top button on his jeans, about to change back into the shorts he'd been wearing before he'd had to rescue Tara, when the cell phone vibrated inside his pocket. He pulled it out and saw the expected name. JACQUELINE. He was in no mood for her. Instead of watching it ring, or hitting IGNORE and then shutting it off, Jace hit the button to answer.

"Dammit, Jacqueline. Stop calling me." Jace disconnected and powered off the phone. With his adrenaline pumping from having done something about the Jacqueline situation at last, he tossed the cell onto the bed.

The sounds of water running and then a drawer closing loud and hard, brought Jace back to the issue at hand. He had to figure out how to deal with this other situation—the one slamming things around in the bathroom.

Sighing, he changed for bed, though he doubted either one of them would rest easily tonight.

*   *   *

The doc and his team, Tara included, walked past where Jace stood behind the chutes. She shot him a glare and kept moving.

Dillon watched her go by. "Things seem a little icy around here."

"Yup." Jace's gaze tracked Tara's progress to the medical room. She didn't have a smile or a word for anyone she passed. At least, it seemed she was giving everyone the cold shoulder, not just him.

"Trouble in paradise?" Dillon asked.

"You could say that." More like trouble in heaven caused by Tara's seven minutes there with Klint.

Dillon glanced at Jace. "She looks pissed as hell at you."

"Yup. She's mad because I pulled her out of the bar last night." Or, more accurately, because he'd pulled her out of the closet before that rookie had a chance to finish molesting her, which apparently she'd wanted to happen.

"Well, you did kind of drag her out of there like she was a child."

Jace stared at Dillon. "Dillon, she's Tuck's little sister. She's barely old enough to be legal to drink, and she's traveling with me. What the hell should I have done? Handed her a condom and sent her over to Klint's hotel room for the night?"

That would happen over his dead body. Jace's gaze swept the riders and spotted the bastard in question. His eyes narrowed.

"You sure that's all it is? You're just taking care of her like her brother would?" Dillon asked.

"Of course." Jace spun to frown at his friend. "What else would it be?"

Dillon shook his head. "I don't know if you're lying to me or to yourself about there being nothing between you and her. But there is definitely something between you two."

"No, there's not. You're crazy. I told you, Dillon, she hates me." Now, more than ever.

"If she hated you that much, she wouldn't be traveling with you. Besides, there's a fine line between love and hate, Jace."

"What are you, some sort of a psychiatrist now?" Jace screwed up his mouth.

"Just calling it like I see it." Dillon shrugged, eyeing Jace with a sweeping glance that traveled down to his boots. "You, uh, gonna put your chaps on? They're ready to flank your bull. You're up next section."

Sure enough, when Jace glanced over, he saw the bull he'd drawn had been brought up by the stock handlers and was ready to be flanked and put in the chute. It stood confined more or less patiently between the metal rails, waiting for him or the stock contractor to loop the flank strap around its hindquarters.

"Crap." Jace had been so distracted by the shit happening with Tara, he hadn't been paying attention. He'd better start.

Only a man who'd lost his mind would strap his hand to a ton of bucking bull when his head wasn't in the game. Dillon was dead wrong about the love and hate thing, but if nothing else, Tara sure did drive Jace crazy.

He strode to where he'd flipped his vest and chaps over the metal rails, and eyed the bull one more time as he swung the chaps around his hips. He didn't know anything about Apocalypse, the bull he'd drawn. He'd normally have asked around and found out what kind of bucker he was—if he'd spin left into Jace's riding hand, or right, away from it.

As Jace buckled the chap straps around one thigh, he saw the handlers were loading Apocalypse into a chute with a left-hand delivery.

Hopefully, the bull would spin left out of the chute when the gate swung open on his left. But if Jace had learned anything over the years, it was that bulls were unpredictable. More than that, contrary to popular belief, bulls were not stupid creatures. They were smart and cunning and, as if they knew it was all one big game, took great pleasure in bucking off a rider. They could get real tricky as they tried to dislodge the man on their back, sometimes changing things up mid-spin. The damn animals could feel the rider's position shift, and would react accordingly to take advantage of it.

Jace was about to enter into a mental and physical battle with an animal ten times his size, and his head was still full of Tara's bullshit. Not good. That could land him in the medical room, where Tara, in her current mood, would probably slip him some cyanide rather than tend to his injuries. He drew in a breath and forced himself to focus.

Five bulls were loaded and ready in the chutes for the next section. Show time. He zipped up the front of his safety vest. He'd yet to put on his glove, or put his bull rope on Apocalypse.

He grabbed the rope from the rail and headed for the chute.

"Give me, dude." Dillon extended his hand to take the bull rope Jace held.

"Thanks." Thank God for Dillon, always there and willing to help. On a normal day, Jace would have handled things on his own. It was not one of those days. Frigging Tara. Enough to make a man lose his mind, she was.

While Dillon leaned into the chute and looped Jace's rope just behind the bull's shoulders, Jace pulled on his riding glove. He flexed his left hand inside the glove to make sure it was on good and tight. With his bare right hand, he pulled his mouth guard out of the pocket in his safety vest and slipped it between his lips.

After clamping his hat lower on his head, he climbed over the top rail, straddling the chute above the bull's broad back. He lowered himself onto the animal. Apocalypse responded to the weight by bouncing a few times in the chute and then leaning against the back rails, pinning Jace's leg in the process.

With his booted foot trapped between the animal's side and the metal rail, Jace wouldn't be able to get into proper position, and the damn animal knew it.

"Yah! Move over." Dillon was there to help once again, waving his hat as he yelled.

The whites of the bull's eyes showed as the animal glared at him. Scary how human the bulls could act sometimes. This one seemed to be telling them all to go to blazes.

Just what Jace needed—a bull with attitude—although a smart-ass bull might be rank enough to earn him a damn good score. He hoped the bull bucked out in the arena as hard as he was leaning on his leg in the chute.

Jace slid his left hand into the handle of his bull rope. One of the stock guys balanced on the outside rail, grabbed the tail of the rope, and pulled. With his right hand, Jace grabbed the length the man passed to him. He wrapped the rope tight around his gloved hand, wove it between his fingers, and pounded his fist tight.

The bull was still leaning against the back wall, pinning Jace's leg. Reinforcements arrived on the chute to help. Justin slid a padded board between the rails and the bull's side, forcing the animal to move over. The moment he felt the weight lift, Jace moved his leg away from the bull rope. To leave the chute with his spur hooked in the rope would mean an automatic penalty. He got his feet positioned, his butt fairly centered and that was all he could do.

With as good a seat as he was going to get, Jace nodded to the gateman. The gate swung wide and Apocalypse spun as he'd hoped, to the left and into Jace's riding hand.

Years of practice and experience had put Jace in the zone the moment his ass had hit that bull's back. Once the gate opened, muscle memory and instinct took over. The arena resonated with the combination of familiar sounds—pounding music, the cheers of the crowd, and the announcer's amplified voice—but he didn't really hear any of it. It all morphed together to become white noise, indistinct as it surrounded him.

He didn't think about his next move, or try to anticipate the bull's. Trying to second-guess a bull was a sure way to hit the dirt before the whistle. Making the wrong call or shifting in the incorrect direction was all it took.

No, this sport was not cerebral; not one you could plan like plays on a football field. There was no time to think about a next move during an eight-second ride. It was a competition based on action and reaction, and the speed of each participant's reflexes, both of the man and the beast.

The world seemed to spin around Jace in a swirl of colors. Apocalypse went left, then dipped low in front while kicking high, almost vertical, with its hind legs. Jace broke at the hips, absorbing the motion, keeping on top of his rope while still leaning back enough to not collide with the back of the animal's boney skull when it whipped up again.

Changing things up, the bull reversed direction. It pushed off with its front legs and went to the right, settling into a flat spin away from Jace's hand. Jace fought to stay centered as the centrifugal force of the spin threatened to push him off the side.

The blare of the buzzer cut through the air, marking the end of the eight seconds. He had covered his ride. Adrenaline pumping, he felt as if he could ride the bull all day. Luckily, he didn't have to. The eight seconds would get him a score.

Reaching for the tail of the bull rope, he tugged and released the wrap. When his hand was free, he flipped his leg over the bull's head and leaped off on the outside of the spin. Bending his knees to absorb the impact, he landed feet first on the arena dirt, as perfect as an Olympic gymnast. In this sport, when the dismount was off a moving animal, that was pretty damn impressive.

He looked for Apocalypse. The horned red bull was still loose in the arena. It would suck to finish a great ride and get trampled by the bull after it was over. Jace saw two of the bullfighters driving the animal toward the out gate. The third retrieved Jace's rope from where it had landed in the dirt after falling off the bull.

The adrenaline continued to pump through his

veins. His hand shook as he reached to take the rope.

"Great ride, Jace."

He pulled his mouth guard out and accepted the slap on the back from the bullfighter. "Thanks, man."

It had felt like a great ride. Still, he looked toward the scoreboard for confirmation. It didn't matter what he thought. It was up to the four judges scoring.

As the numbers appeared on the board, the announcer's voice penetrated Jace's consciousness. "And it's a ninety-point ride for Jace Mills on Apocalypse. That puts him in the lead."

The *lead*. Jace punched the air with his fist. The long round was over. If he held on to the lead for the championship round, if he rode his bull in the short go, he could walk out with the buckle, the winning purse, and the added money, which was nothing to sneeze at.

He could win this competition. Take it all. First place. Maybe there was something to his wearing new underwear, after all.

Two guys offered Jace congratulations for the ninety-point ride as he made his way back behind the chutes, but it was the girl walking past and trying to ignore him who held Jace's attention. The moment their gazes collided, Tara yanked hers away.

"Oh, man. She's still pissed at you." Dillon, beside him, shook his head and laughed.

"Yup. Seems so." Jace couldn't deny that.

Dillon turned from watching Tara walk away and pounded Jace's back. "Good ride, though. You're definitely walking home with that buckle tonight."

"Thanks. Let's hope." The buckle would be nice, but the prize money would be more useful.

Not that either would help make Tara less pissed off. Jace was certain of one thing and that was that she was no buckle bunny. She wasn't interested in his payout for the night or a big showy championship buckle. All she wanted from Jace was a ride and a room. He guessed she hadn't realized his providing both came with strings attached—strings that were proving difficult to keep a hold on. But he could be as stubborn as she could. Maybe more. She was going to have to accept that. Like it or not, Jace was the boss, at least for the next few weeks.

Boy, was she gonna hate that.

Chapter Ten

Now that Tara was working with the medical crew, the events always seemed to fly by. Before she knew it, it was time for the championship round. Her workday was coming to an end, which meant she'd have to get in the truck and go back to the hotel room with Jace, the man she couldn't even look at without her blood pressure rising.

He was in the lead and would win the night if he covered his bull in the short go. Since Jace was footing the bill for their lodging, she should be happy he was going to walk away with the purse, but she was too mad at him.

She'd seen his ride in the long round. Not on purpose. She just happened to be walking behind the chutes during it and turned to see what all the cheering was about.

As much as she hated to admit it, he'd looked good out there. Of course, she'd rather die than tell cocky, know-it-all Jace that.

Tara chose to be more impressed with the younger guys' rides. They might not look as pretty as

Jace did on top of the bull and their moves hadn't been textbook perfect the way his had been, but they'd only been riding a few years. They'd have to have ridden in competition for a decade to be able to look as good as he had.

Jace had enough experience under his belt to hang on through the reversal in direction. He knew that after the bull settled into a flat spin he'd better dress up the ride by spurring with his outside leg and showing a little daylight between him and the bull to impress the judges. But he should ride well. He was like thirty. The damn man had been riding practically forever. That's why it was important to give the rookies more credit for what they accomplished in the arena with their limited years of experience.

In fact, Tara decided to go out of her way to compliment one of the younger guys, just to show her support. "Great ride, Justin."

Justin's eyes grew round when she spoke to him. He glanced behind him and then back to her. "Um, yeah. Thanks, Tara." The words were barely out of his mouth before he turned tail and ran away, faster than if there'd been a bull hot on his heels.

Maryann, the only other female on the sports medicine crew, watched him go. She turned to frown at Tara. "What's up with that?"

Tara let out a short breath. "I wish I knew."

"Maryann?" A male voice drew their attention.

Tara glanced past Maryann to see Klint striding up. "Can I get an ice pack? My shoulder's killing me."

"Hey, Klint." Not real sure how to act around him after last night, Tara forced a smile.

He stopped mid-step when he saw Tara standing behind Maryann. "Um, hi, Tara." He turned his attention back to Maryann. "Can I get that ice?"

"Sure thing." Maryann nodded. "Just give me one minute. I gotta run and tell the doc something, then I'll wrap you up."

"I can do it, Maryann." Tara took a step forward. She had nothing to do at the moment. "Klint, come on back with—"

"Uh, you know what? That's okay. Now that I think about it. It's feeling much better." Klint rolled his shoulder and winced at the pain, but still nodded. "Yup. Feeling much better. Think I'll let it be for tonight." He took off past Tara, looking as if he wanted to get as far from her as he could.

"What the—" Tara let out a string of cuss words that would have gotten her paddled by her momma when she was younger. Hell, maybe even at this age.

Maryann shook her head. "What was that about? Tara, what have you done to these guys?"

"It wasn't me. It was Jace." Tara clenched her jaw. Just saying his name reminded her how very angry she was with him.

"Jace? What did he do?"

"I was hanging out in the bar with Justin and Klint last night, and Jace came storming in. He went all caveman and dragged me out of there like he owned me or something."

Maryann glanced at Jace behind the chutes getting ready for his ride in the short go, and then she focused back on Tara. "And does he?"

"Excuse me?" Tara frowned at Maryann.

"I meant, are you two an item?"

"No." Tara said it with enough force to leave no doubt in Maryann's mind.

"Well, it's obvious those guys think you are. There's no way a couple of rookies are going to get between a veteran rider and his girl."

"I'm not his girl. We're traveling buddies. Nothing more. Jace seems to think because my older brother isn't here, he has to step in and play daddy and protect me from the evils of all bull riders."

Maryann held up her hands, palms forward. "I believe you, Tara. You don't have to convince me, but as long as those two guys think you're with Jace, they're gonna steer clear so he doesn't think they're flirting with you. Once word spreads, all the riders will stay away."

"So no riders are going to talk to me for the rest of this internship because they think I'm Jace's?" Tara didn't know what angered her more about that concept—that once a woman started dating a man she became his property and couldn't even talk to other men, or that she wasn't even with Jace but would still be shunned by all the single men on the circuit, anyway.

"Sorry, sweetie." Maryann shrugged. "Maybe they'll ease up after a while. Sounds like it's pretty fresh, the whole caveman display and all."

"If Klint would rather walk around in pain than let me get him an ice pack, I certainly hope they ease up soon." It was going to be hard for Tara to do her job otherwise.

Though, how cowardly was that? If Klint really liked her, he shouldn't give a crap about Jace. He should go for it with the girl he wanted and to hell with the consequences. That he didn't feel that way—Justin, either—made Tara feel pretty damn crappy.

"Hey. You have to stay late tonight or no?" Jace

had snuck up on her while she'd been busy hating him.

Tara narrowed her eyes. Even if Klint was a big chicken, Jace had caused this mess by acting like he was the boss of her. He certainly was not and she wouldn't give him the pleasure of thinking he was. In fact, she wouldn't even give him the pleasure of answering his question. She turned with a huff and strode toward the medical room.

"Nice, Tara. Your momma would be so proud of your manners." His smart-ass comment followed her as she strode toward the back.

There truly was no getting away from him. Not at work. Not in the truck. Not in the room. How bad an idea this traveling together thing had been was becoming painfully apparent.

Chapter Eleven

"So . . . you, ah, ever going to talk to me again?" Jace asked as they walked into their room after a silent drive from the arena. He closed and locked the door and still she hadn't answered.

It should have been a good night. He'd won the event. Any other time, he would be out celebrating. Drinking away some of the prize money with the other riders. Instead, he was back in his cheap hotel room trying to make nice with a seething Tara.

He'd waited until they'd been alone to even try to talk to her again, anticipating a screaming fight he'd rather not have in public. But as the seconds ticked by with no response, he started to think Tara's snort as she'd stalked past him and into the room was going to be her only reply.

Finally, she spun to face him, her features contorted in anger. "Why? Would you care?"

Jace raised a brow as he moved farther into the room and tossed his truck keys on the dresser. "That depends. If you're gonna throw this shit attitude at me, then I might rather you be silent."

She straightened her spine.

Uh-oh. He was in for a big one. A woman took on a certain appearance and posture when she was about to unleash a good rant, and Tara had that look. He was starting to regret standing so close to her, but it wasn't in him to back up. At least, not until she picked up something to hurl at him, though that was more Jacqueline's style than Tara's . . . he hoped.

"Do you know that Justin and Klint won't even talk to me now? Hell, Klint wouldn't let me get him an ice pack tonight when he was hurting. They're both afraid of *you*." She pointed to him with the hard poke of one finger into his chest.

"Really?" That was an interesting tidbit. One Jace enjoyed a bit too much. The rookies were intimidated by him. Enough to steer clear of Tara.

"Oh, my God. Don't you smile about that, you, you—grrr!" She fisted her hands in her hair. She'd left it down and loose rather than braid it, so there was plenty for her to grab and yank on. It made her display even more dramatic.

Was he smiling? Yeah, he was. Jace ran a hand over his mouth to erase it, equally amused that the two kids were afraid of him as he was at the miracle that Tara seemed to have run out of words . . . or at least out of insults. He'd better enjoy it. He was sure it was only a momentary lapse and wouldn't last long.

She drew in a deep breath. "How dare you even think that you have the right to tell me what I can and can't do? You are not my brother, Jace. We're not even friends."

Nope, not out of words yet. But Jace couldn't sit idly by and listen to her insults like he usually did.

"No, you're right, Tara. We're not family. We're not friends. We're traveling partners."

"Yes, you gave me a ride. That still doesn't give you the right to boss me around. I have two brothers. You don't get to act like the third one because I'm riding in your passenger seat." She folded her arms and turned her head so she was staring at nothing but the stained ceiling above them.

Jace took a step closer. He had her trapped in the corner so she couldn't get away. More than that, she'd have to look at him or shut her eyes to avoid it. In that position, that close, she'd have no other choice but to see him and hear what he had to say.

"Tara, you listen to me and you listen good. You don't know what it means to be traveling partners, so I'm gonna explain it to you. It means we're more than friends, and it's as important as being kin. It means we take care of each other."

"But—"

"You had your say. You're gonna let me have mine."

When she clamped her lips shut, Jace went on. "Being traveling partners means that when I find you drunk and alone in a situation you shouldn't be in, I get you out of there. It's what Tuck has done for me back when we rode together. It's what he'd expect me to do for you now that you and I are traveling together."

Tara drew in a loud, angry breath through her nose. Her body vibrated. Damn, she was pissed. She didn't talk, not even to yell.

Jace took advantage of the silence to try and explain, not knowing if she was even capable of listening to reason. "Tara, don't you understand that I was worried about you? I didn't know where you were. If you were safe or not. Last I knew, I'd made you cry and you were wandering around on foot in a strange town all alone."

"No, Jace. *You* don't understand. I'm tired of men treating me like I'm Tuck's helpless little sister. First Logan. Now even you. You! The one person I expected to not give a shit what I do, suddenly cares and comes riding in to save my virtue. You know what? Justin, Klint, they didn't care whose little sister I was. They treated me like a woman. They were going to make me feel like one."

"You wanted them to take advantage of you?"

"What I want is some experience so the next time I fall in love, the guy doesn't choose a 'ho from New York over me because she knows how to catch a man and I don't." Tara's body still vibrated, but it no longer seemed to be with rage. Her eyes filled with tears that he hadn't been prepared for.

"Ah, shit." Mad at himself for making her cry not once but twice in two days, Jace did the only thing he knew to comfort her. As her shoulders began to shake and the tears came in full force, he reached out and pulled her against him. His arms wrapped around her, he pressed her head to his chest, and felt her tears soak through his shirt. "Listen to me. Emma's not a 'ho—"

Head still buried against his chest, Tara reached out and pounded his arm with one small, surprisingly powerful fist. "Shut up. Don't you defend her."

He smiled against the top of her head at her feistiness even through tears. "Let me finish. I was going to say that Logan's got what? Eighteen? Twenty years on you? Maybe it was just that Emma's older than you are. Closer to his own age."

Tara shook her head. It was a lost cause. It didn't matter what Jace said; she wasn't in the mood to listen.

He still had to make one more point. "You going out and hooking up with random bull riders won't change anything. It won't make Logan not married, or Emma not pregnant."

Tara pulled away. "Was she already pregnant at their wedding?"

"Crap." Jace cursed at the anger he saw in Tara's face. The anger he'd caused. Reminding her about the baby hadn't been a smart idea. Tuck was going to tan his hide for spilling the beans. "Tara, I wasn't supposed to tell anyone—"

"Jace, was she pregnant?" The determination in her words told him not to bother arguing.

"Yeah. I'm pretty sure."

"See?" Tara threw her hands in the air. "That proves my point."

"How?"

"She was obviously giving it up to Logan that weekend she was here for Tuck and Becca's wedding. If I'd gotten to have sex with him first, he wouldn't have—"

"Stop. No, Tara. It wouldn't have mattered. Logan's not the type to go for a woman just because she puts out. There had to have been something there to start with." As much as Jace hated to admit it, he knew that had to be the truth. Logan was a good guy. A damn, annoyingly perfect Prince Charming who made Jace feel like a frog in comparison most days, but still a good guy.

"No." She shook her head. Her eyes seemed unfocused, blind to Jace and the rest of her surroundings. "I'm going to get experience and then I'll be ready. I'll hook up with every bull rider on this circuit if I have to, and next time, I won't lose to any woman."

It seemed to Jace a pretty girl like Tara wouldn't have to resort to letting guys like Klint grope her in a dark broom closet in the back of a bar to get experience with men. Not that he agreed with her plan to get the experience in the first place. But a smart, pretty girl like her should have guys her own age lined up at the door begging to be her boyfriend. Bringing her flowers. Taking her out to dinner.

Then again, Tara was stubborn enough to make even simple things difficult. Jace sighed at the truth of that. "Now you're just acting immature and talking like a child."

"Stop treating me like one! I'm going to go out and be with any guy who'll let me just to prove to you and every other man in my life that I'm an adult. And you know what? You can't stop me." She pounded his chest with both fists and his control slipped.

"Well, Tara, Logan's not here to see you doing that, and it sure as shit won't impress me." Jace drew in a breath, more frustrated than he thought she'd be capable of making him. She was enough to make him want to tear out his own hair. "You really think letting some kid kiss you is the way to prove to everyone you're grown up? Is that what all this shit in the closet with Klint was about?"

"Yes!" She stamped her foot and proved his point that she was behaving like an adolescent.

"Then that just proves what a foolish child you are, Tara. You don't go to a boy to do a man's job."

"I had no one else to go to. You're like a watchdog, chasing everyone away."

The stupidity of Tara putting herself in a compromising position on a whim pissed him off. Deep down, Jace knew she'd do it again—probably every chance she got—just to teach him a lesson for trying to stop her.

"You really wanna be kissed that badly?" Jace's anger made his voice sound husky. Deep and intense.

"Yes, I do." Her eyes flashed with defiance.

"Fine." Jace leaned closer until a crease furrowed Tara's brow.

If she insisted on putting herself into a closet with a kid she knew nothing about because she wanted a damn kiss, Jace would give her a kiss. One she'd never forget. One that would make those rookies seem like kindergarteners. And he wouldn't scrape her face raw the way Klint had doing it. Jace shaved every night before the competition because real men didn't have anything to prove by showing the world they could grow some hair on their chin.

He grabbed the back of her neck with one hand, much as he had when he'd hauled her out of the bar, but his intentions were very different. He pulled her closer until their faces were inches apart.

Her lower lip trembled as her big blue eyes widened. For once, she focused on his face. Jace didn't ask her again. He brought his other hand up, cupped her cheek and took possession of her lips, determined to kiss the childish pout right off them.

It started out hard. He wanted to punish her. Teach her a lesson. Scare the stupid out of her so she didn't try anything so risky again. But she didn't back off like he thought she would. Instead, she kissed him back.

He'd expected her lips to be hard and unyielding,

just like her attitude toward him most days. They
weren't. They were soft and giving, receptive to his
taking. He took a step closer. With one booted foot
between her feet, his thigh fit perfectly between her
legs.

Angling his head, he changed the kiss, worked
her lips as he marveled at how different it felt to kiss
a mouth he didn't know intimately. It had been
quite a while since he'd kissed anyone other than
his ex.

Exploring the new sensations, Jace moved his
right hand down Tara's back, landing on the slender
curve of her hip. At the same time, Tara had gone
from bracing against his chest, to wrapping her arms
around his waist. When she slipped her hands into
the back pockets of his jeans, he had a feeling she
was planning on being there for a while. Fine. A girl
as stubborn as Tara needed a long, thorough lesson.

She opened her lips beneath his. Jace didn't ignore the silent invitation, but he also wasn't going to
rush to give her what she wanted. She needed a lesson in patience as much as—more, actually—a lesson that she shouldn't go into closets to kiss men.

He drew her lower lip between his and scraped it
with a good bit of teeth. She drew in a shuddering
breath that had him smiling against her mouth,
thinking that Klint probably hadn't gotten that reaction from her. Stroking her face beneath his thumb,
Jace decided to give her a bit of what he knew she
wanted. He ran just the tip of his tongue along the
inside of her lower lip, and then repeated it with
the upper one.

Tara opened farther for him and he didn't deny
either of them. He plunged into the wet heat of her
mouth. She met his tongue with her own, stroking

against him in an erotic dance that had him pressing his lower body against hers before he realized what he was doing.

Somewhere, somehow it had gone from Jace proving a point, to him being rock hard in his jeans and ready to take whatever Tara wanted to give.

That realization had him breaking the kiss. But damn the devil inside him, he didn't pull back. He stayed pressed up against her, his mouth a breath away from her face. "That kiss good enough for you?"

"Yes." Tara's gaze moved from Jace's lips to his eyes.

Had her eyes always been such an intense color? As deep as the indigo sky. Jace dragged his attention away from the desire still showing in them and forced his focus back to the situation at hand. "You going to stop this foolishness about hooking up with all the bull riders on the circuit?"

"Yes." She dipped her head in the slightest of nods.

In the small part of his brain that was still functioning, he knew he should be very concerned she was being so agreeable. But with a considerable amount of his blood currently in his cock, there wasn't much oxygen left for thinking.

"I'm going to step away now, and then wash this arena dirt off me and get some rest." Why he was telling her this rather than doing it wasn't clear to him. Maybe it was because he had no desire to step away. "Okay?"

"No." Her compliance had come to an end.

"No?" Jace asked. "Why not?"

"I'm not done yet." Tara pressed her body closer against his.

With her arms clamped around his lower half like a vise, there wasn't much he could do about it. Not that he tried. She leaned in and rose just enough to nip at his lower lip, like he had hers before.

Tara ran the tip of her tongue along the seam between his lips, sending a shudder through him. The student had learned too well. That was just a passing notion before Jace lost his train of thought as Tara kissed him, plunging her tongue between his lips.

On some level he knew he was treading all over the rules. He shouldn't be kissing his best friend's little sister, any more than he should be kissing his traveling partner. His intentions had been good to start—kissing her to save her from acting a fool with the other riders.

That initial rationale had kind of become a moot point when he'd started to enjoy it. He'd deal with the gray areas in his conscience later. It was just nice to know he still had it in him to kiss someone who wasn't Jacqueline and like it. He had begun to doubt that was possible.

Hell, parts of him liked kissing Tara very much. Particularly the part that Tara was rubbing against as she rode his leg. It was making the lesson feel much too real.

Jace pulled back from her mouth. "Tara."

"What?" She sounded breathless.

He realized he was getting a bit breathless himself. "We should stop."

"No."

"But—"

"Jace, if you stop now I'm just going to—"

"Shut the hell up, Tara." He didn't let her finish her sentence. Didn't need to. He knew what the threat was going to be—that she'd go find Klint or some other guy to kiss.

Jace gripped her face harder between his fingers and crashed his mouth into hers.

Kissing was innocent enough. Hell, he'd been kissing girls since middle school. Even the dry humping Tara was doing with his leg wasn't so far over the line he shouldn't cross. As long as their clothes were still on, it meant nothing.

A small sound of pleasure came from her. It cut straight through Jace. Another few minutes and she'd be coming apart. His male pride swelled with the knowledge that he'd caused it.

Jace pulled away from her mouth and brushed his lips against her ear. "I bet Klint didn't make you feel like this. Was he even man enough to make you come?"

Her breath came fast and shallow. "Not sure. Don't think so."

"You're not sure?" He laughed. It couldn't have been very good then.

"No. What does it feel like?"

That panted question stopped Jace dead. He pulled back from working her earlobe with his mouth. "What do you mean, what's it feel like?"

"I never have, so I don't know."

"Never have what? Had an orgasm?" The conversation was ramping up his guilt another notch, while at the same time making him grow harder.

"I don't think so. Would I know if I had?"

Jace cursed under his breath. "Yeah. You'd know."

What the hell kind of men had this girl been with that not one of them had brought her to orgasm? No wonder she was a big ball of need, willing to go to anyone to satisfy her. And Jace could be the first to do it for her.

If he'd thought breathing had been difficult before, it was impossible now. He swallowed hard.

"Unzip your jeans." Even as he thought how bad an idea it was, the words escaped his mouth.

Reaching between them, she did, faster than he'd imagined was possible. Then she went a step further. She pushed her jeans down her thighs and let them fall to the ground where they pooled around her booted feet.

There went his excuse that it was okay as long as they were both fully clothed. Though her shirt still covered her—mostly—and he was dressed. He made a decision. He'd be quick and efficient. Get her off and then go take a nice long shower alone.

Plan set, Jace slipped one hand beneath the hem of her shirt and over warm bare skin until he reached her panties.

He repeated the details to himself. She was mainly covered. So was he. This was no big deal. One quick orgasm to satisfy her and keep her away from the other guys. That's it. With that excuse assuaging his guilt, Jace ran one finger over the cotton covering the juncture of her thighs.

Her eyes closed, Tara leaned her head back against the wall. Ready. Waiting.

It would go faster without the panties in his way. Getting it done quick seemed his only saving grace. His pulse pounding, Jace slid his hand between the flat of her stomach and the cotton of her underwear and kept going until he connected with the heat between her lips. With the tip of one finger he separated her flesh. The moment he touched the sensitive spot hidden there she sucked in a sharp breath.

No turning back now. Setting a slow pace to start, he circled her, first one direction, and then the other. She tipped her hips forward as her mouth opened on a breath. Apparently none of the guys she'd been with before now knew how to find a clit.

Lucky for Tara, Jace was intimately familiar with where it was located and what to do with it. He watched her face as he worked her. As the momentum of his touch built, she reacted. A frown creased her brow as her palms flattened against the wall behind her. All this, from just one finger. How would she react if he dropped to his knees and used his mouth on her? Jace pushed that image away, but not before the wrongness of it hit him hard. Just not hard enough to make him stop what he was doing or make his hard-on go down.

Her mouth opened wider as the furrow in her brow deepened. Jace knew a woman's orgasm face when he saw it. She was close, but not over the edge yet. He leaned close and dipped his tongue into the whorls of her ear. That caused the reaction he was hoping for. A visible shudder ran through her.

He smiled against her ear and said, "Come on, darlin'. Almost there. Just let go."

The soft words had her releasing a moan. Jace heard as well as felt when her orgasm broke. Tara let out a breathy cry as she began to shake. Her hips bucked as she pressed against his hand and came hard. He kept working her, through the first wave, through her strangled breaths and soft cries until she was a writhing mass before him.

If it was going to be her first orgasm, and her last by his hand, he'd make sure she didn't forget it—or go looking to another guy for more anytime soon. He didn't slow down, even when she pulled her hips back. He knew she'd be so sensitive the pleasure could border on pain, but he needed her to feel it. All of it.

He kept direct contact with her clit, but eased off a bit on the pressure. Still, he kept working her until another smaller climax hit. Finally, when she was twitching and gasping for breath, he gentled his touch to let her come down slow and easy.

Feeling the need to recover from Tara's orgasm, Jace braced his left forearm on the wall above her head and let his head fall against it. He tried to regain some semblance of sanity. His dick was so hard he'd come if she even breathed near it.

That wasn't going to happen. Not now. Not ever. Though he didn't miss the fact his hand still seemed to be on her pussy. He pressed her clit one more time and felt how swollen it was from the attention he'd shown it.

A tremor ran through her from the touch.

Enjoying the reaction, Jace smiled and stroked a finger over her one more time before he left her pussy alone and moved to rest his palm against her belly.

He didn't know how long after, Tara let out a shaky breath. "Wow."

He laughed. It seemed she wasn't mad at him anymore and she'd been reduced to one word sentences. If it lasted, what he'd done would have been well worth it.

Still, as much as Jace prided himself on being good in bed—or while standing next to it—he never assumed he was the only man capable of making a woman come. He couldn't seem to wrap his mind around the concept that Tara had never experienced an orgasm before. "I can't believe all the guys you've been with haven't been able to get you off."

"I haven't been with any guys." Her words were spoken so low, Jace couldn't believe he'd heard them correctly.

He leaned back enough to see her face. "You're kidding, right?"

She rolled her eyes. "Why would I lie to you?"

Jace's mouth opened but he had no words. Tara was a virgin at twenty-one? No, older than that. She was twenty-two. He'd always known she had a huge schoolgirl crush on Logan, but never in his wildest dreams had Jace imagined she'd saved herself through four years of college.

She'd saved herself for twenty-two freaking years, but after just a few days traveling with him, she'd already been alone in a closet with a random bull rider, and was standing in a hotel room with her jeans around her ankles and his hand in her underwear. He corrected that situation right quick, pulling his hand away and bracing it against the wall so he could push back from her.

"So now you think I'm a child again?" She scowled at him.

"No. But God almighty, Tara, you should have told me that before, not after."

"Then you would have stopped."

"You're damn right I would have stopped."

"Why? You wouldn't be preserving my chastity or whatever. I already told you. If it wasn't you, it would've been someone else."

Small consolation, that was. *Somebody else* wouldn't have been betraying the trust her brother had placed in him. How had things spiraled so out of control? The one woman besides Jacqueline he'd touched in over a year and he chose his best friend's virgin little sister. Talk about feeling like a piece of crap. He was truly messed up. He'd managed to justify what he was doing while in the midst of the act, but now that it was done, he couldn't seem to.

"I gotta get out of here." Jace reached for the dresser and grabbed his keys, and then turned for the door.

"Where are you going?" Tara kicked off her boots, freed herself from the tangle of pants around her feet and took a step after him.

"Hell if I know." There was nowhere he could run from his own thoughts. He yanked open the door, and then spun back to her as a new concern hit him. "Please, Tara, don't go anywhere."

Not that she ever listened to what she was told, but he couldn't have her wandering around town again, slipping into closets with strange men to prove a point.

Standing before him in just a shirt, she nodded.

His shame doubled at the sight of her. Jace closed the door on the vision of Tara post-orgasm. All bright eyed, pink cheeked and looking concerned as she watched him go. He knew he couldn't drive away and leave her all alone in a cheap hotel in a strange town. He didn't trust her to stay put any more than he trusted himself not to teach her another lesson if she disobeyed him.

The image of putting Tara over his knee and spanking her for her disobedience and for making him worry hit him hard. It ramped up the horror over his own behavior another notch, even as the appeal of the scene sent a tingle through him.

A freaking virgin. Of all the many things Tara

was—obstinate, stubborn, bitchy, contrary, and tempting as all hell sexually—why did she have to be a virgin, too?

He clicked the door locks open and hoisted himself into the driver seat of his truck. There he sat, not moving, not driving. He just sat.

It seemed as if he'd spent a lot of hours in the cab of the truck hiding from a woman, but he never imagined he'd be there with an erection hard enough to drive nails from watching Tara come at his touch.

He'd have thought the virgin revelation would have done in the hard-on from hell. It hadn't. Nope. Now he was horrified and horny, and there was nothing he could do about either feeling.

Jace groaned. "Just great."

Chapter Twelve

Tara peeked between the window curtains. The truck remained parked in front of their room, and Jace was still behind the wheel, but the engine wasn't running. He didn't seem to have any plans to go anywhere.

How long was he going to sit out there? Until morning? He'd slept in his truck the night he'd had it out with Jacqueline in Stillwater. How could kissing her seem as bad to him as that blowout?

She let the curtain fall back into place and made a decision. She'd let him stew for a little while longer, but then she was going out there and getting him.

What the hell was all the hiding about anyway? Men were supposed to want any sort of sex they could get. She obviously didn't know all that much about men, which was the whole point of doing that with Jace.

And holy crap, had he been right about going to a man instead of a boy to get the job done right. Jace had done things to her with the tip of one finger she didn't think seven *hours* in the closet with Klint could have. Forget about the seven minutes they'd planned on.

Parts of Tara tingled, remembering what had happened with Jace. She should have assumed he'd be good. He'd run through enough buckle bunnies when he'd been younger to learn a thing or two. After dating one woman for so long, he'd probably reached a whole other level of familiarity with a woman's body. He was like some kind of savant . . . or an orgasm whisperer.

The memory of the warmth of his breath against her ear as he told her to come right before her body exploded with sensations she could have never imagined sent a shiver down Tara's spine. He was annoying and obnoxious and so many other infuriating things, she couldn't even list them all, but she had to admit, Jace was good with his hands. Probably with his hips, too. She'd watched him ride tonight. She'd seen how his body reacted to every move the bull made. If he was that good on top of a bucking bull, how good would he be on top of her?

A twisting low in her belly told Tara she needed to find out. Strange, since she'd hated him for so long—or at least had enjoyed thinking she did. But the evidence was indisputable. On a physical level, she was attracted to him. Their bodies were compatible even if their personalities were not. That fact made Jace the perfect man to take her virginity. To teach her everything she would ever need to know about making love to a man. About how to catch a man and hold on to him. She could learn it all with no fear of getting hurt because it was Jace. Chances of developing feelings for him and getting hurt were nil.

Add to that the convenient detail that they already shared a room and it was the perfect plan. All she had to do was convince him, which could be the difficult part. Tara eyed the closed door, knowing he was still sitting in the truck on the other side. She hadn't missed his hard-on against her as they'd kissed. He'd felt the attraction too. He'd wanted her. She would have to make sure he gave in to it.

How hard could that be?

The sound of the door lock opening had Tara looking up. Finally. Jace must be over whatever that little self-imposed timeout had been about.

He came in and closed the door behind him. The expression on his face as he glanced at her and then yanked his gaze away told her he wasn't in a better mood quite yet. That was fine. She could wait. They had hours alone together in the truck tomorrow while they drove to the next venue. Locked in a speeding vehicle, he wouldn't be able to run away from the conversation.

Now, however, was a different story. He strode directly to the bathroom, closed and even locked the door before the sound of the water in the shower began. Yup, he could run and hide behind closed doors here, but tomorrow would be another ball game entirely. Tara smiled at the thought.

The sound of the water in the shower quieted and a few moments later the bathroom door swung open. Jace appeared wearing nothing but a towel and an expression of misery. He glanced at Tara where she sat on the bed, and then away.

"Forgot to bring in my shorts." He mumbled that explanation as he pawed through his duffle bag of clothes and avoided eye contact.

He'd tossed the bag on his bed when they'd first

checked in. Before the event. Before they'd made out against the wall. Before he'd shown her a glimpse of what sex could feel like and made her crave more.

Looking at the muscles of his bare chest glistening under droplets of water, Tara turned molten inside thinking about her plan. Maybe it might be easier to talk him into continuing a physical relationship while he was naked and in nothing but a towel. If she could get to him before he disappeared into the bathroom again to cover up with the shorts he slept in . . .

As he headed back toward the bathroom with his clothes balled in one fist, Tara jumped at the opportunity. "Jace."

"What?" His tone was not real receptive as he paused in the doorway.

"Can we talk?"

"Nope." He stepped into the bathroom and slammed the door between them.

What they'd done was really bothering him, but that could be a good thing. It could mean he was thinking about doing it again. If it had been a one-time thing, they'd talk about it and then move on. Yup, Jace was probably in the bathroom thinking about the same thing Tara was thinking about in the bedroom—the possibility of a repeat.

The ringing of her phone for the first time in days had her frowning and searching for where she'd put it. Finally, she located the cell under her bag. She read the display and hit the button to answer. "About time you called me. Real nice, big brother. I could have been dead or kidnapped for all you knew."

Tuck let out a laugh. "I knew nothing bad happened and nothing's going to."

"Oh, really? And how do you know that? Your crystal ball?"

"I know because you're with Jace."

"And because you told him to protect me?" Anger over just the thought had her pulse speeding. Though Tuck telling Jace to protect her would explain his caveman act, and his beating himself up, it still pissed Tara off.

"No, I did no such thing, so get rid of that attitude I hear in your tone, missy. I didn't have to tell Jace anything. Traveling partners take care of each other. Pure and simple."

So that hadn't been a line of bullshit Jace had thrown her way. Hmm. She'd have to think more about that. "Anyway, still nice if you call and check in once in a while."

"That's what I'm doing. Though mostly I called to see how you two were getting along. I figured by now the fur should be flying."

The bathroom door opened and Jace stepped out, dressed in shorts and a T-shirt.

"Jace and I are getting on fine, thank-you-very-much. Sorry to disappoint you."

His eyes widened and he stopped dead in the middle of the room when he realized she was on the phone. He whispered, "Who is that?"

Tara mouthed back silently, *Tuck*.

Jace scrubbed his hands over his face. She shook her head at him. What was he so worried about? As if Tuck could know what had happened between them. Ridiculous.

"Anyway," Tuck continued. "When you coming back this way?"

"Not for a couple more weeks. Why?"

"Uh, nothing. Just wondering. Jace bringing you

to Stillwater? Or are you going to have him take you home or to college?"

This was more interest than Tuck had shown in her plans ever and it made Tara suspicious. "I'm not sure of my plans yet. Again, why do you wanna know?"

"Just wondering. Maybe you could, uh, come here. We could hang out for the night, and then I could drive you home the next day."

Tuck wanted to hang out with her? That was a first. Why?

A horrible thought hit Tara. Tuck must want her to go to Stillwater so he could break it to her about Emma being knocked up. He probably wanted to make sure she didn't do something crazy. Logan could have told Tuck about how she'd shown up at his parents' house the day of his wedding and begged him not to marry Emma. *Lovely.* In fact, Logan had probably asked Tuck to keep her in control.

Tara's stomach knotted. She felt ill just thinking about being sat down by her brother for the big revelation. That was it. She was done with the phone call. "Look, Tuck. I gotta go now."

"But what about—"

"Really, gotta run. Talk soon. Bye." Her heart pounding, Tara disconnected the call.

She tossed the cell onto the bed, then reached for it again. She picked it up and glared at the phone's display to make sure the call was ended. Tossing it down again, she scrubbed her hands over her face.

"What's wrong?" Jace had stayed where he'd stopped midway across the room and was watching her.

She'd been so engrossed in worrying about avoiding Tuck telling her the baby news, Tara had momentarily forgotten Jace was there. "Nothing. Relax. It's not about you."

"Thank God for small favors." Jace blew out a loud breath. Still watching her, he moved a step closer and glanced at the phone. "Something Tuck said got you going. What was it?"

Jace stood at the edge of the bed so Tara had to look up to talk to him. "Tuck's trying to get me to go to his place when the internship's done."

"All right." Jace dipped his head in a nod. "What's so bad about a visit with your brother?"

"Jace. Come on. You know as well as I do that's not like him. I think—" As her stomach roiled, Tara had to take a breath and start over. "I think he wants to break the news to me."

"News?" Jace's brows drew low.

"Yes, the news." Tara opened her eyes wide and stared at Jace, not believing he couldn't figure out what news would have her so upset. "About Emma."

"Oh." He cringed. "Yeah, she's probably starting to show and they're telling people. You might be right."

"Yeah, I think I am, and I'm not ready to hear it. Not from Tuck. Not with Logan and his new bride right there in town acting all happy together." She shook her head. "I'm not going back there so he can sit me down like a child and break the big news to me. I'm not gonna do it, Jace. I'm not."

"All right. Then you don't have to."

She brought her gaze up to meet his. "Really?"

"Really. I'm sure as hell not gonna make you if you don't want to. I'll drop you wherever you want."

She'd figured once the internship was done Jace would dump her at Tuck's with no way to get home, but Tara believed him when he said he wouldn't. "Okay. Thank you."

"Don't thank me." Jace turned toward his own bed with a laugh. "I'm avoiding Stillwater as much as you. Remember? The only thing that's changed is now I have two reasons to not go back instead of one. I get to hide from Jacqueline *and* Tuck. I sure as hell am no more anxious to talk to your brother right now than you are."

Tara had had no idea men thought so damn much about things like kissing—just like girls did. She had always figured Jace was the kind to have sex with a girl, walk away, and never think about it again. At least it had seemed that way back when she was young and Jace and Tuck were on the road together. Before they both settled down.

But Jace was obviously still obsessing over their kiss.

Post-relationship Jace was very different from the younger, pre-monogamous man-whore Tara remembered. Even though he had never married Jacqueline, he might as well have, the way she still had a hold over him.

"You know, you don't have to tell Tuck what happened. I'm not going to, if that's what you're worried about."

"Oh, don't worry. I have no intention of telling him." Jace whipped back the corner of the sheet and sat. When he noticed her watching him, he broke eye contact and reached out and flipped off the light. "Good night."

Just because she couldn't see him didn't mean she was done talking. "Jace."

She heard his sigh through the darkness. "Yes, Tara."

"It's no big deal. It's okay, what you and I did."

He snorted out a laugh. "No, it's definitely not okay."

Tara scowled. "Well, you better get over this stupid guilt of yours and fast. Okay?"

"And why is that?" Jace sounded half miserable, half amused.

"Because we're going to do it again." In fact, if she hadn't gotten so upset over Tuck's phone call, and Jace hadn't been acting like such a woozy-woo over the whole thing, Tara had been planning to get busy with him again tonight.

"Uh no, Tara. We're not."

"We'll see about that."

Tara smiled when he didn't contradict her again.

"You know, if you're tired, I can take a turn driving." Tara glanced at Jace from across the cab.

"You. Drive my truck? Nah, don't think so." Jace was tired, all right, but not so exhausted—or delusional—he'd willingly let Tara drive his vehicle. Not even after a mostly sleepless night when he'd alternated between beating himself up and considering if he should head to the bathroom and beat himself off.

Memories of what they'd done had him hard and throbbing and up, in more ways than one, all night long. It had been torturous. And it had been all his own fault for touching her in the first place. Temporary insanity, he supposed.

"Why can't I drive it?" Her voice sounded so much like when she'd been twelve and begging Tuck to take her to the rodeo with them, Jace felt even worse.

"Because this right here is too much truck for you to handle."

Tuck had told him too many horror stories about Tara's driving lessons the year she got her permit. Besides, he was too antsy to sit in the passenger seat and do nothing. At least driving gave him something to concentrate on.

She turned in the seat to glare at him. "It is not too much truck for me."

"Oh, yeah it is. You know, you can't just hop on up into something this powerful." Taunting Tara put Jace back in his comfort zone. She probably could handle the truck on a flat straightaway like they were on if she stuck to the speed limit, but he wasn't about to admit that.

"That's the best way to learn, isn't it?" Her voice dropped low and the tone changed, sounding almost seductive. It was enough to make him take his eyes off the road and look at her as she said, "Sometimes, I think it's best to jump right in and do it."

He got the impression they weren't talking about trucks anymore, that what she was picturing jumping on was him. Time to dissuade the girl. Make her forget any outlandish ideas she'd gotten into her head about the two of them repeating last night. He had to before he got crazy enough to give in to her.

"Nope. Never a good idea to just jump into anything. That's a good way to get yourself into trouble. You need to take your time. Move nice and slow."

"Nice and slow is good, too."

Yup, definitely not talking about her driving the truck anymore. Tara smirked and had him staring at her lips, remembering the feel of them beneath his.

He swallowed hard. "Anyway, I'm not too tired to drive, so don't worry about it."

"That's good. Then you won't need to take a nap when we get to our room. Then again, maybe heading to bed early isn't such a bad idea." She eyed him.

Jace had seen that expression before. Usually it was on a buckle bunny or the naked model spread across the glossy pages of a magazine. But the woman sending him that look wasn't a stranger at a rodeo, and she sure as hell wasn't in any damn two-dimensional photo he could toss aside and forget about. It was Tara looking at him as if she wanted to eat him alive . . . and he'd be sharing a room with her tonight and for the next couple of weeks.

He calculated how many nights his prize money from the last event could buy him if he booked Tara a separate room. But then she'd be unsupervised and could sneak out in the middle of the night.

It was an impossible situation. One he'd caused himself by getting it in his head that it was a good idea to kiss her in the first place.

Jace wished they lived in the Dark Ages and he could slap a chastity belt on her and be done with it. While he was at it, he should get one for himself, too, since he seemed incapable of making a smart decision when it came to women.

He glanced up to find a small cocky smile bowing her lips as she watched him. Probably waiting for a response or at least a reaction to her never-too-early-to-go-to-bed comment. He had nothing to say about that, so he yanked his focus back to the road. He'd have to eventually address the issue of his having turned Tara into a virgin vixen, but at the moment, procrastination seemed like a good idea.

"You know, Jace—" The ringing of Tara's cell

phone cut off whatever new and horrifying suggestion she'd been about to make.

Saved by the bell. Thank God for small favors. He didn't want to hear whatever came after the words he'd begun to dread. *You know, Jace . . .* In her current mood, he knew nothing he'd like could follow.

Tara pulled the phone out of her pocket and glanced at the screen. "It's Tuck."

The phone continued to ring, loud and annoying. "So answer it."

"I don't want to."

What could Jace say to that? As a man who'd taken to leaving his phone powered off the past week to avoid his own issues, he was in no position to criticize. He and she weren't all that different.

He glanced at her and held out his hand. "Give me."

Her eyes widened. "What are you going to do?"

"I'm going to answer it."

"Don't tell him we'll come to Stillwater. Please."

A *please* from Tara. She truly didn't want to go there.

Jace could sympathize. "Don't worry. Trust me."

Finally, she relinquished the phone to him. He hit CONNECT and pressed it to his ear. "Hey, Tuck."

"Jace? You've got Tara's phone?"

"Seems like." Out of the corner of his eye he saw Tara watching him. "What's up?"

"I was just wondering if you'd be coming back to Stillwater during the break in the schedule after this next event."

"There's a break in the schedule?" Jace was very familiar with the schedule, but didn't consider two rather than just one day between events a break. There was no need for Tuck to know that.

Next to him, Tara's head shaking drew Jace's attention. He mouthed a silent, *shh* to her. He could handle Tuck. He'd been doing it for years.

"Yup, you've got two days. I've got the event schedule up on the computer now."

Tuck. On a computer. This was serious. The man avoided technology like the plague. Maybe Tara wasn't overreacting, after all. Her brother was trying to get her back to Stillwater for some reason.

Luckily, Jace was in the driver's seat, and he had reasons of his own for not going back. "Nope. I hadn't planned on it. We're just gonna stay on the road until her internship is done."

Tuck's hesitation spoke volumes. Then he asked, "Is Tara nearby?"

Jace decided it was time to lie. "Nope. We pulled over to take a break. Grab some grub. Stretch our legs. She's off in the restroom now." He realized the radio was playing loud enough Tuck might hear and added, "I'm waiting for her in the truck."

"Okay, good. Listen, Emma and Logan are finally ready to tell everyone about the baby. I mean Becca, Tyler, and I have known for a while, but they're planning on announcing it to his parents, and Becca's and mine maybe next week. I think it might be best if I break the news to Tara before she hears it from someone else."

Jace glanced at Tara. He saw her breathing fast and shallow. Even if she already knew the news, this girl did not want to hear what Tuck had to say. "I think you're underestimating her, Tuck. She's too busy with school and her internship to worry about this."

"You don't know her like I do. She's going to have a fit, Jace. I need to nip it in the bud before she says or does something embarrassing."

"I think you're wrong, but if you are right and she can't handle the news, then telling her right now isn't exactly fair to her, is it? Just because Mr. Perfect didn't bother to use a condom is no reason to upset Tara in the middle of her internship and possibly cost her the degree she's been working so hard to get."

Yeah, Jace was bitter that Tuck treated Logan like he was infallible but considered him a screwup. He wasn't about to jump to do Tuck's bidding because Logan and Emma had finally decided it was time to go public with what half of them knew already.

Jace's loyalty was to Tara, his traveling partner. The traveling partner he'd had his hands all over last night. One more reason for him not to come face-to-face with Tuck sooner than he had to.

"Jace—" Tuck didn't sound as if he was going to accept Jace's answer.

Time to end the call. "Oops. Here she comes. Gotta go. But no, we're not coming home." Jace hit END, then risked a glance at Tara.

She stared at him, looking pale and kind of in shock.

"Sorry, Tara." He wasn't sure what he was apologizing for, but it seemed the right thing to say. Maybe that he'd spoken for her, or about her to Tuck. Whatever. The end result was the one they both wanted. That was all that mattered.

Her brow furrowed. "Don't be sorry. That was good."

"Really?" Jace thought he pretty much sucked at lying.

"Yeah, it was. Thanks for handling the call and Tuck."

"No problem."

It wasn't finished. Not for either of them. They'd have to go back and face what they were running from, but not today and not after the next event. For now, that was good enough.

Jace realized he still had her phone clutched in his hand and handed it to her. "Hey, let's really stop for a break. I think I could use one."

"Yeah, me too." She took the phone and shoved it back into her pocket. "Jace?"

"Yeah." He glanced at her.

"You're not such a dick all the time. Just most of the time." One corner of her mouth tipped up in a crooked smile.

"Thanks. And you're not such an obnoxious brat all of the time, either. Just most of the time."

Tara tipped her head in a nod. "Thank you."

One step closer to getting back to normal.

Chapter Thirteen

Dillon glanced in Tara's direction and then turned to Jace. "I see things seem to have thawed out a bit between you two."

"What do you mean? Why do you say that?" *Crap.* That reaction had sounded suspicious. Nothing like a guilty conscience to get a man's defenses up.

"Your roommate keeps looking over here, only today, it doesn't seem like she wants to kill you. You two work things out?"

"Uh, yeah. I guess." The last thing Jace needed was Dillon guessing something had happened between him and Tara. Something more than arguing, that is.

Jace glanced up and caught Tara watching him and changed his mind. *That* was the last thing he needed—her eyeballing him with that look that said *wait until we get alone.* He'd managed to deflect her subtle, and not so subtle hints while driving yesterday and even while they were in the room alone, but that was probably because she was still grateful for his handling Tuck's phone call. Jace had a feeling that reprieve was over and she'd be back to the innuendos.

Having to expend all of his energy on Tara on his day off was one thing. Having to give a large portion of his concentration to her when he had to ride was quite another.

From her little looks and comments, it was no secret what she wanted. She was looking for an encore of the other night, and he couldn't let that happen. The thing was, his body seemed to have a different idea from that of his brain. Even as the guilt weighed on him until it felt as if a bull was standing on his chest, parts lower were all for a repeat with Tara.

"You okay?" Dillon asked, bringing Jace's attention back to the here and now.

"Yeah. Just planning out my ride." That was as good an excuse as any. He couldn't tell Dillon he was remembering what had thawed the chilly situation with Tara.

Dillon let out a snort. "Nothing to plan. The only thing predictable about that bull is that he's unpredictable."

That was the truth. Hit the Dirt, the bull Jace had drawn for the night's competition, was aptly named because that's what riders did just a few seconds out of the gate. Add to that the other challenges he was facing—the fact that his head was not in the game thanks to his little travel partner, and that he'd run through all the new underwear he'd superstitiously begun to attribute to his winning to—and he had a feeling the next ride would be the end of his lucky streak. He would have to rely on his experience and instincts and pray for the best.

Either way, whether he made the whistle or not, it would be over soon. He was scheduled to ride in the next section. He moved to the rail where he'd left his safety vest and chaps. Time to suit up and get to work.

Hit the Dirt stood in the chute as still as a statue. Nothing moved on the animal except the eyeball facing Jace as the bull looked in his direction. The bull was checking him out. It seemed only fair, since Jace was checking the bull out as well. It was big. At least two thousand pounds and built strong and solid with muscles that could launch the animal six feet into the air. The bull was unridden in competition. One hundred percent buck-off rate. Jace was crazy to think he'd be the one to break that record, but he still had to try.

The bull didn't mess around in the chute like some did—probably conserving energy for after the gate opened. Jace kept that in mind as he popped his mouth guard in and climbed onto the animal's broad back. He felt how wide the beast was under him.

One of the stock handlers balanced on the rail, pulling the rope tight behind the bull's shoulders, then handed it to Jace. He gave the rope another tug and wrapped it tighter than usual around his hand before weaving it between his fingers. It was referred to as a suicide wrap. Jace tried not to think too hard about the significance of the name.

He flipped his chaps out of the way, made sure his spurs were clear of the bull rope, and then pounded his fist one more time. That was it. He was as ready as he was going to be. He nodded to the gateman and the gate clanged open.

The bull took a giant leap into the air. Dropping its head low, while its hind feet were still airborne put the animal almost vertical. Jace managed to hang on as the bull's feet crashed to the ground and it settled into a spin to the right, away from Jace's hand. The power and speed of the bull's bucking and spinning simultaneously made it hard to stay centered. Jace fought but still felt himself begin to slip into the well. The worst place to be.

His free hand touched the bull's side. With that foul, his ride was officially over, but being disqualified was the lesser of his worries. While the seconds seemed to move in slow motion, he realized he couldn't get to the tail of his rope to release his hand. With his hand still in the wrap, he slid off the side of the bull on the inside of the spin as the animal continued to pound the dirt with its deadly hooves.

He knew he needed to get to his feet and keep trying to release the rope, or be dragged and possibly trampled. The bullfighters were there, but were having trouble getting to him as the bull didn't let up trying to shake the rider still hanging on him.

As he felt something give in his shoulder, Jace made one last-ditch effort, reached for the rope with his free hand, and somehow, miraculously, grabbed it. The wrap released and he fell free to the ground. Shouting at the bull, the bullfighters did their job and drew its attention away from Jace and toward themselves.

Jace crawled onto his hands and knees, intent on getting to the rails any way he could so he could pull himself up and out of the bull's way should it decide to come after him, but one glance told him the bull had no interest in him.

Once the weight of the rider was off, the bull stopped dead in the middle of the arena. The veteran bull knew its job was done. Far more interested in locating the out gate than in pursuing the men in the arena, it turned until it spotted the way out. When the massive animal trotted toward the exit and out, Jace could breathe again.

He rolled to his back and let his head fall to the dirt and lay, staring at the ceiling as the full impact of the pain in his shoulder hit him. Yup, his lucky streak was definitely over, and in a spectacular way.

Doc Chandler and Rick, a member of the sports medicine team, were kneeling on the dirt beside him in seconds.

"I'm okay." Jace tried to sound convincing as he clutched his arm with his other hand.

The doc ignored Jace's self-diagnosis as he prodded Jace's shoulder. "Looks like it's dislocated. We're going to have to take you out and pop it back into place."

"No. Do it here. Right now." It wasn't the pain Jace couldn't handle—he'd been through this before—it was having Tara be there to witness it in the medical room. It had been sheer luck she was in back for his wreck or she'd be hovering over him the way the rest of the medical team was.

The doc's brow rose. "You sure?"

"Yup. Do it."

"All right." Doc Chandler braced his leg against Jace's side, and then with a firm hold, gripped Jace's arm with both of his.

A slow, steady pull on the doc's part and Jace's shoulder slid into the socket. The pain was horrible, but the relief once it was back in place was immediate. Still, he was sore as shit and knew from experience he would be for a while.

He blinked fast a few times and let out the breath he'd been holding. "Thanks, Doc."

"No problem. Come on back so I can get you a sling and something to take."

"Don't need anything."

The doctor pinned Jace with a no-nonsense glare. "Take it anyway."

"Okay. Fine." He'd likely be given an anti-inflammatory. The doc might even try to push a muscle relaxer, if not a painkiller on him.

A little ibuprofen would help the swelling. Jace would take that. No problem. But he wasn't wearing a freaking sling or taking any of that other stuff. If he did, he'd be passed out behind the chutes before the short go. Not that he'd be riding in the championship round with his disqualification at four-point-five seconds, but still, he'd like to be awake for it. Not to mention he had to drive back to the hotel afterward.

"Can you walk?" Rick asked, eyeing Jace still flat on his back on the ground.

"Of course, I can walk." Not that he'd tried but hell, it was his shoulder that hurt, not his legs. He'd walk out of the arena even if it killed him to do it.

"A'ight." Rick grabbed Jace's good arm and hoisted him to his feet.

The crowd's cheer broke through the hush of the arena. They always did applaud as loudly for a fallen rider who walked away from a wreck as they did for a ninety-point ride. In theory, it was to help the rider feel better. It wasn't working. Covered in arena dirt and hurting, Jace had plenty of reminders that his perfect three-event winning streak was good and broken.

* * *

Maryann skidded to a stop in the doorway of the sports medicine room. "Jace wrecked. It's pretty bad."

"What?" Tara spun from the rider she'd been tending to.

"He got hung up in his rope. He finally got free, but he's laid out in the arena. Flat on his back, right where he landed."

"You didn't go see if he's hurt?" Tara's heart clenched with fear.

Jace had been right when he said travel partners had a special bond. Love him or hate him, she had reached another level with him from traveling together.

"Doc Chandler and Rick are with him. But I thought you'd want to know."

"Well, go now. The doc might need you. I'll be there as soon as I can." Tara turned to the veteran rider on the table.

She needed to know Jace was okay, and she realized her concern had nothing to do with worrying she could lose her ride because he was laid up, though that could well be an issue for her if he was broken up bad and couldn't continue on the circuit.

The rider on the table, probably half a dozen years older than Jace, had asked if she'd get him some sports cream to rub into his neck, which had been chronically sore since he'd broken the C1 vertebra a few years ago. There were men who had been paralyzed for life by a similar injury, but this old-timer had worked his way back to the circuit after it.

If Jace had landed wrong he could very well be lying out there with a broken neck. The thought had her knees growing weak.

"Go on out where you're needed, Miss Tara. I can wait." The rider's offer brought her attention back to where it belonged.

"Thank you." The tightness in her throat made it hard to get even those two small words out.

With an urgency that had her pulse pounding, Tara strode through the door of the medical room . . . and smack into Jace.

He hissed when she crashed into his chest. He reached out with one arm to steady her. "Easy, girl. One dislocated shoulder a day is enough for me."

"Oh, thank God." Tara's relief at seeing him upright came out in one big whoosh of breath. "That's all? Just your shoulder?"

As she waited for confirmation, Tara was aware of the doctor walking into the room and past them.

Jace let out a laugh. "That's not enough? You want me more broke up?"

"No, I mean . . . I heard you were laid out."

"Just while I was waiting for the doc here to fix me up. That's all." Jace shrugged, but she noticed he only used one shoulder to do it.

"Waiting on me, huh? Well, now I'm waiting on you to take this." The doctor handed Jace two pills.

"What is it?" Jace eyed the tiny orange tablets in his hand.

"Ibuprofen."

"Nothing else?" He raised a brow.

Doctor Chandler rolled his eyes. "No, nothing else. Would you take something else if I gave it to you?"

"Nope."

"That's what I figured."

Jace popped the pills into his mouth, and then

grabbed the cup of water with the same hand, not using his left arm at all. He was still hurting.

"I'm getting you a sling." Tara turned toward where the supplies were kept.

"Don't want one."

"Too bad. You're wearing it." She pulled a sling out of the cabinet.

"Tara—"

"Jace. Stop." She cut his protest short. "Put on the sling and shut up or I swear, I will nag you until—"

"A'ight." He held up his good hand. "Give me the dang sling."

The doctor smiled at the exchange. Even the older rider on the table wore a smirk. Jace, on the other hand, looked annoyed, and frustrated, and maybe a little bit embarrassed at being ordered around by his friend's little sister. Too bad.

Tara stood back while Jace slipped his arm through the sling.

Riders could be as stubborn as the bulls they rode sometimes. Hopefully, getting Jace to do what was medically advised in spite of his reluctance would win her a good review from the doc.

Tara's satisfaction stemmed from more than wanting a good grade, though. There was much more to it on a personal level. Not only did Jace need the sling he was so opposed to wearing, it was just plain fun making him do something he didn't want to.

As he scowled, but remained quiet while she strapped it around his neck, Tara realized that was the best part.

Chapter Fourteen

Jace stood beneath the pounding heat of the water in the shower until steam filled the room with a thick fog. It felt good on his sore shoulder.

Finally, he flipped off the water and stepped out of the shower stall. Naked except for the towel he draped around his waist, he stood in front of the sink and wiped the steam from the mirror with his good arm.

He hated with every fiber of his being that now he had a *good arm*, because it meant he also had a bad one. His riding arm. He set his jaw at that thought. Pain or not, he was riding tomorrow. It was only eight seconds. He was strong. He could endure anything for that short a time.

"You okay in there?"

He could even endure Tara, who insisted on babying him as if he'd been nearly killed rather than hung up for a few seconds.

"I'm fine. Stop worrying," he called back. Not that he had to raise his voice too loudly, since it had sounded as if she was directly on the other side of the door.

The lack of privacy and knowing Tara was creeping around within earshot had kept him from dealing with the pressing situation beneath the towel while he'd been in the shower. He'd made the mistake of thinking about the kiss and found his cock remembered it fondly. His right arm still worked just fine, but he sure as hell couldn't jerk off with Tara on the other side of the flimsy hotel-grade door.

"You took so long in the shower, I got worried."

He would have been even longer had he taken the time to rid himself of the hard-on that tented the towel he wore. Maybe he should have risked it because even Tara's nagging wasn't making the inexplicably persistent arousal go down. Maybe it wasn't such a mystery. He hadn't *handled* things in that area since being on the road with her. Add to that the new memories of what they'd done together and his suspicions that she wasn't going to let up until they did it again, and it was no wonder he was walking around ready to blow.

"Nothing to worry about. The hot water was helping my shoulder."

"Do you want me to rub it?"

Jace stifled a groan. That was the last thing he needed—Tara rubbing anything. "No. I'm good."

He was picturing her hands on him. He was a sick man, but his cock got harder at the image. He couldn't go out there. He'd have to deal with it. "Go watch television. I'll be out in a minute to join you."

"Okay."

He waited until he heard the sounds of the TV, and then pulled the towel off, tossing it onto the vanity next to the sink. Once free, the erection with the mind of its own sprung up and bobbed, as if mocking him. "Dammit."

Luckily the cheap hotel came with the usual tiny bottles of complimentary products, and hand cream was one of them. He flipped open the lid and coated himself. He closed his fist tight and set to stroking, hard and fast. He'd have to be quick and quiet or Tara would be pressed up against the door again asking if he was all right.

Jace latched on to his lower lip with his teeth to keep any sounds in and tried to concentrate, but the sounds of the hand cream and his fast strokes seemed to echo off the walls. His paranoia convinced him she would hear every pass he made up and down his length.

If he went back into the shower, she'd question why. He turned on the water in the sink to help cover the sounds and went back to work. Eyes squeezed shut, he pictured anything he could think of to finish. The models in the girly magazine he had under his bed at home. The last porn movie he'd watched years ago. He refused to think of Jacqueline, but he couldn't stop the next vision that popped to mind—Tara, up against the wall gasping for breath as she came from his hand.

Desperate times called for desperate measures. As wrong as it seemed, Jace let the memory remain. He was concentrating so hard it was amazing he heard the door latch open, but he did, and when he opened his eyes it was to see Tara standing in the doorway watching him.

"Tara! What the f—" Jace grabbed for the towel with his left hand, but knocked it off the vanity and onto the floor. Reaching out to catch it, pain shot through him. "Ow! Dammit."

"Be careful with your shoulder."

Yeah, because his shoulder was his biggest issue at

the moment. Jace pressed both hands over his nakedness. "Tara, please, please get out of here."

"No." She shook her head and moved a step farther into the room. Reaching for the sink, she turned off the water. "Let me do that."

"Do what?"

"Take care of that." There was no question what she meant when she reached for his hands and tried to pry them away.

"Hell, no." Jace held firm.

"Yes."

"Why?"

"I already told you why the other night. I'm not a child. I'm a woman and I want to experience everything a woman should."

"And this is on your bucket list?" Jace kept talking to distract her for as long as he could. Short of physically throwing her out of the room and locking the door behind her, it was the only idea he could come up with. From now on, he was going to double-check he'd locked the bathroom door.

This idea of hers to help him wouldn't be an issue if the erection from hell would just go away. But dammit, it was as strong as ever and wasn't going down. Damn thing seemed to like the idea of some attention from Tara.

"Yes, it is on my list. Among other things." She ran a finger down his stomach.

His muscles jumped in reaction. His cock beneath his hands did, too.

"It's no big deal, Jace. It's like one person scratching another person's back if they have an itch."

"No, it's not like that at all."

"It could be. You obviously need it, Jace."

"If I do need it, I can take care of it myself."

"But wouldn't it be easier for you if I did it instead?"

"No, it most definitely would not." The entire situation with Tara had made his life harder, not easier. But her suggestion was also making his erection harder, and when she pulled his hands away, he let her.

Smiling, she gripped him in one hand.

The feel of her touch had him reaching for the vanity to brace himself.

"Tara, please." The word *don't* remained unspoken. When she touched him, he seemed unable to say the words to tell her to stop.

She tightened her grip and leaned close to his ear. "Shh."

Her warm breath blew across his skin and sent a shudder through him. He was harder than ever. His balls drew tight as she made long, slow strokes up and down his length. He wouldn't take long, and finishing might be the only conclusion that would satisfy her.

She watched his face with those eyes that had seemed too big for her face when she'd been a bratty pre-teen. Now, they were pools of desire that any man could fall into and drown.

Resolved, Jace drew in a shuddering breath. "Faster."

Tara quickened the pace. That was all it took. A sound of pleasure he never meant to make escaped him. It was followed by another as he got closer. He squeezed his eyes closed and tried to block out everything—his disappointment in himself, his own weakness, the knowledge that every encounter with Tara seemed to take them a bit farther into territory he shouldn't be in.

Somehow none of those thoughts that careened unbidden into his brain affected his body's pleasure. He was almost there when the feel of her hand was replaced by the warmth of her mouth.

Jace's eyes flew open. The sight of Tara's mouth closing over him had his stomach twisting with pure need and tore a groan from his throat.

His mind lost, his resolve long gone, Jace gripped Tara's thick mane of hair with his right hand. He thrust maybe twice more between her lips before he came, throbbing as he shot all he had into her.

The moment it was over, the weight of his actions hit him full force. Horrified with himself, he used the hand that had just held her close to push her away. He popped free of her mouth, but he knew he'd never be free of the memory of having been there.

Tara blew out a short breath. "Next time I'd like to try it without the taste of the hand lotion, but still, that was . . ."

He didn't know what word she was going to say, but he had the correct one. "Wrong. That's what that was. And there won't be a next time."

His face burning with shame, Jace couldn't look at her as he bent and picked up the towel off the floor where it had fallen pre-blowjob. He wrapped it around his waist again to hide his nakedness. Too little, too late. Still, he had to. Knowing Tara, she'd go for another round. He hoped she didn't because apparently he was incapable of stopping her.

"Jace, there's nothing wrong with what we just did."

He couldn't even begin to tell her all he was feeling about what they'd done. None of it good. He shook his head as words escaped him.

The knowledge that he couldn't trust himself to

do what he knew was right, to keep his hands off her, sickened him. He was a weak, broken man. He'd like to blame Jacqueline for his sorry state, but knew he couldn't. It was his weakness that had him going back to his ex over and over. And it was that same weakness that had him doing this with Tara now.

"Tara, I can't do this anymore."

She raised one brow. "That's what you said after last time."

"No, I don't just mean this." He motioned between them, though they couldn't do that anymore, either. "I mean we can't keep traveling together. It's not working. I'll—hell, I don't know what I'll do."

He'd have to think of something. Rent her a car. Give her money for hotels and go back to Stillwater himself. Something. Anything. The girl was too obstinate to listen, and he was too weak to resist, but he wouldn't cut short her internship and ruin her chances at a degree because he couldn't keep his hands off her.

"No! Jace, you can't do that." Her eyes flashed. He couldn't tell whether with anger or unshed tears, possibly both. "What's wrong? Why are you angry with me?"

He'd upset her. What else could he do to hurt her? If he stuck around much longer, he'd be bound to find out.

"I'm not mad at you. I'm mad at myself." Jace softened his voice. He shook his head. "Hell of a friend I turned out to be. I betrayed Tuck. I took advantage of you."

"Everything's not about you, you know." Tara frowned at him. "What about me and what I'm feeling?"

The image of his hand tangled in her hair as he thrust deep into her throat and came was like a blow to the gut. Jace let out a snort. "Yeah, I can just imagine what you're feeling. You probably hate me even more now than you did before since I did this to you."

"You're an idiot." Tara crossed her arms and glared at him with a look of pure hatred.

He didn't blame her one bit. "Go on. Get it all out of your system. I deserve it. Every word. Every insult you can come up with, I deserve."

Tara shook her head. "You're so much of an idiot and so into your own damn self and your wallowing, you didn't even notice I want—I need—what we do together."

"Because you want to grow up and be a woman and learn about men." He rolled his eyes. "I know. I've heard it all."

"You are a stupid, stubborn fool but I like doing this with you and I want more, even if it is with you." In typical Tara fashion, she finished with an insult.

The situation was so ridiculous, it was almost laughable. She and Jace had done nothing but insult each other since almost the day they'd met, yet now she wouldn't keep her hands off him. Wanted him to be her sexual experiment. Her coming of age project.

"You are the most confusing, complicated, annoying doggone woman I've ever met." Jace's string of insults brought a smile to Tara's lips. He shook his head. "That wasn't meant to be a compliment, you know."

"Don't care. You called me a woman instead of a girl." Her smile widened.

"If that's all it takes to make you happy and if it will prevent this shit from happening again, then hell, I'll call you woman from now on."

"That's not all it takes. Will you keep driving me? Can we continue to be traveling partners?"

He sighed. It wasn't her fault he was a weak man. "Yeah. I gave you my word I'd drive you for the full three weeks. I won't back out."

"There's one more thing that will keep me happy." Her narrowed eyes told him what her words left unsaid.

Jace didn't need her to say it outright. He might be stupid sometimes, but he knew enough about women to know what this one wanted from him. "No. Not gonna happen. Nothing more is going to happen between us."

"Sure, it won't." Tara's tone was drenched in sarcasm.

The frustration made him want to rip his hair out. Worse, it made him want to shake her until she got some sense. That image led to the next one, him grabbing her and thrusting his tongue between her lips.

"All right, woman, get this through your head. We are never doing anything like what we just did ever again."

"Uh-huh. Got it." She nodded.

He couldn't deal with any more. It was too much already between the pain in his shoulder from his wreck, and the rock in his gut from what he'd let happen. "It's getting late. Get your ass to bed, Tara."

Her eyes brightened. "Okay."

"*Your own* bed." Jace stressed that point.

They both needed some sleep, not that he believed he'd get any after what had just happened.

"Nah, that's okay. I'm not tired yet. Thanks for your concern."

Contrary as usual. He was beginning to believe she'd say the opposite of anything he said. Maybe he should have told her to blow him. That way she would have gotten that look he knew so well—the look that said *don't tell me what to do*—and refused.

"Can you and I please get back to normal? Can we be the way we used to be before this road trip confused everything?" At this point, Jace wasn't opposed to begging.

"Don't worry about that. We're exactly the way we used to be. I still think you're an idiot and you think I'm annoying. Status quo." She shrugged.

He noticed she didn't say they'd go back to acting as if they hadn't had their hands all over each other and didn't both have the image of seeing the other come seared into their brain.

"This brings up an idea I've been thinking about."

Jace was afraid to ask, but he did anyway. "What's that?"

"Since there's no love lost between you and me, and we're comfortable with our hate-hate relationship, I think we're in the perfect position to take advantage of a risk-free situation."

"You're confusing me again." He had a feeling he was better off not knowing what she was suggesting.

Tara let out a snort. "No surprise there, but I'll explain. You and I, it's the perfect friends with benefits situation."

Jace's eyes widened. "Friends with benefits, huh? Do you know exactly what that term means?"

"Of course I do, you dickhead. I'm not an idiot. It means our relationship will stay exactly as it was, but we have sex."

Oh, hell no. There was no way that was happening. "One problem with that, Tara. We're not friends, remember? Your words."

"We're not. We're more. Traveling partners, remember?"

"Yeah, I remember. And stop using my own words against me."

"You use my words against me. Besides, you shouldn't have said it if you didn't mean it. Did you? Are travel partners closer than friends or not?"

He let out a sigh. "I meant it and they are."

"Anyway, what I'm saying is, it's safe. I get the experience with men I want, without the supposed risk of going out with the other riders since you're so dead set against me being with one of them. It's all of the fun with none of the risk of falling for the guy. There's no way I'm falling in love, so I can't get hurt, because let's face it, it's you."

That hurt more than it should. Jace scowled. "Thanks."

She ignored him and kept going, "And you get to have some fun, uncomplicated sex."

Only a woman who'd never had sex would think that they could be intimate at night, and not have it change things between them during the day. Tara was no buckle bunny. It wouldn't be some post-competition one-night stand before Jace left town and never saw the girl again.

"Uncomplicated sex? Yeah, right." The thought had him snorting out a laugh.

"And maybe," Tara barreled right over his comment, "if you go home satisfied and have been with someone other than your ex, it will be easier to resist falling back into Jacqueline's bed. See? It's a win-win for both of us."

That part made sense to Jace, which was frightening in itself. Tara might be dead-on that the reason he kept falling into Jacqueline's bed was because he hadn't been with anyone else. Or perhaps he had just lost his mind. Either way, there was a small part of his brain—the part that listened to his cock—that was seriously thinking that doing this shit with Tara could be a good idea.

Jace scrubbed a hand over his face. "Crap."

He hadn't meant the cuss to slip out, but it had, and his response had a devilish smile lighting Tara's face.

"You're considering it, aren't you?"

"No." The appalling truth was yes, he was considering it and he shouldn't be. It proved how warped he was in the head thanks to his messed-up relationship with his ex-girlfriend.

His brain spun with more thoughts than a man should have in his head, particularly right after what should have been a damn nice and relaxing act with a woman. But there was nothing normal about what he'd done, so he decided to get while the getting was good.

"I'm going to sleep." Jace turned toward the door and strode to his duffle bag in the bedroom.

He dropped his towel without worrying whether Tara was in the room. Really, why bother? She'd had her hands all over his cock. He'd come in her mouth. What did it matter if she saw his naked ass now?

Jace pulled on his shorts and headed for his bed. He rolled on his side to face the wall, but lay braced for anything. Knowing Tara and her new obsession with becoming an experienced woman, he wouldn't put it past her to drop trou and crawl into bed with him. If she did, then he'd pick her up and toss her right back in her own bed.

Yeah, right. Just like the promise he'd made to himself to never kiss her again. He'd stuck to that, all right. He hadn't kissed her. Her mouth had been too busy for kissing while he'd done so much worse to her.

Jace remained tense as he listened to Tara brush her teeth in the bathroom, and he cringed one more time at the memory of being in her mouth. He heard her pad barefoot across the carpet to her own bed. The television and the light both went off. Still he waited. It wasn't until a good quarter of an hour had passed and he heard her slow steady breaths that he let himself relax.

It might be over for tonight, but he knew tomorrow was another day.

Chapter Fifteen

Jace had been riding some sort of stock since he could walk. First, sheep as a five-year-old. After that he'd moved on to horses, and then, in his teen years, bulls. He thanked the good Lord for those years of experience. The motions he needed to prepare for his ride on the second night of competition in Norman were so ingrained in him, he didn't need his brain to be involved. That was a good thing because his mind was elsewhere. It definitely was not on his bull rope.

"So, you, uh, wanna talk about it?" Dillon's question brought Jace out of his head and back to behind the chutes where it belonged.

Jace glanced over at his friend standing next to him prepping for his own ride. "Talk about what?"

"About what's up with you today." Dillon pointedly eyed the quick, almost violent movement of Jace's gloved hand.

All right, maybe he was using a bit too much enthusiasm working the resin into his bull rope. He released his death-grip and took a step back from the rail where he'd tied the rope. "Nothing's up."

Dillon laughed. "Yeah, right."

"I don't know what you're talking about."

"Don't you?" Dillon's brows rose. "It's pretty obvious to everybody but you then."

When did this kid turn into some sort of psychiatrist? Watching. Analyzing. "All right, Dillon. Stop with the riddles and just spill. What do you think you can see that I don't?"

"Well, for starters, last night she was watching you, but tonight you've hardly taken your eyes off her."

Jace did find himself searching for Tara in the arena, though he wasn't sure if he was keeping an eye on her to make sure she stayed away, or in hopes she'd come over.

Worse than that, every time he thought about being alone again with her in the hotel, he got hard. They had two days off coming up. No competitions to keep them busy. Not a whole lot of distance to cover in the truck, either. It would be just him and her on the road, and then alone in the next town with nothing to do. Maybe he should take her back to Stillwater.

No, he couldn't do that. She'd kill him and he'd made a promise to her he wouldn't break.

Jace realized Dillon was still watching him and repeated, "Nothing's up."

Dillon shrugged. "All right. But if you need to talk, I'm here. Oh, and the wife said that if you want, you and Tara should come visit with us over the break. Said she'd love to have another girl to hang out with."

Great. Now it seemed they were a couple, getting invited over by other couples. And why did Dillon's wife even know Jace was traveling with a girl?

Damned Dillon had obviously turned in his man card and become a gossipy old washwoman when he'd gotten married.

"It's not a break. It's two travel days." Jace scowled and repeated the defense he'd used with Tuck.

"And you'll be traveling right past my house to get to the next venue."

What could Jace say to that? "We'll see." That seemed like as good an answer as any.

"How's the shoulder today?"

A change of subject. It was about doggone time. This Jace could handle. "Sore, but I'm good to go."

"Your travel partner rub it for you last night?"

"What?" Jace's mind immediately jumped to what Tara had rubbed, and how that little episode of weakness on his part had ended.

Dillon shrugged. "Just saying, it must be nice traveling with a member of the sports medicine team. You wake up hurting, she can rub some liniment on you, or wrap you up, or hell, I don't know, hook you up with some painkillers."

"She doesn't bring the medical shit back to the room, idiot. And she couldn't go handing out controlled substances even if she did. She's not a doctor. She's a student." Jace had had just about enough of this conversation. When the hell was this show going to start, anyway?

"I bet she could still give a damn nice massage. Don't they train in that? Sports massage and stuff?"

"I wouldn't know."

"Then you're a fool. If it were me, I'd be taking advantage of anything that girl had to offer."

Jace knocked his hat back a bit to shoot Dillon a look. "You're married."

"Hell, I know that. And you're not. You're single and free as a bird. You do realize that, don't you?" Dillon cocked a brow.

"Yes." Jace said it, but he wasn't sure he had internalized that fact quite yet.

"Then start acting like it, because a pretty girl like her, here on the circuit, won't stay available for long."

"I already told you. She's Tuck's sister."

"So what? That don't matter unless you're planning on being the love 'em and leave 'em type." Dillon eyed Jace with a knowing look. "I don't think you are."

"You don't know as much as you think you do." And that was because Dillon was too young to have been around in the old days when Jace was exactly that type. Tuck, too.

"Whatever. Anyway, I see you're not throwing your other excuse at me."

Jace sighed, tired of the riddles. "What other excuse?"

"That she hates you. Guess you two got past that." Dillon smirked.

"Not exactly." No, theirs had moved from a hate-hate to more of a lust-hate relationship.

He remembered Tara calling him an idiot many times last night. Right after he'd—Jace pushed that image away as his cock stirred. How the hell had this conversation gotten here? He'd need to start hiding until his ride if Dillon refused to shut up.

"Anyway, I see the wife found Tara."

"What?" Jace spun to follow Dillon's gaze.

"Yup, bet those two are gonna hit it off real well. They're about the same age. They both have to put up with our sorry asses. They'll have a lot in common. They can compare notes."

"I told you, she and I aren't a couple. Stop talking like we are."

"Whatever you say." Dillon turned to Jace. "So what do you want for dinner when you visit? Burgers? Ribs? You name it."

As Dillon's wife Cassie and Tara laughed and chatted on the other side of the arena, Jace realized there was nothing he could say to change Dillon's impression. Some battles weren't worth fighting. He began to sympathize a bit more with Tuck and his having to do what Becca wanted. Jace wasn't even with Tara and he was already being made to do things he'd rather not.

If he was going to be mocked anyway, might as well get a decent meal out of it. "Ribs would be good. Been eating way too many burgers on the road."

Dillon grinned. "You got it. Oh, and wait until you have Cassie's potato salad. You're gonna love it."

They were discussing menus for this little couples dinner party thing he'd gotten sucked in to. God almighty, things were good and screwed.

"Can't wait." Without enthusiasm, Jace added, "I guess I'll pick up the beer."

If he was going to be thrown into this thing, he'd better make sure there was alcohol.

"Perfect. I'll tell Cassie you and Tara got the adult beverages covered."

You and Tara. Jace scowled. "Great. You do that."

"So how are you liking life on the road with Jace?" Cassie asked the question while wearing an amused grin.

"Ugh. It's worse than being around my brothers. Jace is so stubborn sometimes."

Dillon's wife laughed and turned toward the refrigerator. "Most men are. Bull riders in particular.
Believe me. I'm married to one of the most stubborn ones there is."

Tara laughed. "Well, I don't know Dillon that
well, but Jace sure is. This morning he was acting as
if he didn't even want to come here today. How stupid is that? We've got nowhere else to be for two
days." She cringed when she realized how rude
she'd sounded. "And I mean besides that, it was so
nice of you and Dillon to invite us to your home for
a barbecue. You two have a really nice place, by the
way."

Jace and Tara had spent so much time in the
truck, sleeping in a new town every other day, and
eating nothing but fast food or stuff from the arena
vendors. Who in their right mind wouldn't want to
spend the day at a real house, and get fed a home
cooked meal?

Tara had jumped at the chance to visit. Besides the
opportunity to spend time with someone other than
Jace, just the sight of the fresh vegetables Cassie had
out on the kitchen island was starting to make Tara's
mouth water. With all the crappy, unhealthy stuff she
ate while on the road, for breakfast, lunch and supper, Tara figured she'd be buying the next larger size
jeans soon if she didn't watch it.

Cassie emerged from behind the fridge door with
a huge container in her hands.

"Let me help you with that." Tara hopped down
from the stool at the kitchen island and reached for
the ceramic bowl.

"Thanks. You can just put it down there for now."
Cassie tipped her head toward the kitchen table,
and then spun back toward the open refrigerator.

"As for Jace not wanting to come here today? I think that had nothing to do with me and Dillon or our place."

"What do you mean?" Tara asked.

"I think it's about you." With two different salad dressings in hand, Cassie moved back toward the island and set the bottles down.

"Me? Why?"

"You tell me." One blond brow rose. "What's the deal with you two?"

How to answer that? Tara hesitated. Other than her momma, she'd grown up with all boys. Her own brothers, Tuck and Tyler, and Logan and Layne next door. She'd always wanted another female to be able to talk to about stuff. Things such as sex and men. Her brand-new sister-in-law Becca, because of her connection to Emma, wasn't proving to be the confidant Tara had hoped for.

But Cassie wasn't involved with any of that mess with Logan and Emma. Cassie knew Jace and she was married to a stubborn bull rider. She was close to Tara's age. She would understand what Tara was feeling.

"Tara, nothing you tell me will get back to Dillon or Jace, if that's what you're worried about. I'm not one of those wives who runs right back to her husband with every scrap of gossip. I promise."

"I believe you. It's just so complicated and messed up, I'm not sure where to start."

Cassie paused chopping lettuce for salad. "Really? Well now, that sounds interesting."

Tara laughed. "Interesting. Yeah, that's one way to put it. Anyway, we've, uh, done some things together." She raised her gaze to Cassie, who was doing a good job of looking casual as she moved on to chopping carrots. Tara lowered her voice to a hiss. "Sexual stuff."

But nothing more since that time in the bathroom. He'd been in such a mood after the last event, Tara had let him be, figuring if she got him mad he wouldn't let them come visiting today.

Her hostess's eyes rose briefly to meet Tara's gaze before Cassie went back to focusing on the knife in her hands. "All right."

"But we haven't done a lot of stuff. Not because of me. I want to, but he refuses. He acts as if he isn't interested in anything, but I know he is." Tara figured the near constant hard-on he'd tried to hide from her the past few nights was one indication of his desire. Not that she knew a whole hell of a lot about men, but that was one sign even she, with her inexperience, couldn't misinterpret.

"Maybe he's trying to be a gentleman."

"I don't think so." She laughed at the thought. Jace? A gentleman. Not so much. "I thought every male wanted sex."

Even as Tara spoke, the words brought up emotions she had yet to bury. Even a man like Logan had wanted sex. He just hadn't wanted it with her. She pushed that painful knowledge away.

Cassie smiled. "Yeah, they pretty much do, and that's probably why he's so freaked out. He wants to, but at the same time he's trying to be respectful of you. Of the fact you're traveling together. Of Tuck."

"That's the excuse he keeps giving me. Tuck." Tara slapped one palm against the top of the kitchen island in frustration. "Why the devil would Tuck care what I do?"

"Tuck's your brother. Of course, he cares. And Jace has been Tuck's friend for a very long time.

You're Jace's best friend's little sister. See how that could cause some conflict?"

Tara let out a breath. "So you think that's what's bothering Jace? His concern about Tuck?"

"I do. Besides the fact that traveling together makes this kind of thing tough."

"Why? I think it makes things easier. We're already in the same room every night."

"Yes, and that's well and good while you two are getting along. But what about when you have a falling out or end it totally and move on to someone new? You and Jace still have to be together twenty-four-seven even if you're arguing."

They already fought like cats and dogs. What difference would it make if they had sex, too? "I don't know. I still think our being nothing more to each other than traveling partners makes it perfect. We can do it without worrying about all the feelings. I would think Jace would be thrilled I want to have steady sex with no emotional attachment."

"Steady sex with no emotional attachment?" Cassie's gaze pinned Tara.

She nodded. "Yeah. It's perfect, right?"

Cassie laughed. "You haven't had much experience in this area, have you?"

Though Cassie probably didn't mean it as such, the insult hit Tara hard. Still, there was no denying the truth. "No, not really."

"It's not a criticism, sweetie. I'm just saying it's pretty impossible for a woman to have sex with a man and not succumb to feelings. Especially when you're around the guy as much as you are with Jace."

"But—"

"Just trust me on this one." Cassie cut off Tara's protest.

Cassie couldn't understand the situation. She didn't realize that the kind of relationship Jace and Tara had was different, but after she spent the day with them, she would see. A picture was worth a thousand words, and a day of watching them fight would be even better proof.

Tara still needed to tap into Cassie's knowledge. "So what do I do? Give up on being with Jace just because he's friends with my brother?" Was she supposed to live like a nun? While Jace wouldn't give her what she wanted, he also wouldn't let her even look at another guy on the circuit.

"No. Give him time and Jace'll give in, eventually. He won't be able to fight it. It's obvious he's into you."

"You think? How can you tell?"

"He keeps looking over here as if he's watching the kitchen door." Cassie glanced through the window at where he sat outside next to Dillon, who was playing with their toddler, Cheyenne.

Tara peered through the same window. "Maybe he's hungry. He's waiting for you to come and say it's time to serve the food."

"Maybe." Cassie shrugged. "Or he's watching for you to come outside."

"Why?" They were together almost every second of every day. He should be happy to have a break from her.

Dishtowel in hand as she wiped down the work surface, Cassie looked up at Tara. "Men become hyperaware of where the woman they're interested in is at all times."

Really? This was news. Although, it made sense. When Tara was into Logan, she'd always looked to see where he was and what he was doing. Those times were over. She buried the thought and tried to concentrate on the issue at hand—getting Jace's hands on her.

"And you think Jace is interested in me?" Tara had been missing out on having a female she could talk to about men. Cassie seemed to know everything.

"Yeah. Play it cool. Let him come to you. He'll come around."

Tara wasn't good at sitting around and doing nothing, but Cassie seemed so convinced, it might be worth giving it a try. "All right."

Cassie picked up the bowl of greens. "Can you grab that potato salad? We can take this stuff on out. The ribs should be done on the grill."

"Sure." More aware after her talk with Cassie, Tara noticed when Jace's attention whipped to the back door the moment it swung open. He stood and strode toward them.

"Let me grab that." Jace went to Cassie first. As he should, Tara supposed, since she was their hostess.

Cassie shook her head. "Nah, I'm good. This is light. Take the potato salad from Tara. That's the heavier of the two. Can't run out of tater salad. Dillon would never forgive me." She laughed and sent Tara a knowing look as Jace tipped his head in a nod.

"A'ight." He turned toward Tara and their eyes met for a heart-stopping second as he took the bowl from her hands.

Tara swallowed as he relieved her of the burden. "Thanks."

"No problem." He smiled. The expression reached all the way to his eyes. "Did *you* help with all this?"

"No, Cassie had most everything done already. And what was that supposed to mean? I can cook." Tara frowned at the tone he'd used, as if insinuating she couldn't have helped.

"Yeah, right." Jace laughed. "I seem to remember the year a fire extinguisher appeared in your momma's kitchen. If I'm not mistaken, it was because of a certain incident while you'd been trying to cook something alone."

Tara sat on the bench next to him because there wasn't a spot anywhere else. If there had been, she would have taken it since he was in annoying mode again. "Not my fault that I didn't know water makes a grease fire spread."

"Uh, yeah, I think it is. Don't they teach you that in like middle school?"

"Oh, shut up." Tara scowled. If this conversation didn't prove to Cassie that there was no potential for feelings with Jace, nothing would.

"Salad?" Cassie handed her the bowl of greens, drawing Tara's attention away from the pointless and frustrating argument with Jace.

Tara glanced up to find Cassie and her husband looking amused. Stupid Jace. Embarrassing her in front of her new friends. She'd have to keep her head down, eat and pretend nothing was wrong in front of their hosts, and then yell at him later in private. "Yeah, thanks."

"How's the shoulder feeling, Jace? Dillon told me you dislocated it the other night." Cassie set Cheyenne in her lap. The little blonde girl dove in fist first and began to eat potato salad off her mother's plate.

"Eh, it's fine. As good as I could expect, anyway."

With his right hand, Jace took the bowl Tara thrust at him. He wasn't wearing his sling because he was a stubborn fool, but he was still favoring his left arm and not using it as much as usual. He glanced up at Dillon. "Is there a Big Mart anywhere between here and the next venue?"

"Yup." Dillon nodded. "Right off the highway in the next town. You can't miss it. Why? You need something?"

Jace sipped at his beer. "Yeah. Nothing important. Just thought if we passed one, I'd stop."

That had been evasive. Tara frowned. "What do you need?"

They'd stopped at a store not long ago and picked up whatever they'd been missing.

Jace looked as if he'd rather do anything than answer her. Finally, he said, "Underwear."

"Underwear? Last time we did laundry you had like eight or nine pair." The fact she knew that wasn't lost on Tara. Travel partners certainly were close. A bit too close.

"Doesn't matter. Don't make a big deal out of it, Tara." His eyes cut to her as he lifted the bottle of beer to his lips again.

"Why? What's going on? Where did all your underwear go?" The more Jace tried to avoid answering, the more Tara needed to know.

"Relax. Nowhere. I still have them."

"Then why do you need more?"

Jace let out a breath. "I had an unopened three pack when we started out. The three events I rode in while I wore a brand-new pair, I finished in the money. We stopped and did laundry. Remember? So I'd washed those three, and on the fourth night I was wearing a pair I'd already worn. That's the night I dislocated my shoulder. Yesterday, too. A used pair of underwear and I bucked off at six point nine seconds."

Tara frowned at the surreal conversation. "Yesterday proves nothing. You rode for almost seven seconds."

"Yup." Dillon nodded. "And if he can hold on for seven, he should have been able to hang on for eight."

"Exactly." Jace raised his bottle to Dillon.

"You're an idiot." She scowled at Jace's logic. "Yesterday's buck off and the one the day before had nothing to do with your underwear. You dislocated your shoulder because you got hung up on a bull that's unridden in competition. You bucked off last night because your riding arm is injured."

Jace shook his head. "That don't matter and you know it. We all ride injured."

"Yup. We riders keep you sports medicine people in business. You're welcome." Dillon grinned.

Tara ignored the comment and stayed focused on Jace and this newfound underwear superstition of his. "Whether you think you can ride through the pain or not, your riding arm was still sore and weak. Subconsciously, you knew that and you didn't push yourself as hard. Yesterday's buck off had nothing to do with your underwear."

"You don't understand." Jace shook his head.

She looked at the others at the table. "Are you two hearing this?"

"Yeah." Dillon nodded. "And I happen to agree with Jace."

Faced with the overwhelming stupidity of the

men, Tara turned to Cassie for support. "Do you even believe them?"

"I do."

Blown away, Tara frowned at Cassie. "You buy into this superstitious stuff?"

"In part." Cassie shrugged. "Bull riding is as much a mental sport as it is physical.. Whether it makes sense or not, if Jace thinks new underwear will make him ride better, then it will."

Tara sighed. She couldn't fight that logic, as ridiculous as it sounded.

Cassie laughed. "Tuck doesn't have any riding rituals?"

"I don't know. Maybe." Tara had been pretty young when Tuck lived at home and rode full-time, before he'd enlisted in the army and gotten married to his first wife.

Back then Tara never paid much attention to what underwear her brother wore to ride bulls. Ick. That would have been far too much information. But whatever Tuck had done, it had nothing to do with her feelings about Jace's underwear obsession now.

"Fine, Jace. We can stop at the store if it'll make you happy."

"Thanks." Jace shot Tara a sideways look. "That's generous of you, given it's my truck and my gas and I'm driving, and all."

Tara rolled her eyes. Cassie was way off in her theory. There was no way Jace was interested in Tara personally. Interested in mocking her, yes, but anything else? Nope. She annoyed him as much as he annoyed her. Whatever else was between them was purely physical. An itch that needed scratching.

Cassie thought Tara couldn't have sex with Jace without feeling something? Okay, Tara would agree with that theory. She and Jace had feelings between them, all right, and most days that feeling was loathing.

Chapter Sixteen

"No, Jace, I insist. You and Tara are sleeping here tonight." Dillon shook his head.

"I couldn't impose on you like that." Jace rose from his seat on the bench.

Tara watched the exchange from her side of the picnic table. The night was still warm enough that they'd stayed sitting outside long after supper was over.

Still seated, Dillon frowned up at Jace. "What imposition? You're more than welcome to stay the night."

"Thanks, but we'll just get a hotel."

"But why spend the money when you don't have to? We've got an extra room. Hell, we've got two rooms. One for each of you if that's how you want it. Cheyenne's taken to sleeping in bed with me and Cassie, so her bed is empty if one of you doesn't mind sleeping on a twin-sized mattress with pink sheets and pictures of princesses all over them. The other room has a nice big sofa and a television. A pillow and a blanket and you're good to go."

"Seriously, I'll just—" Jace hooked a thumb toward the driveway where the truck was parked, their bags inside.

Cassie pushed through the kitchen's screen door. "No, Jace. You've had a few beers and I won't let you drive."

"I'm not drunk, Cassie."

"That doesn't matter. There's alcohol in your system, so why be silly and risk it? Besides, Dillon's right. Cheyenne's already dead asleep in our bed. Her room is empty and so is the TV room. I already pulled the extra pillow and blanket out of the closet for you."

"All right. I guess we'll stay." Jace turned to look at Tara. "You okay with that?"

"Me? Heck, yeah. I'm not passing up sleeping on pink princess sheets after all the crappy bedding at the places we've been staying." Tara's joke had Jace shaking his head.

She wondered if his protest was really because he didn't want to impose on the McMahans' hospitality, or something else. Like maybe he wanted privacy for the two of them. Tara had been watching him. Judging by the number of times she'd caught his eyes on her, Jace seemed to be watching her, too.

Cassie could be right about him. Maybe he was hyperaware of Tara and hopefully that was because he was ready to stop fighting the physical attraction. Ready to give in and let the sparks fly. Tara had no doubt that if he ever stopped holding back, they'd set fire to the sheets together. She couldn't blame him for not wanting those sheets to have princesses on them, though.

"I'll go get our bags, then."

"Need help?" The bags weren't big, and Tara was

pretty comfortable where she was, but she figured she should offer.

"Nah, I got 'em." Without making eye contact, Jace spun on a boot heel and headed for the drive.

Once they'd all gone inside, and Cassie had made sure Jace and Tara had whatever they needed, they said good night. Dillon and Cassie headed off to their bedroom and their sleeping daughter.

Inside the pink room, Tara changed into fleece shorts and her oversized T-shirt. It was too warm for her sweatpants. Not that it mattered too much, since she had every hope of not being in them much longer if things went well with Jace across the hall-way.

Grabbing her toiletry bag, she figured she could wander over to his room under the guise of wanting to say good night after brushing her teeth. Not a great plan, but it was the best one she had at the moment.

She found Jace already in the hallway between the two rooms they'd be staying in. He'd changed out of his jeans and boots and was in the shorts she'd become used to seeing him in.

He paused in the middle of the hall. "Sorry, Tara. You can have the bathroom first."

"No, that's fine. You can go before me." She glanced in the direction the McMahans had gone. "They have a bathroom off their bedroom. Cassie told me. So this one's all ours."

" 'Kay." He didn't move to go in, just looked at her as if he was waiting for her to do something.

She scrambled to make conversation so he wouldn't say good night and disappear into the bathroom. She tipped her head at the other end of the hallway. "So that whole situation must put a real damper on their sex life. You know, the kid sleeping in bed with them."

"Yup. Probably."

Tara swallowed hard when she noticed Jace's intense gaze remained on her. A day of sitting in the warm sun drinking cold beer and plotting how to get Jace into her bed had ramped up her neediness. Maybe it had done the same for him. "So, is your room nice?"

"Go on and take a look if you want to." He pushed the door wider and stepped inside before her.

Tara followed him in, sidestepping the duffle bag on the floor. "Cozy."

"Uh-huh."

"You want the bed and I'll take the couch?" she offered, for lack of anything else to say. "So you'll be more comfortable with your arm and all."

"You don't have to do that. I'm fine. I've had enough beer, it don't hurt so bad. I won't even know I'm on a sofa once I'm asleep." Jace's gaze dropped to the skin exposed by the deep V neckline of her T-shirt, and then grazed over the bare legs framed by her shorts.

He was thinking about something, but it wasn't sleep. For all his fighting and denying it, he wanted her and she was sure the beer he'd drunk only helped her case.

Tara took a step closer and laid a hand on his shirt. His gaze dropped to where she touched him and he drew in a breath that had his nostrils flaring. When his eyes rose again, they were heavily lidded. He was teetering on the edge. One push would send him over to where she wanted him—in bed, or at least on the sofa, and ultimately, inside her.

She reached out and pushed the door to the hallway shut, waiting for him to protest. When he didn't, her heartbeat sped up. It was going to happen. She tossed the small bag in her hand on top of his duffle and took a step closer.

"What are you doing?" Jace planted his hands on her hips.

"Nothing."

"Doesn't feel like nothing." His voice sounded low and sexy.

"Neither does this." Tara reached between them and stroked a hand over the bulge beneath his shorts, taking great pleasure when he drew in a sharp breath. She pressed closer.

With a tight grip on each of her hips, Jace held her away from him. She used the space between them to her advantage and stroked him again through his shorts. When he didn't stop her, she slipped her hand inside the waistband and touched his hard, silken flesh.

"Jace, I want this."

"I know."

"Then let's do it." Tara grasped him tighter in her hand.

"No."

Why was he so stubborn? "Jace—"

"Tara, please stop arguing with me."

"Then give me what I want." She traced a fingertip over the slit and the slick moisture beading there. She remembered the taste of him from the other night.

Jace closed his eyes. A frown creased his forehead as she stroked his length. That he hadn't pushed her hand away had to be a good sign. She pressed closer to him and ran her tongue along the outer edge of his earlobe, delighting when a tremor went through him.

Tara was planning her next move when he opened his eyes and hoisted her up. Shocked, she wrapped her legs around his hips. She straddled him, putting him right in line with her, and right where she wanted to be. He could play domineering caveman as long as she got what she wanted in the end.

Things looked promising until he dumped her onto her back on the sofa.

"What are you doing?" she asked, concerned he might just leave her there and go take the princess bed.

"I am gonna give you what you need, Tara. Just not everything you want."

"What does that mean?"

"I suggest you stop asking questions. Lie back, shut up, and let me handle things before I change my mind." He yanked her shorts down her legs and drew in a deep breath when he found she wore no underwear.

"Okay." She could be quiet if whatever was about to happen required she be naked from the waist down.

With a hand on each of her ankles, Jace spread her legs wide and positioned himself on his knees on the floor between them. When he dipped his head low and she felt the heat of his mouth connect with her core, her hips jerked off the mattress. "Oh, my God."

Jace's eyes crinkled in the corners as he smiled and looked up at her from between her thighs. Then he no longer looked amused as he went back to concentrating on torturing her with pleasure she'd never imagined.

His tongue filled her channel and Tara pushed closer to the sensation. The wet heat stroked in and out of her while his thumb moved, rubbing a spot that had her muscles clenching. He gave her a small taste of what she craved and slid one finger inside her.

"Yes." Tara pressed her hips closer, seeking more.

He sucked hard, sending tingles to her very core and bringing her close but not over the edge. It made her want to crawl out of her skin as the ultimate pleasure eluded her. He slipped in a second finger and stroked, working her from the inside all while his mouth tortured her from the outside.

She pushed against him as frustration warred with anticipation. As she wiggled, seeking what, she didn't know, Jace lifted his head. "Brace your feet on my shoulders."

Tara did as told and pulled her bent knees back. The position gave him more room to stroke inside her, even if it was his fingers when what she wanted was all of him. He went back to work with his mouth while he pressed the spot inside her that had her breath coming faster.

Jace reached for the bed pillow on the sofa next to her with his left hand. He shoved it next to her face just as Tara's muscles clenched and the orgasm broke like a rubber band snapping.

He'd known she was near the breaking point, and while she'd forgotten there was a family just down the hall, Jace hadn't. Grabbing for the pillow, Tara buried her cries against it as the orgasm sent wave upon wave of unbelievable pleasure through her.

It lasted for a long time, though time seemed to have stopped making sense to her. Jace didn't ease up for what could have been a minute, or ten minutes for all she knew. Finally, he gentled his touch, bringing her back to reality slowly. One last flick of his tongue against her had her twitching like she'd been electrocuted.

He pulled away and plopped down on the end of the sofa. "Better? You satisfied now?"

"A little."

Jace's brows rose. "Sounded pretty satisfactory to me."

She dropped her gaze pointedly to the bulge in his shorts. "For one of us."

"Don't worry about me."

"I'm not worried." She rolled bonelessly toward him, then lifted a knee to straddle him.

"What are you doing?" His eyes narrowed.

"Thanking you."

"No thanks necessary." Jace settled his hands on her hips.

"I disagree." Tara leaned low and drew his lower lip into her mouth, before sliding her tongue between his lips.

They hadn't kissed since that first time they'd been together. Too bad, because she liked this part. She half expected him to pull back and tell her they shouldn't be kissing. He didn't. Instead, he kissed her back. Interesting. Maybe, just maybe, he was giving in. She leaned more heavily against him.

With only the fabric of his cotton shorts between them, Tara could feel the outline of his cock pressing into her. If he was naked and in this position, he could slip inside her with no effort at all. As they were, the friction of the fabric covering his bulge was enough to have her rubbing harder against him . . . and enough to have him trying to stop her.

Jace tightened his grip on her and held her still. When she still pressed against him, he leaned away from the kiss. "Stop."

"No."

"Then you'll have to go to your room."

"If I stop I can stay?"

"Not all night, you can't."

"Why not?"

"Because little kids wake up early and so do their parents. I don't want anybody finding us in here together."

"So if I go to sleep in the other room later, we can do more now?"

"Not what you're thinking about, we can't."

"You don't know what I'm thinking."

"I think I do." He glanced at where Tara was making sure the tip of him rubbed against her.

As long as he was on to her anyway . . . she slid her hand beneath the elastic waist of the shorts and exposed his erection.

Jace covered her hand with his. "Not a good idea."

"I think it is." She trailed a fingertip through the glistening moisture at his tip, noticing he didn't stop her.

"Tara, go back to your room."

"Why?"

"Because we're not doing this."

"Do you really think Tuck won't be upset that you had your hands and your mouth all over me just because we didn't do anything else?"

"No, you're right. And thanks for reminding me how inappropriate this all is." His expression turned angry.

That logic had backfired. "Stop. That's not what I meant at all. I mean . . . I don't know what I mean. I just want you to stop denying yourself."

"It makes me feel better."

"Denying yourself makes you feel better?"

"Yes."

"So if I leave you here, like this, then what?" Tara glanced down between them.

"It'll go down."

"If it doesn't?"

"Then I'll deal with it."

"Why can't I help you deal with it?"

"Because it's wrong."

"You help me deal with things," she pointed out.

Jace cocked one brow. "You need the help. I don't."

"Oh, real nice. Thank you so much, Jace, for helping poor little inexperienced Tara who can't even—"

Jace covered her mouth with his in a rough kiss and cut off any further rant. Tara was tempted to ask if she'd won the fight, but figured that was a bad idea. As long as he kept kissing her, as long as his hard length remained trapped between her thighs, she'd consider it a victory.

His hands moved to cup her face as the kiss became more intense. Without him holding her hips still, she could move, gyrating until he groaned against her mouth.

He pulled back just far enough to say, "There's gonna be some rules."

Tara wasn't much for rules, but she figured she

could always stretch his rules until they broke. "Like what?"

"We're not having full-out intercourse and you stop trying to get me to." Jace's breath was coming fast and shallow.

"But we can do everything else besides that?"

He drew in a breath. "Yes."

She'd work on pushing the boundaries of the deal later. A smile bowed her lips. "Deal."

Jace glanced across the room. "Lock the door."

Tara jumped up and for once didn't mind following Jace's instructions since it meant they were definitely going to get down and dirty. By the time she got back to him, his shorts and T-shirt were on the floor and he was laid out, bare before her on the sofa.

Tara moved to straddle him as she'd been before, but he shook his head. "Spin around."

"What? Why?"

"You want this, you do as I ask."

"Fine." She did, which had her kneeling over him and facing his feet, which seemed a pretty unproductive position until he grabbed her hips from behind and guided her backward so she was braced above his face.

A gasp escaped her as Jace pulled her hips down over his mouth and drew her clit between his teeth, while his erection thrust skyward just below her.

He pulled back just far enough to say, "Feel free to suck on that if the urge strikes you."

That was all the conversation before he went back to working her already sensitive bundle of nerves. She leaned low and slid his length into her mouth. Jace tensed beneath her. Tara grabbed his shaft in one hand and ran her tongue up one side, and then over the slit, tasting him. He paused between her legs. She felt his hot release of breath against her skin. She slid all the way down to the base of him as he thrust his hips up to meet her.

Tara might not know much in this area because of her lack of experience, but what she was doing seemed to be working for Jace. She set a steady up and down pace with her hands and mouth and after a few strokes, Jace's hold on her hips tightened and he attacked her with more vigor than before.

Yup. This was a pretty good compromise they'd worked out between them. Of course, she'd continue to pursue the end goal, losing her useless virginity.

Her muscles clenched around the fingers Jace thrust inside her as he sucked her core, all while she tasted him in her mouth.

For now, yeah, this would work just fine.

Chapter Seventeen

"See? Now don't you feel better?" Tara treated him to her usual smug smile and all he could think of was how those lips had just been wrapped around him.

"Yes. Thank you. You were right. I feel better." Jace rolled his eyes. "That what you want to hear?" A war waged within him between guilt and post-orgasm euphoria.

"I want to hear the truth. I think it's good for you to have sex with someone else besides Jacqueline."

Tara had to go and say that name, just when he'd been happily not thinking it.

"Is this a therapy session? Because I don't remember making an appointment for one." Jace hoped to redirect the conversation with a joke.

"Can I ask you something?"

He sighed. "Could I stop you?"

"No. Not really."

Oh, well. It had been worth a try. "Fine. What?"

Why the hell not let her ask him a personal question? They were collapsed on top of each other, exhausted and satisfied after doing one of the most intimate things two people could, although not *the* most intimate thing. But Lord help him, they got a little closer to that final act every time they were together. That was one thing he could not let happen.

"Why didn't you and she get back together? I mean you said you'd broken up a bunch of times. She'd thrown your shit out on the lawn other times, but you always stayed together in the end. So what was different this time? If you two were still having sex and you're still into each other, why not get back together? Move back in."

She wanted to talk about Jacqueline? If Tara didn't keep trailing the tip of her finger down his stomach as if she were fascinated with the line of hair leading down to his cock, Jace might have minded the conversation more. As it was, the way she touched his happy trail was making him hard again even though he'd just come. It seemed what she lacked in experience, she made up for in sheer enthusiasm. And how he hated knowing that about his best friend's little sister.

Maybe the depressing conversation about his past with Jacqueline was exactly what he needed to keep his burgeoning erection at bay before Tara noticed it and came up with some creative plan to deal with it.

"I'd had enough of the bullshit that night. I don't know what made that time different for me but it was and I drove away rather than stand there until dawn to talk her into letting me back inside. And when I didn't stay, when I left, she got pissed off."

"Pissed that after she threw all your shit out on the lawn, you had the nerve to pick it up and leave?" Tara laughed.

He shrugged. "Yup, because all the other times I

hadn't left. Even if it took all night, I always stood outside and waited for her to calm down."

"And begged."

"Yeah, I guess you could say that." His male pride stung that Tara had called it so accurately. That was exactly what he had done. Begged Jacqueline to open the door. To stop being silly. To let him prove to her she was the one he wanted. "But not that time. Or since."

One dark brow rose. "Good. Make sure you don't do it ever again."

Tara could be a real hellcat. To see her fire turned to protect him, rather than fight him was a shocking switch, and it affected him more than he'd like to admit. He let out a breathy laugh. "Yes, ma'am."

"You know I took a psych class. We learned about mental disorders. The way you describe her—with the very high highs and the very low lows—it sounds like Jacqueline could be bipolar."

Jace rolled his eyes. "No need to say she's a psychopath or whatever just because she's my ex."

"I'm not, Jace. I'm serious. It used to be called manic-depressive years ago, but now they call it bipolar. It just means really violent mood swings. There's pills for it and everything."

Violent mood swings didn't begin to cover it, but Jace couldn't deal with this conversation. "Can we not talk about this any more right now? It's kind of strange to be discussing my ex-girlfriend's psyche while lying here with you naked."

Although truth be told, he was the only one naked. Tara still wore a T-shirt, and now that he thought about it, he'd like to have that gone. He ran a hand up her thigh, enjoying the fact that at least she was naked from the waist down.

"Why is this weird? We're friends with benefits. Friends talk to each other about anything."

"Oh, really?" Jace raised one brow. "One thing wrong with that theory, darlin'. We're not friends. Remember? Your words. Not mine."

"You're right. We're not friends. We're much more. We're traveling partners. Your words. Not mine."

Tara always did love to turn his words against him. He couldn't even argue. He gave in, which he seemed to be doing a lot of with her. "Yeah, we are."

"So I have this theory . . ." she began.

"That worries the shit out of me."

"Shut up." Tara smacked his chest. "Just listen. I think that every time you come with another woman, you move farther along in your recovery."

Tara had taken one too many psych classes at school. She fancied herself a freaking therapist. Jace laughed. "My recovery?"

"Yeah, in getting over this physical addiction you have to Jacqueline."

"That's your plan, huh? Cure by orgasm. Sometimes the way your mind works is frightening."

"Good. I like keeping you a little afraid of me. It gives me the upper hand." Tara trailed her finger lower, sweeping it over his cock so it jumped beneath her touch. She had the upper hand, all right. No doubt about it.

Hell of a plan she'd come up with, but they'd already crossed the line so many times and in so many ways, he might as well do it some more. He rolled onto his side to face her. "Take off that T-shirt."

Tara frowned. "But it's kind of cold in here."

"Not that cool and I'll have you warmed up soon enough." He pushed the hem of her shirt up. "Besides, don't you want to help me in my recovery? It was your idea, remember?"

"Fine." Tara rolled her eyes, but he didn't miss the smile. She pulled off her shirt to expose two small, rounded globes.

Jacqueline's fake tits had been nice for a while, but Jace had been missing the good old-fashioned kind. The ones that were just a mouthful and so sensitive a little work had the girl writhing beneath him. That's the kind he hoped Tara had. Jace tested it by sucking her nipple into his mouth. Her back bowed in response.

Yup. Nice and sensitive. He smiled "Good?"

"Yes. Now, shut up and do that again." She palmed his head and pushed his mouth down over her peak.

He'd work her until she came, then send her off to her own room. He was hard enough to cut diamonds and she knew it. She'd already wrapped her fist around him and was stroking him, long and slow. Maybe he'd let her finish him off, and then shoo her to bed.

Good thing tomorrow was another day off. They were going to be tired as all hell in the morning. Him especially because a guilty conscience—and Jace knew once the endorphins were gone, all there'd be left was guilt—was not conducive to a good night's rest.

As he worked her breast with his mouth while sneaking a finger down her belly to land on her clit, she threw her head back against the sofa cushion. She tightened her hand around him, and his cock anticipated another round.

Yeah, they were gonna be exhausted, but man would it be a good kind of tired.

* * *

"You look chipper." Dillon grinned, looking much too awake and energetic for Jace's liking.

"Uh, thanks." Jace drew in another sip of coffee in an attempt to get chipper, since that's what his friend seemed to think he was. Meanwhile, Dillon's persistent grin had Jace feeling uncomfortable. Finally, he just came out with it and asked, "What? Why are you looking at me like that?"

Dillon gave a half shrug. "Let's just say my house has thin walls."

Realization hit Jace hard. Dillon must have heard him and Tara going at it in the guest room last night.

"God almighty." Jace hung his head, more disappointed in himself for letting it happen than embarrassed Dillon had heard. And his wife and daughter must have heard, too. They were all in that room together. "I am so sorry, man. I don't even know what to say."

"Don't be sorry."

"But Cassie. And Cheyenne." Jace scrubbed his hands over his face. The knowledge they'd all heard was enough to make his brain bleed.

"Cheyenne was sound asleep and I haven't seen Cassie so happy in a long time. She wants to see you and Tara together so badly, I'm surprised she didn't grab her old pompoms from high school and run in there to cheer you on."

The image was so ridiculous, Jace couldn't help but laugh. "Still. I'm sorry. It was wrong." On so many levels.

"It's fine. Really. I'm happy for you. It's about damn time you two are together."

"We're not together." But he had given in to her.

Again. Jace shook his head. Things that seemed like a good idea in the dark never could stand up to the light of day.

"Uh-huh. Sure, you're not."

"No, really."

"So you busted up that little party she was having with Klint and Justin at the bar because you're not together?"

"I did that to protect her because Tuck's not here to do it."

"All right. And so what I heard last night was for what then?"

Certainly not for Tuck. The rock in Jace's gut doubled in size. He sighed. "Tara decided that we should be travel partners with benefits."

Dillon broke out into a hearty laugh. "Man, if I were single, I'd have to try that line out myself."

"It wasn't my idea." Jace scowled, but he couldn't blame Dillon for laughing.

Tara's theory sounded like bullshit to Jace, too. It was the kind of thing a guy might come up with to get into a girl's pants without setting up any expectations. But it was Tara who'd proposed it to Jace. As he'd thought a good hundred or so times since the road trip had begun, she always did enjoy being contrary.

"Whatever you want to call what you two have, it's working for you. I haven't seen you look this good in years."

"What are you talking about? I look like crap." Jace had gotten a peek at himself in the bathroom mirror this morning. He had circles under his eyes deep enough to drive a truck into.

"Well sure, you could use a few more hours sleep, but look at you. You're relaxed. Lounging here with me, enjoying a cup of coffee with not a care in the world. You haven't rubbed your shoulder once all morning, so you must be feeling better. Do you even carry a cell phone anymore? Back just a month or two ago, you'd look at your phone like every three minutes. No joke. Here, I haven't seen you do that once."

Dillon was right. Things had changed. "I'm, uh, trying to disconnect a bit from technology." *And from Jacqueline.*

"Good. Keep it up. Like I said, it's working for you, dude."

"Yeah, I guess it is."

But shutting off his cell phone wouldn't work forever. Eventually he'd have to deal with that loose end back home. For now though, the phone would remain off so he could pretend Stillwater and Jacqueline didn't exist. Dillon was right—he did feel relaxed for the first time in years—though there was no way in hell he'd give the credit to Tara's cure by orgasm theory.

As Jace pondered the situation, Tara walked into the room—the other thing that, beyond all explanation, was also working for him. She cradled a steaming mug in her hand, blowing on it before she took a sip.

"Got your tea?" Jace asked.

"Yup." She smiled and plopped down in the chair across the room while he tried not to marvel at how he knew she preferred tea over coffee in the morning.

That was something a boyfriend would know about his girl. Then again, it was also something a travel partner would know, so maybe things weren't as screwed up as he assumed. But as a travel partner he shouldn't know how Tara tasted, or the little noises she made when she was close to orgasm, or how she bit her lip trying to be quiet while she came.

"So what's the plan for today? We driving to the next town by way of the store to buy you some lucky bull riding undies?" Tara smirked.

Dillon laughed and Jace couldn't even get angry. She was a funny girl. If it weren't at Jace's expense, he'd be laughing, too.

He let the smart-ass underwear comment go and nodded. "Yup. That's the plan."

"Why don't you stay another night?" Dillon glanced from Tara to Jace. "We can all head out in the morning and make it to the next venue in plenty of time for the event."

Jace was more than aware they'd already imposed on this family enough. "No. Thanks for the offer, but we gotta get going."

"Oh, couldn't we stay, Jace? Cassie was talking about taking Cheyenne to the mall in the next town. I haven't been shopping anywhere but the Big Mart in forever."

"I don't think—"

Dillon interrupted Jace's protest. "Just stay. Your stuff's already inside."

Yeah, as if that was a good reason.

"Let her stay and come shopping with me." Cassie's voice came from the kitchen and Jace knew he was outnumbered.

"All right. We'll stay." In what he feared was becoming a pattern he'd have to put a stop to before he did something he'd really regret, he gave in to Tara one more time. But tonight she'd play by his rules.

No more sixty-nines on the McMahans' TV room

sofa. She'd sleep in her room and he'd sleep in his. A man had to draw the line somewhere.

"Thanks, Jace." The way Tara's smile over being able to go to the mall lit her face made him feel a little better about buckling under and doing what she wanted once again.

How could he have said no when something this simple made her so happy?

Jace felt that line he'd drawn slide a bit.

Chapter Eighteen

Jace had snuck off to bed in his room while Tara was in the bathroom brushing her teeth. The door was closed, but that had never stopped her before. With a glance down the hallway to make sure the McMahans were all still inside the master bedroom, she reached for the doorknob. It turned in her hand. He hadn't locked the door. That was an invitation if ever she'd seen one. She pushed the door wider, stepped inside, and quietly closed and locked it behind her.

"You really have no respect for a closed door, do you?"

The room was lit by nothing but the television screen, playing softly in the corner while Jace lay stretched out on the sofa.

"Nope." Tara crossed the room and crawled on top of him, straddling his legs.

He moved his hands to her hips. It was beginning to feel natural, his hands on her. His mouth on her, too.

She really liked Jace's mouth on her. Reaching for

the hem of her T-shirt, she pulled it over her head and dropped it to the floor so she sat on him topless.

"What are you doing?" he asked.

"Getting naked. I suggest you do the same."

"We can't do this. They heard us last night."

"I know. Cassie and I discussed it today while we were shopping."

"You did?" He tensed beneath her. "Wonderful."

Tara reached down and covered his hand with hers, then moved it up to her breast. "Yup. We did. It's not a big deal."

"Yeah, it is."

"You are such an old fuddy-duddy. Relax. Sex is natural. We're two single adults—"

"Imposing on the hospitality of our friends, who also happen to have a small child who could hear us." As he spoke, telling Tara all the reasons they shouldn't do anything, he also brushed his thumb across her nipple. He could lecture all he wanted, but actions spoke louder than words.

"We'll be quieter this time."

He laughed. "Easier said than done."

"No. It's not too hard if both our mouths are busy." Tara waggled her eyebrows up and down.

Jace shook his head. "I've created a monster."

"Yup, you made me. Now deal with it." Tara leaned low and nipped at his lower lip. "And don't act like you're not interested. I can feel you, you know. You're hard."

"That doesn't mean anything. Men can get hard if a strong wind blows against them."

"Bullshit." While brushing her lips over his, Tara snaked her hand between them, down beneath the waistband of his shorts until she made contact with the part she wanted. She stroked up and down his length, and noticed he didn't stop her. His hand was too busy rubbing her nipple. "Cassie gave me some pointers."

"What?" His hands stilled on her.

"Yup. Some tips."

"God almighty, you told her details about us?"

"No. Okay, a few. But mostly it was her telling me what she does with Dillon. A few little wifely tricks she's learned that she uses on him, or used to before the kid started sleeping between them."

"I really, really don't want to know what Dillon and his wife do together in bed. Please, Tara, don't tell me any more. I have to face this guy."

"Oh, I don't plan on telling you, silly." Tara stood and slid her shorts down her legs so she was bare from head to toe. "I'm going to show you."

Jace's gaze traveled over her bare skin. When she bent at the waist, grabbed his shorts and yanked them off, he didn't stop her. Nor did he protest when she straddled him backwards like she'd done the night before. She leaned low and ran her tongue over his length, and tasted the slick pre-come already at the tip. He didn't fight her on that, either. He pulled her hips down lower so he could reach her with his mouth.

She was definitely making progress, and she intended to progress even further tonight.

"I'm surprised no one's called or texted you lately." While trying not to relive the memories of the last two nights on the sofa with Tara, and concentrating on the highway ahead, it was surprising Jace realized her cell phone had been dead silent for days.

"Hmm?" She turned to him as if she'd been day-dreaming herself.

"Your phone. Mine's off but yours is—" Jace took his eyes off the road long enough to see the guilty expression settle on Tara's face. "Your phone is on, right?"

"Um . . ."

"Tara. What if someone needs to get a hold of us?"

"Your phone's not on either." Her tone sounded defensive.

"I know that. That's why we agreed to keep yours on."

"But Tuck kept calling. I didn't want to deal with it while we were having such a nice time at Dillon and Cassie's place."

Jace let out a breath. "I know."

How could he argue with that? He didn't want the outside world to find them any more than she did. They had had a good time the past two days. And nights. A time he wouldn't forget anytime soon.

"That was pretty amazing last night, huh?" She smiled.

Jace's eyes opened wide. "God almighty, Tara. We're not talking about that while I'm driving."

"Why not?"

"Because—" He couldn't come up with a reason other than he might drive off the road if he thought too much about how Tara sticking her sneaky little finger into his butt during the blowjob last night had made him shoot off like a damn geyser. "Just because. That's why."

She continued to look amused at his expense. "All right."

As it was, he'd never be able to look at Dillon and

Cassie again without knowing that they'd heard him and Tara, and that Cassie had been teaching Tara that little *wifely trick* she used on Dillon. Good God, that was more than any man should know about another. His face heated just thinking about it. He sure as hell hoped Cassie and Tara hadn't discussed over tea this morning how he'd reacted to what she'd done. The idea of that was horrifying.

"Turn on your phone," he ordered, not just to change the subject, but because they needed to have some way for people to contact them.

"Then you turn on yours, too."

"Fine." Jace reached onto the dash and tossed his phone at her. "Turn them both on."

"Fine. I will." She scowled at him and turned her attention to the phone that had landed in her lap.

Good. He could handle pissy Tara better than this new sexual explorer she had become. He truly had created a monster.

"I don't understand why you're acting like this about the other thing. You obviously enjoyed it—"

"Tara, I swear. Quit it."

"You can do it to me if you want. I won't mind. You liked it so much I want to see what it feels like."

He bit back a cuss far too foul for her ears, and looked for an escape from the conversation. As embarrassing as it was that he'd let her do it, the memory of the feel of that finger, slick with her saliva, sliding into him sent tingles up his spine.

Escape came in the form of a truck stop he nearly sped by. Jace flipped on the blinker and hit the breaks hard enough that they jolted forward as he swung into the entrance at the last moment.

Tara braced one hand on the dash in front of her. "What are you doing?"

"I need to take a break." One look in the mirror told him that Dillon, who was following behind them, had made the turn, too.

As Jace swung open the driver's-side door, Dillon pulled his truck into the spot next to where Jace had parked. Great. Maybe they could all discuss their sex lives together, as if they were in one big touchy-feely commune.

Dillon walked around to Jace's side of the truck. "Hey, what's up? Need a break?"

"Yup." Jace nodded, happy to leave it at that.

"No, he's mad at me," Tara elaborated, giving Dillon info he didn't need to have.

That was why a man should only have another man as a traveling partner. Females talked too damn much about the wrong things.

Dillon's brows rose. "Okeydoke. Well, as long as we're here, I'm getting something to eat and hitting the head."

"I'll come with." Tara thrust Jace's phone back at him. "You have a bunch of messages on there."

He had no doubt. Jace took the phone and silently cursed all women as he hoped Tara didn't decide to discuss her new sex trick with Dillon on the way to the bathroom. Then again, Dillon deserved to be as embarrassed as Jace. Let him share the misery. His wife had started it.

With that in mind, he drew in a deep breath and faced whatever hell his phone would bring. No surprise, a good number of the calls had been from Jacqueline, though she didn't bother leaving a voicemail. He'd just hear her angry breath before the call disconnected. Fine with him. One was from the guy taking over his lawn jobs, letting him know everything was fine. And then there were a couple of texts from Tuck. More than Jace would have expected. Tuck was still trying to get Tara to Stillwater for the big baby reveal.

Jace left the phone powered up, but on silent. He hopped up in the seat and tossed the cell under the dash, where he intended to leave it. When he'd crawled back out of the truck, it was to see Tara and Dillon on their way back to him. Dillon said something and she laughed, feeding into Jace's paranoia that they were talking about him.

"Something funny?"

"Yup." Tara smiled and handed Jace a cup and a bag. "I got you sweet tea and some onion rings."

Apparently she had learned as much about what Jace liked during her short stint as his traveling partner as he had about her likes.

She knew his addiction to sweet tea and how he preferred onion rings to French fries, just as he knew she liked diet cola over regular and loved ketchup, the more the better. He also knew that kissing that one spot on her neck just beneath her ear drove her a little crazy. His gut clenched at the memory.

Shit.

"Thanks." He grabbed the bag and drove those thoughts out of his head. "So would you like to share with me what you two are having such a good time discussing?"

"Sure. I was telling Tara how the Big Mart is off the next exit . . . and how I'm fixin' to buy me some of those underwear you're getting."

"Ha. Funny." Jace forced a fake smile.

They could mock all they wanted, but Jace had

seen riders do stranger things than wear new underwear in the name of superstition, and so had Dillon. The kid was enjoying teasing him in front of Tara.

He knew how to put an end to that. He set the cup and food bag on the truck's hood and turned toward the building. "I gotta take a piss. Tara, while I'm gone why don't you tell Dillon all about that little bedroom trick his wife said he enjoys so much."

Jace didn't know if she'd do it or not, but the look of fear on Dillon's face was enough to have him smiling all the way to the urinals. Ha! That'd teach Dillon to make fun of a man's riding rituals. It was true what they said. Misery did love company, and Jace loved that Dillon got to be miserable right along with him over the fact that Cassie and Tara were talking about private shit that should stay private.

As for little Miss Tara giggling over his underwear, when Jace got back to the truck, he'd make sure her phone was on. His was and fair was fair. They'd both have to suffer through the unwanted calls from home. Good traveling partners did those kinds of things together. It was the other things he and Tara did together that were wrong.

But dammit all if her orgasm therapy wasn't starting to work. He hadn't felt a thing seeing the messages and texts from Jacqueline. Not guilt. Not a desire to see her again. Nothing. If only this orgasm stuff would work to get rid of his guilt over Tara being Tuck's little sister, he'd be good to go . . . but that was Jace's issue to get over on his own. Somehow.

When Jace got back from the bathroom, Tara was nowhere to be found.

Dillon noticed him looking. "She decided she couldn't live without a shake for the road."

"A shake. A'ight." Jace grinned. He loved how Tara put food away like a bull rider.

"As for that other thing, I'm not real sure where we go from here." Red-cheeked, the usually cocky Dillon was having trouble maintaining eye contact.

"You mean now that we both know stuff about each other we shouldn't?" Jace asked.

"Yeah."

"I tell you where we go from here. We never breathe another word about it to each other or another living soul. That is *after* you tell your wife to please stop giving Tara advice in that particular area."

"A'ight." Dillon shook his head. "I still can't believe Cassie—"

"Eh! Nope. Not another word."

"Okay." Dillon drew in a deep breath, visibly regrouping. "So, uh, you know anything about the bull you drew for tonight?"

A change of subject. Good man. "Actually, I do. Tuck had him last year in Perkins. Flat bucker. He scored lower than he should have."

"You're gonna have to dress it up for the judges."

"Yup. That's what I figure. Though with the shoulder not at a hundred percent, I might rather have a bull that's not gonna challenge me too much."

"Sure. I agree."

This was good. Just two men shooting the bull and not thinking about women. Or blowjobs. Or how after last night's embarrassing incident, while they were still naked and the feel of her finger inside him was still much too fresh in his mind, Tara had forced Jace to hear all about how Cassie had explained, in horrifying depth, the benefits of male prostate stimulation during oral sex.

Good God almighty he might never get her words out of his head, but he had to try. He'd get hard if he kept thinking about it. Worse, Jace suspected if Tara tried it again, he'd let her do it.

He swallowed and glanced at Dillon. "So, what about your bull for tonight?"

Chapter Nineteen

The announcer's amplified babble bounced off the arena walls pretty much nonstop once an event began. Tara ignored it, mostly. Between the echo and the pounding music, it was nearly impossible to understand what was being said unless you were paying close attention to the action down on the dirt. But she found herself halting mid-step in her path behind the chutes when she heard Jace's name spoken over the loudspeaker.

". . . the original bull Jace Mills drew has been scratched. Instead, Mills will be aboard Beast Master tonight. This bull's been ridden only three times in fourteen outs this season, with two riders scoring in the nineties. If Jace can cover this ride, he'll move onto the leaderboard and head to the short go."

As the announcer went on to review the current event leaders, Tara glanced at the group of riders huddled over one of the chutes and knew Jace must be in the middle of them, climbing on top of Beast Master for a ride that would either help move him toward the win or dump him in the dirt without a score. As much as she hated to admit it, she was glad

he had on his brand-new pair of Big Mart underwear since, crazy though it seemed, it gave him confidence. He might need that mental boost to ride a
bull with a record that good, especially since Jace's
shoulder must still be sore.

Whatever item she'd been headed back to get
fled her mind. She'd remember once she got back
there, but that could wait a minute until after she
watched Jace's ride. That was the beauty of this
sport. A qualified ride lasted eight seconds. It was
pretty convenient that she could see Jace's entire
ride, and then get back to work, all in under a
minute.

The bull was giving Jace trouble in the chute. Tara
could see that even from where she stood. She
couldn't glimpse much more of Jace than just the
top of his hat, but that was bobbing up and down as
the bull danced beneath him. Dillon straddled the
rails over Jace, reaching in to hold on to his vest.
The chute was the most dangerous place to be, with
nowhere for the rider to get away from the bull,
whose bulk filled the space.

Tara held her breath, willing Jace to nod to the
gateman and get out of the chute and into the arena
where the bull had space to move and the three bullfighters could do their job and protect the rider.

Finally, the gate clanged open and Jace spun into
the ring on top of Beast Master, who was living up to
his reputation of being a ninety-point bull. Tara took
a step forward to get a better look as the animal
bucked hard and high. Jace stayed firmly seated
even through the worst of the moves. It looked as if
he'd cover the ride and get a hell of a score doing it.

Eight seconds seemed an eternity. She was about
to look for the clock to see how long it had been

when the animal dropped low in front, then whipped its head back. Jace couldn't react fast enough.

The crack of skull hitting skull cut through the air, and Tara was running toward the entrance even before Jace's body hit the ground.

Doc Chandler grabbed her arm before she could open the gate. "Wait."

"He's unconscious." That was obvious as Jace lay crumpled and unmoving while the bull continued to spin next to his body, missing him by mere inches.

"Let the fighters do their job. Tara, you gotta wait until they get the bull out of there."

"But—" She didn't have to finish her protest. Between the mounted safety man and the fighters, they herded the bull through the out gate.

"It's clear." Tara wasted no time. She pushed past the doctor and ran to Jace. His hat had been knocked off. She saw the amount of blood pouring from the gash in his forehead. "You should be wearing a damn helmet. Stupid, stubborn—"

The doctor kneeled next to her in the dirt. "Lecture him when he's conscious and can hear it."

Tara knew he couldn't hear her, but it made her feel better to yell at him, even unconscious.

Doc Chandler signaled for a body board, and the bile churned in Tara's stomach. Jace was lying in a horrible looking position. His body twisted and awkward. What if he'd broken his neck? What if he was paralyzed? The possibilities seemed endless, one worse than the next.

The arena went deathly quiet, a sign the crowd knew it was bad, but the silence didn't help Tara think. All her training, everything she'd learned in school, fled as she looked down at Jace.

She was used to him cocky, full of life and laugh-

ter, even if it was at her expense. This—this was unbearable.

Maryann and Rick arrived with the body board
and kneeled on the other side of the doctor. "The
ambulance is out back. We ready to move him?"
Maryann asked.

The doctor hissed in a breath. "I can't tell how
bad it is. I'd rather he be conscious so I can get some
idea."

Tara knew what the doctor wasn't saying. He
needed to know if Jace had broken his back or neck
before they untwisted his body and strapped him on
the board.

One of the most famous bull riders in history had
broken his back not once, but twice. With time, he'd
recovered and gone back to work in the arena with
nothing more than a sore neck to show for the injury. Tara repeated those facts silently to herself as
the doctor slapped Jace's cheek.

"Jace. Wake up."

Rick handed the doctor smelling salts. He
cracked the tablet open and waved it under Jace's
nose. He woke with a start.

"What happened?" His voice wasn't strong, and
he sure as hell wasn't coherent, but hearing him
speak was the best sound Tara had heard all night.
His eyes opened. His gaze swept past the doctor
leaning low over him, and settled on Tara. He
turned his head and hissed in a breath. "Ow."

"Try not to move just yet," the doctor instructed.
"Can you tell me what hurts?"

Jace's eyes moved back to the doctor. "My head.
Neck. Shoulder."

The doc nodded. "Well, you landed on your head,
after cracking it against the bull."

The blood ran in a steady stream down Jace's face, past one eye and over his nose. Maryann leaned low with a piece of gauze, but Tara was closer.

"I can get it." She held out her hand for the gauze.

Maryann handed it over and Tara blotted at the blood. He'd need stitches to close up the wound, but knowing him, he probably wouldn't want to get them.

"Can you feel your legs?" The doctor continued the evaluation as he probed the back of Jace's neck with his fingers.

"Yes." He moved one foot as proof.

"Can you squeeze both my hands?" Doc Chandler asked as he laid his fingers beneath Jace's.

"Yes." Jace tightened his fingers around the doctor's as proof.

"Good. Now, how many fingers am I holding up?"

He squinted. "Four. No, three, I think."

The doctor put down the two fingers he'd been holding up, and took out a penlight. He flicked the light across Jace's eyes. "Do you know what day it is, Jace?"

"Um." A frown creased Jace's bloody forehead.

"You might want to try another question," Tara told the doctor. "He doesn't know what the day is even when he hasn't fallen on his head."

Doctor Chandler nodded. "All right. Jace, what's this pretty lady's name next to me? Who is she?"

Jace's attention moved from the doctor to Tara. "Tara Elizabeth Jenkins. She's my traveling partner."

For some reason his answer, complete with the middle name Tara would have never guessed he knew, choked her up. She forced back the tears and put on a smile. "That's right."

The doctor flipped off his penlight. "Well, it looks as if you've got yourself a nice concussion, but I think that's the extent of it. We're gonna get you on the board—"

"No, I can walk out." Jace winced as he pushed himself up with one arm. His eyes focused on Tara. "Help me up."

Tara looked to the doctor for confirmation. He raised a brow. "He wants to walk out, he can, but not without help."

Cheers exploded throughout the arena when the fans saw Jace being lifted to his feet. The doctor moved to support him, but Jace reached out and grabbed for Tara's arm. He pulled her to his side, wrapping his right arm around her shoulder.

"All right. Tara can help you." With an expression that spoke more than his words had, the doc led the way toward the back.

Jace leaned so heavily on her that if Rick hadn't slipped beneath Jace's left arm to support him, Tara might have crumpled and taken both of them down to the ground.

As Jace's weight crushed against her, Tara took one staggering step after another. "Careful, Rick. That's the shoulder he dislocated in the last event."

Rick snorted. "A sore shoulder is the least of his worries right now, but I'll do my best."

"Damn new underwear didn't work." Jace's grumbled words took her by surprise.

Tara couldn't help but laugh, even as tears of relief stung behind her eyes. Happy he was with it enough to be a smart-ass, she had no problem humoring him. "Nope. They sure didn't. Maybe I'd better tell Dillon to ditch his before his ride. He'll have to ride commando, instead."

A crooked smile tipped Jace's mouth up as they made their way slowly but surely toward the back.

"I'm seeing two of you. You're gonna have to drive my truck back to the hotel." He was feeling mighty poorly to suggest that.

"It's okay. I'll ask Dillon to drive it, if you're worried about me."

"Not worried. I trust you." He let out a labored breath. "Damn, I hurt."

Jace trusted her. Enough to drive his truck, which was a total one-eighty from the last time they'd discussed her driving his vehicle. Tara had to recover from that pronouncement before she could respond to his other admission—equally amazing for a stubborn bull rider—that he was in pain.

"Will you take whatever pills the doc gives you without arguing?" she asked.

He nodded but the move looked painful. "Yeah."

That settled it. Jace had gotten one hell of a knock on the head. He'd changed his mind about most everything he'd been so adamant about before.

"All right, then. I'll see what he prescribes for you."

"Thanks." They'd reached the hallway leading to the medical room when Jace turned his head. "Somebody get my hat?"

Tara realized he was going to be fine if he was worried about his hat. "Yeah, Maryann grabbed it. But it's gonna need a good brushing after rolling around in the dirt. I'll clean it up for you when we get back to the hotel."

He let out a short laugh. "And I'll let you."

Dealing with a compliant Jace was a new experience, but so far, injury aside, she kind of liked him that way.

Had he been compliant and healthy—man oh man, she'd have him doing everything she wanted. Anywhere. Everywhere. That thought had her body tightening with need. But his weight across her shoulders making every step an effort for all three of them was a very real reminder he was hurt.

"Do you think he needs to go to the hospital? Get a CT scan?" The double vision concerned Tara enough to ask.

"No hospital." Jace answered Tara's questions before the doctor could.

Doctor Chandler blew out a breath. "I'd love to get a brain image and make sure there's no swelling or bleeding, but you heard him. I guess we won't be using the ambulance after all."

"No need. I feel fine." Jace stumbled, making him look not so fine.

The doctor watched his progress critically. "Jace, hospital visit or no hospital visit, it doesn't matter. I'm not letting you ride tomorrow. You realize that, right?"

"That's fine. I'll sit out tomorrow." Again, he agreed.

Doctor Chandler continued. "There's a good chance you're out for the next week."

Tara realized the full implications of Jace being injured. Yes, she was very worried about her travel buddy. Head injuries were nothing to mess around with. There could be internal bleeding, or swelling of the brain, or hell, any number of things. But in addition to all that, Jace was her ride. If he couldn't compete, he wouldn't be going to the next event.

"I'll be fine by the next event. You'll see. I feel better already, Doc."

Stubborn as ever, apparently. She'd been worried prematurely. Knowing Jace, he would keep driving to the events out of sheer stubbornness and the hope the doctor would give in and let him ride.

But right now, he wasn't looking so good. The doctor glanced at Tara. "You two are traveling together. Can you check on him a few times during the night?"

Tara opened her mouth to say of course she could since they shared a room, but now that they did more than just share a room, she decided to keep that detail to herself, just in case it wasn't already common knowledge. "Sure. No problem."

"All right." The doctor dipped his head in a nod. "Then we'll do what he wants. You have my cell number?"

"I do." Tara answered quickly because they'd reached the medical room and Jace was already reaching for the exam table.

Rick let him go and Jace swayed as he reached for the table's edge, missing it by a solid inch. His perception was way off.

Luckily, Tara still had a grip on him. He held onto her as she helped him sit. "Lie back."

"Nope."

"Why not?"

"Makes me feel sick. Like getting the spins after a night of too much drinking." He didn't quite focus on her face as he said it.

Nausea was common with concussions, but the last thing she needed was Jace taking a tumble off the table because he didn't want to lie down. Later, she'd have to prop him up in the bed with pillows. Maybe she should sleep in bed with him to make sure he didn't fall out.

Jace swayed again and she stepped closer. "Just hold on to me."

"Okay. Sounds good." He propped his hand on her shoulder and blew out a breath.

"Take these." Doc Chandler handed him two pills and a cup of water. Jace swallowed without argument.

More compliance. Too bad he was hurting. She sighed at the thought of what he might agree to if he was in this mood but physically feeling well.

She managed to get Jace to stay in the medical room, sitting down so he didn't fall down, for the remainder of the event. It was a bit like babysitting a child. Every time she got called away to do something else, she held her breath until she could get back to make sure he hadn't done anything to injure himself while she'd been gone.

Talk about nerve-wracking. If Tara could have strapped Jace down to the table, or even better, drugged him so he'd go to sleep, she would have. Rest was the best medicine for a concussion, but they couldn't give him anything that would make him sleepy. Throughout the night, she would need to make sure he was responsive. If he were drugged, she wouldn't be able to do that.

The doctor had given Jace some acetaminophen to make him more comfortable with the promise of a muscle-relaxer tomorrow if the discomfort in his neck or shoulder was too much for him. Since he refused to go to the hospital, and his symptoms weren't severe enough they could make him, that was about all they could do.

All in all, it looked as if Tara was going to get quite a bit of round-the-clock, on-the-job training thanks to Jace. Since the doctor had put her in charge of caring for him, he had to listen to her and do what she said. She liked that idea. However, once Jace began to feel better and realized she was in charge, he would absolutely hate it.

Tara liked that idea even better.

Chapter Twenty

"**B**ut I'm bored."

"I'm sorry, but you need to rest." Tara sounded like a mother coddling a two-year-old.

"I rested last night, except when you were poking me to wake me up all night long." Jace tried to ignore how whiny he sounded. He had a right. Being stuck in a hotel room sucked.

"I had to make sure you were all right since you refused to go to the hospital for a CT and I had no idea if your brain was bleeding."

Having Tara in charge of his medical care and apparently every other aspect of his life was enough to make a man's brain bleed. "Why can't I just go and sit behind the chutes? What difference does it make if I'm sitting here or I'm sitting there? The doc's not gonna let me ride anyway."

"You won't just sit there. You'll be up on the chutes helping the other guys take their wraps. Or hopping up and down yelling for their rides. I know you."

"So I'm just supposed to sit here? And do what?"

"Watch television."

"I hate television."

"You do not. I heard you talking to Tuck about that show with the guys with the long beards who hunt ducks or whatever."

"Fine, I like one show. What if that's not on tonight? Then what?"

"Find something else to watch." Tara shook her head. "I swear. You're worse than a child."

"Am not. I'm just bored."

Tara laughed. "Pouting doesn't help your case any."

"I've seen you pout plenty." Jace knew he was acting like a baby but being laid up was torture. Being laid up in a cheap hotel room with Tara as his warden was a nightmare. "What if I promise to sit and not leave my seat at the arena?"

"I have to work. I don't have time to watch you."

"I don't need a babysitter."

"Yes, you do." She planted her hands on her hips and looked too much like a young version of his mother. If Tara used his full name while yelling at him, he'd be traumatized by the likeness forever.

At least this new version of Tara, deep in caretaker mode, had stopped trying to attack him in bed. Not that he would have been able to perform in any way even if she had tried. He'd been too out of it.

The dull ache in his head was still present, and the even worse ache in his neck was nearly unbearable. Of course, he would never admit that to her. The force of the collision with the bull's skull had probably given him whiplash, but he would bet the bull wasn't feeling as crappy today as he was. Damn hardheaded creatures had skulls like freaking iron.

"Do you need anything before I leave? Food. Drink."

"No." He'd filled up on the pizza and pop they'd had delivered an hour ago.

"You sure? Jace, I want you to promise me you won't go anywhere after I leave."

"How could I go anywhere? You're taking my truck, aren't you?" He scowled at the idea of being trapped.

"No, uh, Dillon's coming to get me."

Jace frowned, which hurt his head. "Why?"

Tara pulled a face, which made him even more interested in the answer until a horrible thought crossed his fuzzy brain.

His eyes widened. "You didn't wreck my truck last night, did you?"

Had he been that out of it he didn't notice they'd gotten in an accident? Maybe she'd gone out again to get something when he'd fallen asleep and wrapped it around a phone pole trying to park. God almighty, he loved that truck.

"No, I didn't wreck it. It's fine. Right outside in the same place I parked it last night."

"Then—"

"It's too big for me, okay?" She let out a frustrated huff. "You were right. I hated driving it. It's too much truck and it scares me. Happy?"

He really was. Tara had admitted he was right about something and that rarely happened. He decided to take the high road. "I'm sorry you had to drive me last night and that it scared you."

"It's okay. I lived through it and so did your truck, so it's fine. But as long as Dillon is staying at the same hotel we are, and going to the same place, it seemed foolish not to text him and ask for a ride. You just rest and get better so I don't have to drive it again tomorrow to the next town. Okay?"

"Okay. Promise." He tried to control the smile brought on by the sheer satisfaction of being right.

She eyed him more closely. "How's your vision today?"

"Fine."

Tara moved to perch on the edge of his bed. She thrust two fingers in front of his face. "How many fingers am I holding up?"

"Two."

"Good." She nodded, happy because she had no idea he was lying. Or at least he hadn't told her the complete truth.

He saw two, all right, but they were so blurred they looked more like two hummingbirds in flight rather than two still fingers. The blurred vision would go away, and soon he hoped. Otherwise, traveling tomorrow would be a real challenge, since Tara wasn't getting behind the wheel of his truck again.

The sound of an engine outside had her glancing toward the door. "That'll be Dillon."

"Go on. I'll be fine."

She stood. "Keep your cell phone on—and not on silent, either—so I can call to check up on you."

"You keep yours on, too," Jace ordered.

She let out a huff. "Mine is on. You made me turn it on yesterday. Remember? Call if you need anything. Or if you feel dizzy or nauseated or—"

"Good-bye, Tara. Have a good day at work." If he didn't give her a little verbal push out the door, he had a feeling she wouldn't get there on her own. He didn't need Dillon knocking and then coming in and seeing him laid up in bed like a damn invalid.

"Okay, I'll see you later." With one final glance, Tara grabbed her bag and headed out the door.

The room felt different without her in it—as if all

the energy had seeped out the door along with her. It must be the boredom making him feel so alone. He'd dare say lonely. The side effect of being with someone twenty-four hours a day, he supposed.

Jace reached for his cell on the nightstand and pressed the volume control up from silent to vibrate. He didn't think he could handle it ringing, especially if Jacqueline continued to blow up his phone with calls and messages.

While he had it in his hand, he decided to kill some time. He couldn't deal with going through whatever new messages Jacqueline had left for him, but he would enjoy making Tuck jealous he wasn't there by telling him about the epic wreck on Beast Master.

The television was the only light in the room when Jace awoke with a start. He must have fallen asleep. No surprise. He was bored out of his mind.

The sound of water running in the bathroom gave him a clue as to what had awoken him. Tara was home. The event must be over. He hoisted himself up a little higher on the pillow and winced at the pain in his neck. He'd have to go to the bathroom after she came out, and sneak something out of his shaving bag. He never traveled without ibuprofen to dull the aches and pains.

Jace waited until he heard her walk out of the bathroom and slip into her own bed before he slid out of his. He brushed his teeth and swallowed a few pills for the pain with water right out of the tap.

When he came out of the bathroom, Tara was sitting up. "Hey, how do you feel?"

"Fine. How'd tonight go at the arena?" He padded slowly toward his bed.

"Good. Klint won."

"Klint?" Jace turned his whole body rather than just his stiff neck to glare through the dimness at her.

"Yes. What's the problem?"

"He's a frigging rookie." Jace climbed into his bed, but chose to lie on top of the covers. His anger was making him hot.

"Rookies can win an event sometimes, too."

Rookies who'd taken Tara into a closet to molest her shouldn't win anything. Where was karma or whoever was supposed to take care of such things? He was still scowling when she swung her feet over the edge of her mattress and covered the short distance between their beds. She climbed onto his bed, and kneeled, straddling his legs.

"What are you doing?" he asked, though he supposed he could guess.

"You're acting pissy so you must be feeling better." With her thighs spread wide, Tara ground against his pelvis, waking up his erection.

He felt her warmth clear through his shorts. Frowning, he slid his hands up her thighs and beneath the hem of her T-shirt. Bare skin greeted him. "When did you stop wearing shorts to bed? And underwear, too?"

"When you agreed we could fool around."

"I never agreed to that."

"Uh, yeah, you did. At Dillon's house, the first night. You said that we could do everything but fuck."

He frowned. Yeah, he kind of remembered saying that, but he didn't like foul cuss words coming out of her mouth. "That is too filthy a word to be coming out of your pretty little mouth."

"Then you'd better keep my mouth busy so you won't have to hear it again." She leaned low and brushed her lips over his bruised forehead. "I'm glad you have a hard head."

His head wasn't the only thing hard. As Tara grabbed the waistband of his shorts and pulled them down, his cock sprang free, bobbing, greeting her.

"I bought something the other day while you were buying your bad-luck underwear." She stroked his length while she spoke, her fingers soft and cool against his heated skin.

"You did? What'd you get?" Considering how strange their situation was, talking about shopping while she stroked him didn't seem as weird as it should.

"Lube."

He'd been going along with her small talk and enjoying the feel of her hand on him until that single word stopped him in his tracks. *Lube.* God almighty, he truly had created a monster.

The thought of Tara trolling the lubricant and condom aisle at the Big Mart while he wasn't looking had his face heating even as she reached for the drawer in the table between the beds. She emerged with a tiny plastic bottle.

"Please tell me you didn't have that stashed in there next to the Bible." Cheap hotels in Oklahoma didn't provide much in the way of extras, but they always came with a copy of the Good Book.

"Um. Okay, I won't tell you." She flipped open the lid and looked down, concentrating on the thin stream of clear gel she drizzled over his length. Glancing up, she caught the expression of horror on his face. "What was I supposed to do? There's only one drawer."

That clinched it. They were going to hell for sure. "I don't know. Keep it in the bathroom. Don't buy it to begin with."

"You're going to be very happy I bought it." Tara stroked her fist over his slick hard-on, and Jace didn't have much breath—or incentive—to argue any further.

As it was, he was having trouble keeping his eyes from rolling back in his head. His lids drifted shut from the sensations rocketing through him. All the times he'd touched himself, and there were many since the break-up, it had never felt as good as it felt with Tara's slick, firm hold on him.

She leaned low. He felt her breath against his ear as she said, "Feel good?"

"Yes."

As if she had to ask.

Jace realized he wasn't doing anything for her in return, but that was easily remedied. He slid a thumb between her lips and pressed on her clit. She made the noise in her throat that always sent tingles down his spine.

"I love when you make that sound."

"I love when you touch me there. Don't stop."

"Wasn't planning to." Not stopping was no problem. He could continue all night, especially if she kept up what she was doing to him.

"Would it hurt you to take off your shirt?" She slipped her fingers under the hem of his T-shirt and traced a path over his stomach that had his muscles jumping beneath her touch.

"I think I can manage that without doing any bodily injury." Jace was always willing to indulge a lady.

Especially one who wanted him naked so she could touch him.

With her help, they divested him of his shirt. Once he was bare as the day he was born, Tara leaned back and pulled her T-shirt up and over her head. The sight of her naked above him had Jace moaning, even before she reached for the lube and sent another stream careening over his very happy cock. She rose above him and adjusted their position, and he felt the pleasure of stroking between Tara's ass cheeks.

"This feel okay?" She asked the question while running her palms up his sides.

"Yes."

"Good." Tara lowered her mouth to tease his nipple. She drew the peak between her lips, scraping her teeth over the sensitive flesh until the fine hairs stood up on his arms.

Somewhere through the haze of pleasure Jace realized Tara was awfully concerned with his pleasure. He had a feeling her focus had nothing to do with his injury. His suspicions told him he'd better watch her or, as slick as he was from the lube, she might try to slide him into her and take what she wanted before he had a chance to stop her.

Tara ran the tip of his cock from front to back, running it over her pussy and up between the cheeks of her ass, before she reversed and then repeated the motion. It felt great and he should be happy, but it was Tara, who on a good day did the opposite of what she was told. With her on top and in control, one thrust and he'd be fully seated inside her. And damn if that didn't have him tingling just thinking about it.

It wasn't as if Jace had any peace of mind with all

the guilt over what they had been doing, but the one thing he could still say was that he hadn't stolen her virginity. He intended to hold on to that, at least. "Careful there, darlin'. Watch what you're doing."

"Relax, you prude. I'm not doing what you think I'm doing." She leaned low to scrape his other nipple with her teeth and sent a tremor down his spine.

Fair was fair, he supposed. He'd spent a considerable amount of time torturing her with his mouth the other night on the sofa. He'd worked her into one hell of an orgasm with not much more than his mouth on her tits and a few well placed fingers between her legs.

He wrestled his mind back to their conversation. "You sure about that?" He wouldn't put it past her to bend the truth to get what she wanted.

"Mmm, hmm. Now hush up and kiss me." She wrapped her arms around his neck and kissed him like she meant it, plunging her tongue against his.

Tara's mouth was a distraction, but not enough of one that he wouldn't notice her breaking the rules. If that was her plan, it would fail, but, damn, the friction of sliding his cock between the globes of her ass felt so good, he could come just from that.

She pulled away from the kiss far enough to ask, "You sure you're okay?"

"Never felt better." That wasn't even a lie.

"Good." Her lids drifted low over her eyes as she rocked back against his cock.

Jace enjoyed the view as she rose over him like a sex goddess. She didn't have the exaggerated hourglass figure of a centerfold, but her athletic build sure worked. She was long and lean and healthy, and enjoying being naked on top of him. He knew how to make her enjoy it more.

He slid two fingers inside her and located her G-spot while continuing to work her clit with the base of his palm. A low groan told him Tara approved of the change. Her breathing quickened as she moved against him while riding his hand. He had to admit as he slid between her cheeks that she was right. The lube did make it better.

Her rhythm slowed as she adjusted her angle and then he felt it—Tara pushing the head of his slick cock against the insanely tight entrance to her ass. His hand stilled on her as he tried to decide what to do about that turn of events.

"Don't stop. I was close to coming." A frown drew her dark brows low as she used her body weight to try to force him inside. She was right. Coming would help her.

Was he really going to let her continue? As his chest tightened right along with his balls in anticipation of what was to come, Jace knew the answer was yes. He started working her again, harder as his other hand settled on her hip and held her still. "Don't hurt yourself, Tara. Take it slow."

She laughed. "I notice you're not fighting me or telling me to stop."

God help him, no he wasn't. He'd feel bad about that later. He considered asking if she were sure about trying this, but that question seemed stupid. Tara was clearly in charge. She was the one on top.

As he worked her with his hand, her muscles clenched, tightening for her impending release. Jace watched her expression change. He could see when she moved from pain to pleasure. Her eyes closed and her mouth opened on a breathy moan.

He knew the moment she tipped over the edge into orgasm. He surely felt it as she slid down to en-

gulf his length. He didn't ease up with his hand because he sure as hell didn't want her climax to end
anytime soon as her body milked his cock with
spasm after spasm that shook her.

It wasn't easy to move his hips with her weight
pressing down on him, but as she moved over him
Jace managed a few small thrusts. Three times was
all it took before the sensation of being sunk deep in
her tight heat while her muscles gripped him was
enough to send him careening to completion right
along with her.

The whole thing seemed kind of surreal once it
was over. She remained on top of him, panting and
silent. The silent part was what made it so strange.

Spent, he softened and slipped from her body.
There was going to be a mess for her to deal with
shortly. In typical Tara fashion, she probably hadn't
thought that far ahead when she'd decided to do
this thing with him.

He ran his hands up her back. "You go clean up
in the bathroom first. I'll wait to get in the shower
until after you're done."

She nodded, but didn't move. She was silent for
long enough that he started to worry about her.
Maybe he'd hurt her. He'd just opened his mouth to
ask if she was all right when she leaned back far
enough to look at his face. "Is that what it's like?
Real sex, I mean?"

He hated to tell her what they'd done had been
very real, but he knew what she meant. How to answer that was the big question.

Sure, buried inside her he'd felt every pulse of
her body around his as she came. And yeah, he'd
gotten to see every reaction—both the good and the
bad—cross her face as he sank past her pain and

into her tight body. But there was a level of intimacy reached when making love that seemed so much more *real,* to use her word, than this had, despite how amazing what they'd done had felt. Damn, it had felt amazing. It had been so long since he'd indulged in that particular pleasure, he'd forgotten how much he enjoyed it.

As Tara watched his face, Jace decided on an answer to her question. "No. Not exactly."

"Why not? How is it different?" She didn't look happy with his answer.

Jace might not have taken her actual virginity, but he was certain he'd been her first in what they'd just done. That fact seemed huge. He felt the weight of it on him. It made saying the right thing seem doubly important.

Stroking her face with his thumb, he said the only thing he could think of. "It's even better."

Her expression softened. "Then let's—"

"Nope." He'd walked right into that trap. He'd have to learn to be more careful with his answers or she'd somehow trick him into agreeing to take her virginity, just as she'd somehow gotten him to agree to do everything but that the other night at Dillon's.

She frowned down at him. "But if it's—"

"Tara, I said no. Now go get finished in the bathroom so I can get in there." He waited and still she didn't move. He could see the gears working in her brain, concocting new plans and schemes to get him to have sex with her. Time to nip it in the bud and at the same time show her how *real* what they'd done was. "Tara, what I shot inside you is going to come out. I'd rather it not be on my bed."

That did it. She sat up with such a deep scowl on

her face, he had to hold in his laugh. But she didn't call him a pig, which he'd totally expected her to. She got up and strode naked to the bathroom. He could have sworn she clenched her butt cheeks the entire way. He smiled as she slammed the bathroom door behind her.

She finished in the bathroom pretty quickly, and then Jace got to indulge in a long hot shower that he hoped would ease the stiffness in his neck and shoulder muscles.

When he emerged from the steam of the bathroom, he found Tara back in her own bed and in her big T-shirt, flipping through a magazine she'd bought at the store, apparently along with the lube he'd just found out about.

Things were back to normal. As if they hadn't just come as close as two people could to having the real sex she kept pushing for. As if Tara hadn't been the first woman besides Jacqueline that Jace had come inside in the last eight years—a pretty monumental milestone to him, adding to the stress of the already awkward situation.

Given all that, he couldn't help thinking how weird the separate beds thing felt after what they'd done together. He didn't like it, though it was for the best since things were confused enough without him spooning her all night in his sleep.

Damn, he missed spooning.

Reconciled to the way things were, he grabbed his shorts off the floor, pulled them on, and crawled into his own bed. He'd just settled back against the pillows when he remembered he'd forgotten something in the bathroom.

"Crap." Jace flipped the sheets back again with a

sigh and a wince as every motion sent a twinge through him. Funny, he'd managed to ignore the pain pretty good while buried inside Tara.

"What?" Tara glanced up from her magazine.

"I wanted to take another ibuprofen before I went to sleep."

Her eyes popped wide. "You shouldn't be taking ibuprofen. That could increase the risk of internal bleeding. You're supposed to take acetaminophen after a severe head injury."

"I already took some ibuprofen before. I'm fine. I don't have any internal bleeding."

"How many did you take before?" She kept him pinned with her stare.

"Two." He should have lied and said none before she had him in the emergency room looking for the nonexistent bleeding she was so worried about.

"When did you take them?"

"Right before we—you know." Jace tipped his head toward the mattress and let it go at that.

"Why do you need more so soon? What hurts? Your head? How's your vision been?" She was up and out of her bed like a shot.

Kneeling on his mattress, she frowned at him, clearly in doctor mode. That was one way to get them both back into one bed. Not the most ideal way . . .

Time for damage control. "Tara, relax. It's not my head. I had a dull headache when I woke up but the ibuprofen helped that. It's my neck."

The blue pools of her eyes widened one more time. "Could you have injured your vertebrae?"

"No, it's muscular. I'm just sore. That's all."

"You sure?"

"Yes, I'm sure." Jace had literally had a head-on

collision with something that weighed as much as a small car. Of course there'd be some soft tissue damage from the impact. "It's just my muscles. I promise."

She paused a second while he waited for the results of the debate he could see going on inside her head. Finally, she stood. "I've got some Midol with me. It's marketed to women for cramps, but it's the formula without ibuprofen. It'll help your muscle aches. Will you take it if I give it to you?"

"Yes, ma'am. If you give it to me, I'll take it."

"Yeah, I noticed that before." Tara's expression turned on a dime, and the she-devil was back.

The change in her demeanor was enough to give him whiplash all over again. Still, he couldn't help but smile. He watched her pad barefoot around the room in her floppy T-shirt, getting the pills, filling a plastic cup with water from the sink, and then she was back.

"You really shouldn't take these so close to the ibuprofen."

Jace thrust his hand toward her. "Just give me. Do you know how many pills some riders take just to get through the day? And prescription shit, too. Not over-the-counter, lady cramp pills." He waited with his hand out.

After another internal debate, she gave in. "All right, but you need something in your stomach with these."

"Okay. Whatever you say." The cold leftover pizza they'd had delivered as an early dinner before Tara left for the arena wasn't looking too appetizing, but he was willing to humor her and let her think he'd eat it.

She watched him swallow the pills, and then was

up and moving again. "I forgot that Dillon stopped to eat on the way back from the arena so I got you these. Your favorite cookies."

He smiled as she held up the small white bag. "Aw. Thank you."

"Anytime."

He truly was touched. She'd remembered that every time they stopped for a sub sandwich he'd order the chain's hot, fresh baked cookies. Sex and cookies—Tara had really perfected the travel partners with benefits role she'd invented for herself.

When she kneeled on the edge of his bed to deliver the cookies, Jace reached out, wrapped his hand around her arm and drew her to him. "You're pretty handy to have around. You know that?"

Tara looked surprised for a second, then she leaned back and settled into the space beneath his arm. "Thank you."

"You're welcome." He gave her the satisfaction of eating one of the oatmeal raisin cookies so she wouldn't worry that her two girly pills would eat a hole in his stomach.

He spotted his cell phone on the table and decided he'd better tell her what he'd done while she'd been at the event. Jace ran his hand up and down her arm hoping to soothe the blow that he'd called the brother she'd been trying to avoid because he'd been bored and felt like talking. "So I, uh, talked to Tuck on the phone tonight."

Tara stiffened against him. "And?"

Trying to make light of it, Jace shrugged, and then after the fact remembered how much that motion hurt. "I told him about my wreck."

"Which means he knows you're out until the doctor clears you to ride again." Her lips formed a tight, unhappy line. "Did he ask if we're coming right home?"

"Yup." In fact, Jace had noticed how Tuck had jumped right on that assumption, sounding almost happy about the injury. No doubt about it, he hoped Jace's being on the injured list would get Tara back in town so Logan and Emma could break her heart again with the news of their baby.

"What did you tell him?" The tension in her body increased.

Jace felt it radiate off her, but it was in his power to relieve her worry.

"I told him that it don't matter if I'm hurt or not. You still have to finish your internship and there's what? More than a week of it left? And I told him I wouldn't be coming home anyway because I'm fine and I'll be back riding in another day or two."

"So basically you lied to him about that last part."

"No. Shut up." Jace felt her relax and smiled, deciding a lighter topic of conversation was in order. "So, I'm kind of afraid to ask this, but here goes. Did Cassie put the idea for this—what we did tonight— into your head?"

Tara smiled. "Nope, I thought of it all myself."

"Well, thank God for that." He didn't need any more crap in his brain than he already had regarding Dillon and Cassie's sex life.

"I read on the Internet that we needed lube so I got some."

Tara was reading about anal sex on the Internet.

"Great." With a sigh, Jace settled in lower against the pillow. He'd had enough talk. It was all too disturbing. "Let's get some sleep."

"You want me to sleep here? In your bed?"

Jace wanted to say *yes, please stay*. Wanted to tell

her he hadn't slept well since he'd gotten his own place and had started sleeping alone over a year ago. What he said was, "Sure. If you want to."

"What do you want?" She twisted her neck to glance up at him. "It might be more comfortable for your stiff muscles if I went to my own bed and gave you more room."

"I want you to stay." Jace didn't miss how that bit of honesty slipped out of him a little too easily.

Truth was, he missed having someone else in the bed. That wasn't to say that he missed Jacqueline. Not at all. He just hadn't gotten used to sleeping alone again after seven years of sleeping with a warm body next to him. That seemed as good a reason as any for why he couldn't sleep for shit. Most nights it took a nice big shot of whiskey before bed to get him to fall into a sleep that he'd wake from before dawn, anyway.

"Okay, I'll stay here." Her voice sounded soft. Peaceful. Not at all Tara-like. It was kind of soothing and nice.

"Good." Jace closed his eyes, then thought of one last thing. "Oh, and I'm never opposed to being woken up with a blowjob. Just an FYI."

She let out a short laugh. "In your dreams."

With her pressed up next to him after all they'd done? Probably. He smiled, pulled her a bit closer, and then felt himself start to drift off.

Chapter Twenty-one

Tara woke to the sunlight creeping through the crack between the curtains, and a hard, warm body pressed against her back. One part in particular felt harder than the rest as it nudged against her rear while she lay on her side. Somebody was awake.

"Good morning to you, too." She laughed.

"Hmm?" Jace's arm tightened around her waist as he sounded more asleep than awake.

"Your morning hard-on is poking me in the butt."

"Mmm." His low rumbling groan vibrated through her back where they were pressed together. "That's because it, like me, has remembered how much we both used to enjoy morning sex."

He pulled her tighter against him and kissed the side of her face. Nothing sexual. It felt more like a good morning kind of peck—or it would have if his cock wasn't still making the tiniest little thrusts against her flesh. Almost as if Jace, or the erection with a mind of its own, hoped she wouldn't notice . . . if the movements were small enough.

"The lube is right there if you wanted to, you know, do again what we did last night."

Jace and his morning wood went dead still. "You're not too sore?"

"I think it'll be okay." Honestly, Tara had no idea if she was sore down there or not.

She hadn't moved more than her mouth to talk since becoming conscious, but even her mention of the lube had Jace breathing a little faster. That he wanted her so much his body reacted to just the thought of having her was a huge turn-on. After all the nights of fighting his damn honor code or guilty conscience, she wasn't about to pass up doing more with him when he was finally willing. Enthusiastic, even.

Jace's weight crushed her into the mattress as he reached past her and grabbed the lube from the table on her side of the bed. He rolled on his back and flipped open the lid. As she glanced over her shoulder, she saw him yank off his shorts. He drizzled a long stream of lubricant over his length, then spread it with his fingers.

She'd had him in her hand last night and had marveled at how he was hard as steel but covered with skin as soft as velvet. She'd never thought much about the mechanics of the male penis, but it truly was a pretty amazing instrument.

Tara pulled her T-shirt off and dropped it to the floor and moved to roll over, figuring she'd straddle him like she'd done last night.

"No. Stay like that. On your side."

"Really? That will work?" She rolled back to her original position.

Jace ran one slick finger between the cheeks of her ass, pressing just the tip inside. "Mmm, hmm. It'll work fine. Trust me. Bend your top knee, darlin'."

When he spoke, low and close to her ear like that, it never failed to have her insides clenching with need. Outside of bed, Jace telling her what to do gave her hives. But in bed, with his giving her instructions she knew would bring them so much pleasure, she had no problem following his orders. None at all.

"This okay?" He pushed deeper and rotated his finger.

A tremor ran through her from the combination of his words near her ear and his finger moving inside her. "Yes."

He slid out and then back in with what felt like two fingers. He pushed deep and then held still, making her feel stretched and full as her body adjusted to the new addition. "How about now?"

"Fine." She heard the lube snap open again. His fingers disappeared, then she felt breached with something wider.

"Still just my fingers. Three this time." Jace moved slowly and gently, letting her body adjust.

She nodded. His talking her through it was hot as hell. So was the way he took such care with her body. His behavior with her, and his concern, was far from that of the wham-bam-thank-you-ma'am player she'd assumed him to be.

He pulled his fingers out and she had a hunch what would be next, even before he lined up the blunt tip of his erection with her entrance. "This is me now. Okay?"

She heard the tension in his voice and felt it as he held his breath and pressed against her. "Okay."

He snapped open the lid on the lube one more time and a cool drizzle hit her butt, then she felt the wide, flared head of the penis she'd become so familiar with recently push inside, breaching her. She hissed in a breath. Maybe she was a little sore from last night, after all.

Jace swallowed hard enough for her to hear it. "I know this first part hurts, but it'll be better as soon as I push past it."

She nodded and he pressed deeper. She drew in another sharp breath. He eased back a bit and brushed a kiss against her ear. "Listen. When I push inside again, try and use your muscles to push me out."

"Why?" Tara frowned even though, uncomfortably stretched to her limit, pushing him out sounded like a pretty good idea.

"Trust me. Do it."

"Okay." She did trust him, and did as he'd said, bearing down when he pushed forward one more time. Inexplicably, it worked and what felt like it wouldn't fit before, slid inside.

"That's my girl." He held still while breathing heavier than before.

So was she.

Last night hadn't seemed so difficult. Then again, last night she'd been so excited he hadn't refused her, she couldn't have cared how tight the fit was. And damn, it was a tight fit.

Jace slid a hand beneath her knee and pulled her top leg over his hip, spreading her wide so he had complete access to her, which he took full advantage of by finding her clit. He began rubbing her, hard and fast, waking up nerve endings that really enjoyed the attention he gave them.

That was another difference she hadn't thought of. Last night she'd been coming when he entered her. If he kept this up, she'd be coming again soon.

Her muscles bore down around him. He felt it and pressed deeper with a hissed, "Yes."

His entire body felt tense, as if he was holding back. She didn't want him to hold back. "You can move, Jace. I'm okay."

"You sure?"

"Yeah. It's better now."

That was obviously all the permission he needed. He plunged deep, before pulling almost all of the way out and then thrusting inside again. The motion was slow, but firm, forging through the tight space between muscles that were hell-bent on keeping him out. At the same time, he worked her harder, circling her clit with the rough pad of his finger.

He moved inside her faster, harder compared to the gentleness of last night when he'd lain almost totally still while she did all the moving. He'd seemed to hold himself in check. Totally in control. Not so this morning. She'd never seen him let go except maybe on that night he'd given in and first kissed her.

His breath was loud and fast. His left arm kept a tight hold around her, anchoring him as he rocked into her. His fingers on her clit seemed to have one purpose, to push her over the edge as quickly as possible.

Tara might have been afraid of the change in him, of the speed and intensity with which he took her, if he didn't already have her so close to orgasm. Every thrust seemed to push her nearer to the edge. She knew he'd slow down, or even stop if she needed him to, but she didn't ask.

As foreign as the invasion to that part of her body felt, she loved having him inside her. Loved how he lost himself in her. She let him take her how he needed to and trusted that he'd know what she needed, as well.

Jace pressed two fingers inside her, filling her virgin channel as his palm pressed hard against her clit. He stroked her with his fingers while continuing to plunge his cock into her ass. Her body clenched around him and he groaned, long and low. The sound pushed her one step closer to completion.

She turned her head on the pillow and caught sight of his expression. His eyes were squeezed shut and a frown creased his bruised and battered forehead.

He sensed her watching him and opened his eyes, but the lids remained heavy as he gazed at her with an expression so intense she'd never seen it on him before.

He hauled her tighter against him with the arm she'd been lying on and crashed his mouth into hers. Jace kissed her hard, plunging his tongue into her mouth with as much enthusiasm as he used to plunge his cock inside her.

The knowledge that he filled her overwhelmed Tara. Between tongue, fingers and cock, Jace, the man she'd spent half of her life hating, or at least really disliking, possessed her completely. The thought gripped her, sending her over the edge. She came harder than she had the night before.

He became more frenzied as Tara rode out the waves of the climax that seemed as if it would go on for as long as he did. Ridiculously long and incredibly hard, the orgasm had her making sounds she didn't recognize as her own. His name might have even escaped her lips once between the keening that sounded barely human.

His speed built until he came loud with one deep,

hard thrust. She held still and felt his release throbbing.

Not moving, they stayed just as they were, panting, still connected, their limbs intertwined. She felt him semi-hard inside her. He didn't make any move to pull out. He didn't move his hand, either. He still cupped her. His fingers, hooked inside, idly pressed against a spot that enjoyed the attention. The motion had her muscles clenching. A bit more and he'd have her coiling for another release even though less than a minute ago she'd come harder than she ever had in her life.

"Thank you, Tara." His breathy thanks surprised her.

"For what? The morning butt sex?" She craned her neck on the pillow to see his face.

"You have such a way with words, but yeah, I guess as ridiculous as it sounds, that is what I'm thanking you for. That and your insane orgasm therapy." A crooked smile tipped up one corner of his mouth. "I can't believe we're making this work. This crazy traveling partners with benefits thing you came up with."

"I told you it would work. Both the traveling partners with benefits thing *and* the orgasm therapy." She'd faced head-on the Jacqueline tattoo over his heart—an indelible reminder of exactly how much he needed what they were doing. They both needed it to get over the past and to move forward.

"Yeah, I know you did, but I didn't believe you." He moved his left hand over her belly and up to her chest, where he rolled her nipple between his thumb and forefinger, shooting a bolt of pleasure straight from her breast to between her legs.

Curiosity got the best of her and she asked, "Did you used to do this with her?"

He let out a short laugh. "Do what? Have anal sex with Jacqueline?"

"Yeah." Now that he said it, she wasn't sure she wanted to hear the answer.

"No. Tried to once. It ended badly. I made the attempt again maybe twice over the years, but she was too scared of it by then. Cried, yelled, accused me of being selfish and wanting to hurt her. I never tried again after that." Jace shrugged as if it didn't matter.

Tara had a feeling it mattered very much. Not so much the missing out on the butt sex, but the fact she'd accused him of wanting to hurt her. "You didn't hurt me. Maybe it was a little uncomfortable in the beginning, but once we got going, it was fine. For not having done it, you're pretty good at it."

"Uh, thanks." He laughed. "But I never said I'd never done it. Your question was did I used to do it with her."

"Oh. Yeah. You're right." Tara felt silly for making that assumption out loud.

Of course he'd done it before. He'd probably had all sorts of kinky sex with a hundred women before dating Jacqueline. For some reason, the thought of Jace burying himself inside some buckle bunny's ass bothered Tara. More than it should considering the last time he'd been with anyone other than his ex for any kind of sex at all had to have been like eight years ago.

It was crazy, but she'd hoped it would be their thing. Something only they had done together. A lot to ask, she supposed, since Jace was a thirty-year-old man, not some inexperienced kid. No, Jace was definitely not that.

He was still inside her, no longer hard, but definitely not soft. He tipped his hips forward, pressing deeper and holding there as he leaned down and brushed his lips against her neck.

"You think you have one more orgasm in you this morning?" The warmth of his breath against her throat sent a tingle down her spine, as his finger strummed her clit. "I promise I'll leave you alone after that. I'm just not ready to pull out quite yet. You feel too good."

"I'll give another orgasm a try. You know, for the good of our travel partnership, and all." She smiled as she felt him laugh behind her.

"Thanks, Tara. You're really taking one for the team." Then there was no more laughing as Jace's left palm held her breast, and he circled her already sensitive bundle of nerves with his right.

She tightened her muscles around his length and felt him move, growing inside her. "Amazing."

"What is?"

"I can feel you inside me." She squeezed him one more time.

He groaned in response. "I certainly hope so."

Jace latched on to her earlobe with his teeth. The wet heat of his mouth on her ear sent another thrill through her as he worked her clit harder. She could definitely come again if he kept it up.

"Gonna stop at the next sex shop and buy you a vibrator." He spoke low. His voice, a deep rumble against her ear, sounded full of need and desire.

"Why?" Tara didn't want a piece of plastic inside her. She wanted him.

"So I can work you with it while I'm inside your ass."

That thought had her clenching tighter around him.

He reacted. His breath caught in his throat. Hard

again, he started to stroke inside her as her body gripped his. "I can feel you squeezing me."

"I certainly hope so." She turned his own words back on him.

He groaned just as her cell phone started to vibrate on the bedside table. Breathless, Jace held her tighter. "Ignore it."

She had no intention of doing anything else as his thrusts grew more frenzied and he grunted with every frantic stroke.

Jace plunged his tongue into her ear and that was it. Tara tipped over the edge and cried out with the orgasm that gripped her. Behind her, he thrust deep and held there. His whole body stiffened as he groaned, deep and long.

Tara couldn't keep herself from thinking, even as the waves of pleasure wracked her body, how he was already planning their next time together after a visit to the sex shop. The idea seemed to double the intensity of her orgasm, before it finally slowed. A stray aftershock twitched inside her as Jace pulled his hand away and pressed his palm to her stomach, holding her tight against him.

With his head resting on the pillow behind hers, he said, "Remember how last night you asked me if this was what having actual sex was like? And I said no."

His cock went slack and slipped out of her. The demands of his morning hard-on had been satisfied, she guessed. Not that she was complaining. Waking up with multiple orgasms every morning wouldn't exactly be a hardship. He made no move to loosen his arms, wrapped tightly around her and she wasn't about to ask him to.

"Yeah, I remember."

"This time, it was. At least, it seemed pretty damn close."

She'd felt it too, the difference. It was as if a part of Jace she'd never seen before had been exposed. Bared to her. Like he'd opened up and shown her a piece of his soul. And as if he'd touched something deep inside of her, too.

"Thanks for telling me." Tara swallowed hard, feeling the enormity of the feelings hurtling through her. "I think I'm going to jump in the shower."

"Okay." Jace rolled off her and she escaped to the bathroom.

Needing a little time alone, she indulged in a longer than usual shower. After she started to feel guilty for hogging the bathroom, she went back out so Jace could get in there.

As they passed in the middle of the room, Jace grabbed her arm. "You can start packing if you want. We're heading out today." He gave her a smile and a quick kiss, before disappearing behind the closed door.

Yup. Things definitely felt different. Cassie's words echoed in Tara's head. *It's pretty impossible for a woman to have sex with a man and not succumb to feelings.*

As Jace took his turn in the shower, Tara sat on the bed she hadn't slept in and tried not to admit that some sort of shift had happened between them. She spotted her cell phone on the nightstand and remembered the missed call. Might as well get it over with. It was as good an excuse as any for not thinking about what they'd done. She sat on her bed, still nice and neat, and grabbed the phone. The display read MISSED CALL, but it wasn't from Tuck. It was Tyler.

Frowning, she hit the button to retrieve the voice-mail.

"Sis, pick up your phone. I've got a surprise for you. I'll be at your hotel in an hour and you two had better still be there. Call me back."

Tyler was an hour away. Why? How did he even know where they were?

She surveyed the disaster around her. There was one bed messed up in a room with two. The bottle of lube was somewhere in Jace's sheets, and she was pretty sure she could detect the scent of sex in the air, though that might be her paranoia.

Jace emerged from the bathroom, looking jolly and freshly satisfied and that clinched it—Tyler was going to take one look at the two of them and all the evidence and know they'd spent the night and the morning doing things no brother should even think about his sister doing.

"What's wrong?" Jace halted halfway across the room, naked.

She guessed they'd moved past the towel-wearing stage in their relationship. *Great*. Just when her brother was an hour away. And wait, he'd left that message a while ago.

Had he called during round one or round two of the morning sex? She couldn't remember. Either way they didn't have much time. "There's a voicemail from Tyler. He's on his way here. He'll be here any minute."

"Tyler? Why? Did you talk to him? How does he even know where we are?"

"Hell if I know. Maybe Tuck told him. He could have looked at the event schedule. There's one hotel in this town. Wouldn't be that hard to find us. It doesn't matter." She stood and tangled her hands in her hair, trying to figure out what to do first. "We have to clean up in here."

Tara moved to Jace's bed, pawing through the sheets to find the bottle of lubricant. She realized some had spilled on the sheets and of course, this being her first lube purchase, she'd made the mistake of buying the scented kind. Anyone familiar with it would recognize the odor and realize exactly what had been going on. She was considering stripping off the sheet and hiding it in the closet when Jace came up behind her. He turned her around to face him.

"What? There's no time. I have to straighten your bed. And mess up mine." Too much to do and not enough time to do it.

"Tara. Relax. I'll help. We'll get it done. And when he gets here, he doesn't have to come in. We'll meet him at the door and take him out to breakfast. Okay?"

It was a smart plan. Jace wasn't just a pretty face. As Tara wondered at the fact that she'd just thought of him as both pretty and smart, which had never happened before, he raised her chin with his thumb and forefinger so she had to look at him.

"Okay?" he repeated.

She swallowed, realizing she'd never answered him. "Yes."

"Good. Now pick up your phone and call him back. Make sure you got the message right. And while you're at it, ask him why the hell he's coming here."

Another good idea from Jace. The world truly was upside down. She grabbed her phone and with shaking fingers, pressed to return Tyler's call.

Chapter Twenty-two

The knock on the door had Tara jumping in the desk chair she'd insisted on sitting in rather than on her bed. As if her brother seeing her watching TV from a bed would make him assume she'd been having sex in it.

She'd gone crazy after Tyler's call, but that might be a good thing. Maybe she'd finally appreciate Jace's position. How hard it was for him that she—the girl he'd spent last night and this morning inside—was his best friend's little sister.

Now that Tara felt the same about Tyler finding out as Jace felt about Tuck, he doubted she'd mock his concerns again. Irony was a beautiful thing.

Jace swung his legs over the edge of his mattress and headed for the door since it was obvious Tara had become glued to the furniture. One look through the peephole revealed a familiar cowboy hat. He flipped the lock and swung the door wide. "Tyler. Good to see you."

"Same here. My sister here?" As Tyler tried to glance past Jace's shoulder a frown drew his dark brows low over eyes that reminded Jace of Tara's.

He smothered the memory of how often he'd stared into her eyes recently while doing things Tyler wouldn't approve of. He tipped his head toward the bedroom. "She's inside. Too lazy to get up and answer the door herself. You know her."

Tyler laughed. "Oh, yeah."

"Shut up." From behind Jace, Tara's annoyance came through loud and clear.

Good. The best way to keep her from acting as if they had something to hide was to keep her good and pissed off. Still in the doorway, Jace turned. "Then prove me wrong and get up here and see your brother. He drove all the way here for some reason."

That reason had yet to be revealed since Tyler hadn't divulged it during the phone call with Tara.

"Yeah, get your butt out here, girlie. I've got a surprise for you," Tyler called into the room.

So far the biggest surprise had been Tyler's unexplained appearance in a town two hours from his home on a day Jace and Tara were scheduled to travel to the next venue. But apparently, they were in for more surprises.

Tara crept up next to Jace. He moved out of the doorway and gave her a tiny push forward. He left his hand on the small of her back for a few seconds longer than necessary, letting her know he was right behind her.

"So, I was talking to Tuck a while back and he told me he was going to junk your car, so I said, what the hell. Let me take a shot at it." Tyler looked giddy, like a kid with a secret. He started backing away from the door, toward the parking lot as he talked. "And it took a bit of doing but . . . surprise. I fixed it." With a big, shit-eating grin, he held up a set of keys.

"You fixed it?" Tara's gaze swept the parking lot.

After a moment, it landed on her car, parked a few spots away from the door. Her handy brother sure as hell had fixed it, because there it was.

Jace stared at the car. "That must've taken some doing. It was in bad shape last I saw it." Why did he feel sick to his stomach? Tara had her own wheels. It should be a good thing.

"Eh, I got a friend at the junkyard who had all the major parts I needed. The rest was just elbow grease and time and a few things I picked up at the auto parts store." Tyler's focus shifted back to Tara. "I figured you can consider it an early graduation gift, but Tuck was dead set against me giving it to you. Y'all know of any reason Tuck would get pissed when I told him I was bringing you the car? He tried to talk me out of it."

Jace knew why. If Tara had her own wheels, she could drive directly to school after the internship and not go back to Stillwater so Tuck could ambush her with the baby news.

Tara shot Jace a look, obviously thinking the same thing. "Uh. No. No idea. Maybe he thought it wasn't safe or something." She moved forward, took the keys from Tyler, and delivered a sisterly hug. "Thank you, Tyler. I really appreciate your fixing it and taking the time to bring it here."

"You're welcome. When I heard Jace was out injured, I figured you'd need it since you couldn't travel with him anymore."

That right there, in a nutshell, explained why Jace's stomach had fallen the moment he'd seen that piece of junk was running—it meant the end of his life on the road with Tara. No more excuse to not go back to Stillwater and face his demons. No more hurtling down the highway together with both phones turned off as they tried to pretend life back home didn't exist. No more traveling partners with benefits, either.

Or maybe not . . .

Jace reviewed the facts. Tara had no money. She couldn't afford gas for the car and a hotel room and food. He grasped at the hope, though he had a feeling she wouldn't want to admit to her brother how tight money was.

He took a step forward. "Actually, Ty, I was thinking of staying with the circuit."

"Hmm." Tyler's brows drew lower. "All right. I was kind of hoping you'd be willing to drop me back home on your way to Stillwater, but if you're staying, then I guess I'll call one of the guys from the ranch to come get me."

"Sorry about you wasting a trip, but yeah, I'm staying. Tara can keep traveling with me, and you can drive the car home so you won't need to call for a ride. No problem."

Tara turned to Jace. "I have about a week left of this internship and you're going to be out of competition at least that long. It's crazy for you to stay on."

He dismissed that with a wave of his hand. "Nah, I'm sure the doc will ease up and let me ride this next event once he sees how good I'm doing."

Tara was going to be stubborn about his riding, but if he could somehow get rid of the car, she'd need him to stay with her, if only for the ride. He glanced at the vehicle he'd thought was dead and buried. He needed to convince Tyler to take it back home. "You sure she's running all right, Ty?"

"Drove it here, didn't I? She purrs like a kitten now."

For better or worse Jace knew that Tara purred

like a kitten, too, when he touched that one spot . . . Tyler and the car needed to leave.

"All right." Jace cringed, hoping to appeal to Tyler's protective, brotherly side. "I just wouldn't want Tara stranded along the side of the road all alone."

"I stand behind my work, Jace." Tyler shook his head. "Toss him the keys, Tara. Let the man start it up for himself."

"All right." Jace nodded and held up his hand for the keys. Hopefully the damn thing would overheat if he started it and let it run long enough.

Tara turned, drew her arm back like a softball pitcher and let the keys fly. Jace reached out to catch them in mid-air, and missed them by a mile. They landed on the driveway with a jangling noise that seemed to echo around him.

"Do you still have double vision?" Tara strode toward him.

Jace frowned. "No."

She peered into his eyes until he was convinced she'd see right through him and his lies. Truth was he had no depth perception, next to no peripheral vision, and things dead ahead were still a little blurry around the edges. But hell, that didn't mean he couldn't ride. Didn't need to see clearly to hang on to a bull rope, did he?

"You can't ride. If you get another concussion on top of this one, which is worse than you're letting on, it could mean permanent damage."

"Tara, I missed the keys. Relax. It's nothing. I wasn't ready. That's all." When she didn't look convinced, he turned to Tyler. "Tell her it's not a big deal."

Tyler's brows rose. "I'm not getting in the middle

of this. And if I was gonna tell her something, it's that I've never seen you miss catching anything . . . ever. Hell, you were trashed at Tuck's bachelor party and you caught that beer bottle I tossed you from across the room."

He sent Tyler a look meant to wound, if not kill.

Tyler shrugged. "Sorry, man. Just telling the truth."

Jace sighed and turned back to Tara. "All right. So I won't ride in the next event, or even until the doc says it's safe, but that still doesn't mean I'm going home."

Tara opened her mouth, then closed it again, her teeth latching onto her lower lip. She turned toward Tyler. "I'm just gonna talk to Jace inside alone for a second. Okay?"

Tyler laughed. "Uh-oh, Jace. You're in trouble. You take your time lecturing him on riding with a concussion, Tara. I'll be out here, admiring this truck of his that I guess I'll be driving him back home in so we don't end up wrapped around a pole."

Jace rolled his eyes. "I'm fine."

"Come on inside." Tara led the way back into the room, and turned to him the moment the door closed. "I know why you don't want to go back home."

"You do?" Jace always had been pretty transparent but still, he didn't want Tara knowing he was getting used to their arrangement. Hell, more than that, he was really starting to like it—and her. Her stupid jokes. The companionship on the long drives. And with her in his bed last night, he'd slept better than he had in a year.

Tara nodded. "It's Jacqueline. You don't want to face her yet. I understand. Believe me, I do. But it makes no sense for you to stay with the circuit knowing you can't ride."

"It does make sense, because I promised I'd get you through this internship and it's not over yet."

"But now I have a car."

"But do you have the money in the bank to pay for the gas and the hotels and the food?"

A frown crossed her forehead even as a smile tipped up her lips. "You want to stay on just for me *and* you're willing to keep paying for everything? Even knowing you can't ride?"

"Yes. We're traveling partners. That's what we do."

"Yeah, we are. But you don't have to do that, Jace. I'll be fine."

"How? You get a sudden windfall I don't know about?"

"Actually, yeah. What day is the first of the month?"

He was too upset to figure that out, so he just shrugged. "I don't know. Soon. Two, three more days, maybe."

"My parents deposit spending money for me into my account the first of every month. If it's a few days away, I have enough money to last me 'til then."

"Oh. Okay." It was starting to sink in that Tara didn't need him anymore. That, too, should be a good thing. Why didn't it feel that way?

She strode forward and reached up, depositing a kiss on his cheek that felt much too sisterly considering recent events. "You really are a sweet guy. And if you tell anyone I said that, I'll deny it, and then kick you."

"I won't tell." Even her joking didn't cheer him up. This really was over. He hadn't wanted it to begin with, but now that he had it, he wasn't ready to let it go. "Tara. Promise me something?"

"Sure. What?" She stood close enough he could smell the fruity shampoo she used on her hair.

"After I leave, don't hook up with any of the rookies." He didn't want her with anyone, but Jace was most worried about Klint and Justin.

"Why would I go to a boy to do a man's job?" She smiled.

His words turned back on him almost lightened his mood. In this case, they were good words. He even managed half a smile. "I'm glad I taught you something during our time together."

"You did. I learned a lot."

Whether she was talking about sex or life on the road, he wasn't sure and didn't ask. It was truly over and delaying the inevitable wouldn't change anything.

Jace blew out a breath and glanced around the room they'd shared. "I guess I should pack up my stuff. We can all go out and grab something to eat and then hit the road so I can get Tyler home. You going to be okay driving to the next venue on your own?"

"Yeah. I'll stop by the gas station and pick up a map."

"You should get a GPS."

"Maybe I will. *After* the first of the month when I get some cash." She smiled again.

"All right." It felt like now or never, so Jace reached out and looped an arm around her neck, reeling her in close. He brought one hand up and cupped her face before leaning low. He delivered a slow, thorough kiss to remind her she shouldn't settle for less—such as seven minutes in the broom closet with Klint.

Tasting her for what he realized could be the last time nearly undid him. It made him want to throw her onto the bed and take what he'd been denying them. More than that, it made him want to stride outside and tell Tyler to take the car and go because he and Tara were a couple.

Problem was, they weren't. And, dammit, when had he started wanting them to be?

Jace realized the answer to that question was this morning, when after spending two weeks day and night with this girl, fighting, laughing, confessing, he'd woken next to her and they'd made love, twice, even if technically she still was a virgin.

He couldn't help himself. He kissed her for longer and with more intensity than he'd intended, stroking her tongue with his, holding her to him like he'd never let her go.

When he could bring himself to pull back, she stayed close, her eyes meeting his. "I had a good time."

"So did I." Wasn't that the biggest understatement of the year? Jace drew in a deep breath and let it out. "Go tell him the plan. I'm gonna pack up."

She didn't move for so long he wondered if she had more to say. Hoped, more like. Something to make it not end . . . such as asking him to stay with her.

Tara took a step back. "I'll tell Ty the plan. Then I'm gonna go check out my car."

"Okay." Jace swallowed away the sick feeling. Then she was gone, out the door to her car and her freedom, and damn if he didn't feel her absence.

He packed his stuff and loaded it into the truck, and then they went out for breakfast even though he didn't have much of an appetite.

Under the watchful eye of her brother, Jace couldn't even kiss Tara good-bye. He settled for a hug that lasted a little too long but hopefully looked platonic. Before he knew it, he was in the passenger seat of his own truck with Tyler behind the wheel heading for home.

Tyler glanced across the cab. "So given your condition, I guess I'll take you to Stillwater, then get Tuck to drive me back home to my parents' place."

"No. That's nuts. Go home. I can get myself from there to Stillwater."

Tyler sent Jace a glance full of doubt that pissed him off more.

"I'm fine. I could've driven, but I know Tara would have flipped the hell out if I had."

"She is going to school for this shit. Sports injuries and stuff."

"And she's too new at it to realize that bull riders more hurt than me ride and drive every damn day."

Tyler bobbed his head to concede the point. He rode bulls and broncs, and worked raising stock on a ranch with other guys who also rode, both amateurs and professionals. He knew the deal. A rider did what he had to do, and usually did it while hurting.

"All right. I'll head home. Maybe you'll hang out there for a bit. Stay the night, and then see how you feel tomorrow. Unless you're in some rush to get back to Stillwater tonight."

Thinking of what waited for him there, Jace let out a snort. "Nope. No rush."

"Okay, good. It'll be nice to have some male company in the house. Momma's got Daddy so involved in her stuff, I'm surprised he hasn't started to grow tits. She had him taking a wine making course with her. I mean, what the hell? Making moonshine or brewing beer, fine, but wine? I blame Becca for that one."

Jace laughed. "All right. I'll stay. A guys' night out sounds good. Thanks."

Maybe a night with Tyler would remind him what it was like to be carefree and young again. Concerned only with where your next piece of ass or the next big payout could be found. No drama. No worries. Those were the good old days.

"Not a problem. Thank *you* for chauffeuring my sister around the past couple weeks. And congrats on not killing each other."

"It wasn't as bad as we assumed it would be." Jace gave a half-hearted shrug and felt the tug of sore muscles, but his injuries were much better than yesterday.

His body was healing. It was the rest of him he was worried about. What the hell were these feelings he was having about leaving Tara? And why did he panic at the thought of her following the circuit without him?

The answer to that was pretty clear. He didn't trust her not to do what she'd done that night in the bar. The thought of another guy's hands on her—or worse, giving her what Jace had refused to—made him insane.

What the hell was between them? A rebound relationship? More? Or no kind of relationship at all? Just traveling partners with benefits, like they'd agreed?

Whatever it was, Jace knew one thing—Tara shouldn't be with any of those guys. Hopefully, they'd continue to assume he and she were together and steer clear, but just in case, Jace decided to take out some insurance. He pulled his cell out of his pocket. It was on because, crazy ex-girlfriend turned stalker or not, he wasn't about to turn off his one connection to Tara.

He punched in a text to Tara's number.

Stop by that sex shop we saw on the highway. Get a vibrator. Use it next time you feel the urge to go into the closet with a rookie!

He started to question the text the moment he hit SEND, until her reply came through.

I will if you promise no more booty calls at Jacqueline's!

He smiled. Maybe he was a little messed up, but so was Tara. They were damaged goods. Could be why what they had worked.

"Your girl?" Tyler's question reminded Jace he wasn't alone in the truck.

"Eh, not exactly." He shook his head at himself for grinning from ear to ear over a text message.

"Ah, gotcha." Tyler nodded knowingly. "I bet having my sister as a roommate put quite a damper on your social life, if you get what I mean."

He did. Tyler figured the text was to some buckle bunny Jace had hooked up with. Jace decided to let him believe that. "Not as much of a damper as you'd think."

"Good to hear. I was feeling bad for you, being saddled with her, but maybe Tara's cooler than I gave her credit for."

Tyler had no idea. Jace let out a short laugh. "Yeah, she definitely is."

"So, what d'you wanna do tonight? You shouldn't be drinking with the concussion, but we can go hang out somewhere. The bowling alley's got good food."

Jace ran a finger over his chest, just over his heart. He hadn't missed Tara glancing at his Jacqueline tattoo more than once while they'd been together. It was long past time to get it taken care of. "I do have one idea. Do you know of a good tattoo parlor?"

"Sure do. You thinking of getting a new tat?" Tyler took his eyes off the road long enough to glance across the cab.

"Cover-up for an old one, actually."

Tyler's brow rose before he nodded. "All right. Sounds like a plan. Know what you want yet?"

"Nope, but I guess we got a couple hours' drive to come up with an idea." Jace looked forward to it. Step one in moving on. Though maybe the cover-up wasn't the first step at all. Tara had been.

She was alone on the road without him. With that fact uppermost in his mind, Jace punched in another text. This one to Dillon.

Heading home to recover. Keep an eye on Tara for me. She's traveling alone now.

A man could never have too much insurance when it came to protecting something important to him.

The phone vibrated a few seconds later and Jace read the incoming text.

You got it.

Dillon's reply helped a bit. At least enough that Jace could turn his attention back to the issue at hand. "I was thinking of maybe something bull riding related for the tattoo, but I'm not sure."

Chapter Twenty-three

There were two things that occupied Jace's mind on his drive to Stillwater after leaving Tyler at his parents' house—maybe three, because first and foremost he had to concentrate on the road so he didn't crash and prove Tara right that he shouldn't be driving. The other two issues were seeing Jacqueline and Tuck again. As the highway brought him closer to home, and the new tattoo on his chest began to itch, he kept playing things out in his head.

Seeing Jacqueline would be the hardest. He'd have to confront her to settle things between them. Seeing Tuck would be easier, but it wasn't weighing any less on his mind, since he'd be keeping a huge secret from his best friend.

Could Jace act as if nothing had happened between him and Tara without Tuck seeing through him? Maybe. Tyler hadn't suspected and he'd spent time with them together. Anyone who knew the two of them would be unlikely to guess that Jace had hooked up with Tara given how well-known the animosity between them was.

Still, keeping something from a friend as good as

Tuck sucked, but Jace figured he'd brought it on himself. He'd reaped the benefits of his and Tara's strange relationship, and now he had to deal with the consequences.

So, who to face first? Jacqueline seemed the answer. Despite being a big college town, news traveled through Stillwater with the speed of a wildfire. She'd hear he was back and come looking for him. God only knew where she'd catch up with him. Probably someplace nice and public where she'd make a huge scene.

Best to have the reunion on his own terms, where he could control things. He'd drive to her house and see if she was home. For the first time since the break-up, heading to her place didn't hold any potential for a booty call. There was no way he'd end up naked. First, it was midday. He usually succumbed to her at night. More important, when he did let himself think about sinking into a woman, it finally wasn't Jacqueline who came to mind. For better or worse, it was Tara he thought of.

Last, but not least, was the cover-up tattoo. One look at it would bring on a screaming fit from Jacqueline, he was sure. Best insurance he'd ever had that he wouldn't ever get naked with her again and worth every penny.

Next issue was what to say. What could he say that he hadn't said before? He'd told her until he was blue in the face that though a part of him would always love her, he wasn't in love with her anymore. He had to make her realize they'd be so much better off moving on so he could start rebuilding his life outside the shadow of his years with her.

Something Tara had said about Jacqueline tugged at his memory. About very high highs, and very low lows and how it was an actual condition and there were pills to control it. Looking back at some of Jacqueline's inexplicable mood swings, it made sense.

His brain spun and landed on a ray of hope. What if the answer for all the issues Jacqueline had was as simple as popping a pill? How tragic was it that they had both suffered for years, when it hadn't been necessary.

Jace had to find out if what Tara had said was true. How? The answer hit him like a bolt of lightning. He did yard work for a pretty well-to-do family. The husband was some sort of surgeon, but the wife was a therapist. In fact, he'd just talked to her on the phone a few weeks ago to tell her his guy would be filling in for him and to give her his number.

Slowing to a stop, he pulled onto the shoulder and reached for his cell. It wasn't the time to multitask and drive and dial at the same time. Not when he was so excited he was shaking and his vision was bad enough he'd probably fail an eye test. He scrolled through his outgoing calls and there it was, the number he needed.

He hit the button to dial and she answered after a few rings. Jace swallowed, his heart pounding "Hi, Mrs. Bowman. It's Jace Mills. I was wondering if I could talk to you about something personal . . ."

Less than an hour later, armed with a lot more information and an appointment for a counseling session for him and Jacqueline, Jace drew in a deep breath and raised his fist to knock on Jacqueline's door. Her car was in the driveway, so it was no surprise when she answered.

She glared at him, her eyes zeroing in on his forehead. "Nice bruise."

The bruise had moved into that lovely yellow

stage bruises always turned before fading away. Jace pulled his hat a bit lower over it.

"Yeah, but you should see the other guy." He decided to move on when she didn't laugh at his joke. "Anyway, can we talk?"

Hope you haven't been in any more closets. Are you being a good girl?

Tara read the text from Jace and rolled her eyes. They'd been messaging back and forth since he'd gone home over a week ago. She was getting pretty tired of him throwing that in her face every other time they talked. Tara punched in a text of her own.

Yes! And quit with the closets. It was one time! How's your big hard head feeling?

Jace's reply came back less than a minute later.

Fine. I should be riding. Would be if you hadn't made me come home.

Tara could imagine his face as he'd typed that. She smiled as she punched in her reply.

Oh stop your pouting. I didn't want you to lose what brains you do have.

Always good to keep him in his place with a healthy dose of insults. Such was their relationship since he'd left. She just had to finish up tonight's event and she was done with her internship. The three weeks had flown by, probably because Jace had been with her for the first twelve days of it.

Being alone had sucked after she'd gotten used to having company. She'd considered asking Maryann if she wanted to share a room, as much for the company as to save on expenses, but it had become apparent that Maryann and Rick were having their own private event every night. So Tara slept alone with the door double locked and her cell phone right next to her, jumping at every noise from the parking lot and holding her breath when someone walked past her door.

She missed Jace, though she'd never admitted that to him in any of her texts. She missed more than having a man there for protection. There were other things she missed about him, too, and that was just ridiculous. She was never supposed to get attached to him as a person. It was only recently she'd started to think of him as a decent human being, forget about someone she wanted to spend time with.

She had to finish school, look for a permanent position, and then, maybe, she'd take a trip to Stillwater. Maybe visit Jace and see if he was a friend and more, or if she'd been delusional for those two weeks.

The phone vibrated in her pocket again. She glanced up to make sure the doc wasn't around. They were coming up on the short round and there were things she should be doing besides texting, but she opened Jace's text, anyway.

Last night then you're done, right? Where you heading after?

Home to parents then to college. NOT coming to Stillwater. Don't tell Tuck that.

In spite of more calls and texts from Tuck, none of which told her the truth about why he was pushing her to come to Stillwater, she wasn't going there. Why should she? So he could sit her down like a child and tell her Logan and Emma were having a baby? Screw that. Tara was moving on with her life.

The phone she'd forgotten in her hand vibrated and she glanced down.

Not gonna tell. Sorry to not see you though. Kinda miss you, brat. Must be the head injury.

Tara smiled.

Kinda miss you too, idiot. Must be lack of air in this broom closet.

She grinned as his reply came faster than she'd thought possible.

You better not be in any closet!!!!

Not one, but four exclamation points from Jace. Her text had hit home. Laughing, she decided to relieve his anxiety.

Just kidding. Short go starting. Gotta run. Leaving right after for home. Rather drive in the dark than spend another night alone in hotel.

Tara had checked out of her room earlier in the day and all her stuff was in the trunk. The car was full of gas, and she'd already looked at the map. She knew how to get home and she'd made sure her parents knew she'd be arriving late.

Maybe there'd be leftovers from dinner in the fridge when she arrived. Some home cooking would sure be good after being on the road for so long. Either way, it would be nice to sleep in her own bed, no matter how late she got there.

Another text vibrated the cell in her hand.

BE CAREFUL DRIVING. Text when you get home.
Don't care how late.

Tara punched in *OK,* then added a smiley face and sent the reply.

Three weeks ago, if someone had told her that she and Jace would be friends, she would have called them insane. She shoved the phone into her pocket and headed for the chutes, thinking what a difference three weeks made.

Chapter Twenty-four

Tuck turned when Jace walked up to him in the practice arena. "Where the hell have you been hiding since you've been back? Barely seen or talked to you in the past week."

There were a number of reasons for that, none of which Jace wanted to discuss with Tuck here and now. Maybe not ever. He shrugged. "Been busy."

"Busy at what?"

Jace sighed. "I've been going to joint counseling sessions with Jacqueline every day."

"Really?" Tuck's brows rose.

"Don't give me that look." Jace could see Tuck assumed he was back with Jacqueline.

"No look. Your life. Your choice. Anyway, I appreciate your help tonight."

He should explain, but it wasn't his place to tell Tuck that Jacqueline had been diagnosed and was being treated as bipolar. Or that part of that treatment was therapy along with medication and the only way he could convince her to go was to promise to keep going to the sessions with her.

Nope. Jace had to stand there and let Tuck judge him. Hell, it wasn't the first time, and it wouldn't be the last.

Jace had promised to help Tuck out with a rodeo team practice since his assistant coach, Carla, needed the night off. "Happy to help out. What're we working on with them tonight?"

"Roping. You remember how?" Tuck sure was cocky for a man who'd long ago traded in life as a cowboy to join the army.

Jace snorted out a rude noise. "Yeah. *You* remember how, soldier boy?"

"Yup. Like riding a bike. Anyway, before this thing starts, I wanted to ask you something. You hear from Tara lately?"

"Um, yeah. Once in a while. Why?" Jace had been texting Tara out in the parking lot before he'd come into the arena. He hoped she didn't send him another one in the next few minutes.

"She's not answering my calls or my texts. She's got to have been gone three weeks by now. The schedule says tonight's the last competition before they go on a long break, so this event must complete her internship. Right? She should be coming back now?"

"Uh." *Crap.* Jace should have gotten his lies in order. Sad day when a man had to do that, and with his best friend, too. "Tuck, I'm not her travel partner anymore. You've got to talk to Tara about her schedule."

"That's what I'm telling you. She won't talk to me." Frustration radiated off Tuck.

"Maybe that's because you keep trying to strong-arm her into coming back here."

"Why wouldn't she want to come here? She and I get along fine. So do she and Becca." Tuck eyed Jace, looking for an explanation.

"Maybe she doesn't want to come to Stillwater because this is where Logan and Emma are living out their happily-ever-after. You think of that?" Jace hoped Tara had gotten over Logan, her tarnished Prince Charming, but he understood if she didn't want his fairytale ending rubbed in her face.

Tuck drew in a deep breath. "Yeah. You're probably right. Crap. I've really got to talk to her. Logan and Emma are at his parents' place right now telling them about the baby. I wanted to get to Tara first before my momma tells her. You know how women talk."

Jace's eyes widened. "Logan and Emma are there now with his parents?"

Right next door to Tara and Tuck's parents' house, where Tara was driving to straight from the event. God almighty, she was headed directly toward the thing she was trying to avoid.

"Yup. Emma had some superstition that she refused to tell anyone else, not even their parents, until after she'd reached three months in the pregnancy. Thank goodness that passed because she's starting to puff up. Can't be hiding it anymore." Tuck was so busy bitching about things, he didn't notice Jace was ready to crawl out of his skin at the news.

Good thing Tuck wasn't being all that observant, because a casual friend shouldn't be as concerned as Jace was about Tara. He had to stop her. "I'll try texting Tara and see if maybe she'll answer me."

He punched in the text and hit SEND before Tuck could see what he'd written.

Don't go home! L and E there.

He hoped Tara saw it before she hit the road and ended up blindsided.

"Thanks for doing that, Jace. Appreciate it. In the meantime, I guess we better get these kids moving."

He followed Tuck toward the group of kids who made up the Oklahoma State University rodeo team, but his mind was no longer on the practice. It was miles away with Tara. Where would she go if she couldn't go to her parents'? College? Did she even have a place to stay there this semester? He hadn't asked about her lodging situation. They'd been far too busy doing other things.

Jace checked his phone in case he'd missed feeling the text alert come through. Nothing. She hadn't replied, which made him nervous, and the unease increased with every minute that ticked by.

As soon as the damn practice was over he was going to find a way to get in touch with her. And if he couldn't . . . then what? He didn't know. He'd text Dillon. If she'd already left, then Tyler. Hell, Jace would wait until morning and call her parents' house if he had to. Seeing Logan and an ever-expanding Emma face-to-face was going to throw Tara into a tailspin. She'd need somebody with her who'd understand.

Strange as it would have seemed before their little trip, that person was Jace. He might be the only one who understood.

Tara woke in her own bed and stretched. She squinted across the room at the red glowing numbers on the dresser clock. It was still kind of early,

but she should get up. Her phone had died sometime after she'd sent that last text to Jace and her
charger had been buried somewhere in her bags in
the trunk.

She threw her legs over the edge of the bed and
pawed through her bag, digging out the charger.
She plugged it into the wall and the phone into it.
She'd never gotten to text Jace last night that she
was safe so she powered the cell on to do it.

It started to vibrate in her hand the moment it
came to life. The display read INCOMING CALL FROM
TUCK. That figured. He was still looking for her to
come to Stillwater. Well, it was too late now. She was
already home.

Tara hit the button and anticipated saying exactly
that to her pain in the ass brother.

"Tara, where are you?" he asked instead of good
morning or any other nicety.

"Home."

"Home where? At Momma and Daddy's house or
at school?"

"School isn't home, Tuck. School is school. I'm
home as in the house where our parents and our
brother live." Being a smart-ass was extra fun now
that she'd heard how pissed Tuck sounded.

He let out a huge breath. "Crap."

"What's wrong, big brother?" She smiled, loving
when she frustrated Tuck so much he cussed.

"You talk to anyone yet this morning?"

"No, I just woke up."

"I tried calling you and texting. Even Jace tried
getting in touch with you. You didn't get back to either of us."

"Sorry." Tara saw she had a bunch of unread texts
in her inbox but she hadn't had time to open any

with Tuck calling and yelling at her first thing in the morning when she'd just woken up.

A beep in her ear told her she had another call. Perfect timing. "Ooo, gotta go. I'll call you back later."

"No, Tara—" As she hit the button to accept the incoming call, she heard Tuck's protest and smiled as she cut it off.

She pressed the cell to her ear. "Hello?"

"Tara. Thank God. Why haven't you called or texted?" Jace sounded all out of sorts, too.

Jeez. What was the big deal? "I know. I'm sorry I didn't text when I got in last night. My battery was dead and the charger was buried and I was just too tired to deal with it. Okay?"

"That's not why I'm upset. Listen to me, Logan and Emma are there. Right next door, right now, to make the big baby announcement to his parents."

Tara took a second to absorb that as breathing felt harder than it should. Her escape plan hadn't worked out so well, after all. She sat down in the chair next to her bed. "Wow."

"You need me to come there and be with you? Hell, you wanna come here instead? You can stay in my apartment."

Jace's offer sounded really good. Get in her car, drive away, and not face anyone. She could probably sneak out without her parents even seeing her. Cowardly, yeah, but way easier. Then again, she was going to have to face this eventually. "I don't know, Jace. I don't know what to do."

"Okay, well listen. I'm going to have to turn my phone off shortly for about an hour, hour and a half, but right after that, I'll turn it back on and I can do whatever you need me to do."

"What are you doing that you have to turn your phone off?" Tara knew he'd turned it off for days at a time during the whole ex-girlfriend thing while they were on the road, but to specifically mention it would be off between an hour and an hour and a half seemed odd.

"I've got to go to a therapy session with Jacqueline. Long story. I'll tell you all about it later. But after that, I'm free and available. Okay?"

A therapy session with Jacqueline. Like as in couples counseling? It seemed that, contrary to what Jace had just said, he was neither free nor available. Jace and Jacqueline were back together. That hit Tara harder than the news that Logan was next door with his pregnant wife.

"Uh, yeah, thanks but I'm fine. Your traveling partner responsibilities are over so don't worry about me. I gotta go." Tara disconnected the call with shaking hands.

What the hell had happened in a week to make Jace go back to Jacqueline after all the hell she'd put him through? Sex? History? Traumatic brain injury? It had to be something, but it didn't matter. It was done.

When it rained, it poured. Logan and Emma next door. Jace and Jacqueline back together. Heart pounding, Tara set her jaw and stood. She glanced down at the cell phone still clutched in her hand. She'd considered powering it off after hanging up on Jace, but no, she wasn't going to do that. No more running and hiding. Time to face the demons. Maybe Jace couldn't move on from his past, but Tara could and she was doing it today.

She showered, dressed, and ignored a bunch more incoming texts and calls. Proud that she didn't

even look to see who they were from, Tara continued to get ready for the day, taking the time to blow
dry her hair and throw on some lip gloss. She didn't
let herself think she was trying to look good for the
confrontation with Logan. She decided she needed
to look good for *herself*. She needed all the self-con-
fidence she could get.

Her pulse still beating faster than it should, Tara
strode into the kitchen, ready to face the world. It
turned out, the only person she had to face was
Tyler.

"Hey." She frowned. "Where's Momma and
Daddy?"

"Who knows? They're like newlyweds. She's got
him going all sorts of places with her. When did you
get here? I didn't hear you come in last night."

"Late. I drove straight from the event."

"How's the car running?"

"Perfect. Thank you again. It was a lifesaver." Although she had to think that if Tyler hadn't delivered it, Jace would have stayed safely far from
Jacqueline. Tara pushed that depressing thought
away. "So, I heard Logan's visiting."

"You heard right." Tyler poured himself a glass of
sweet tea, then put the pitcher back in the fridge.
"You, uh, talk to him lately?"

He watched her as if she was a horse ready to bolt.
Real nice. Did none of her family think she was adult
enough to hear that Logan was about to have a
baby? "No, I haven't. I was about to go over there
now."

Tyler's brow rose. He put his cup down. "Oh. All
right. I'll go with you."

Tara frowned. "Why?"

"No reason. Just being friendly." He shrugged,

then glanced down at his phone on the table. "Hm. Text from Jace."

"Jace is texting you? What's he want?"

Tyler read the display and she watched his eyes widen. He punched in a reply that seemed to be about one word long, then looked up. "Uh, nothing. Just saying hey is all."

Tara had known her brother all her life, and she knew when he was hiding something. When he shoved the phone deep into his front jeans pocket, she was sure of it. "That's all?"

"Yup. That's all. Ready to go next door?" He pressed his lips together and waited. His lips were sealed on the matter, literally.

"Yeah. Fine. Let's go." She turned for the door. If her brother chose to follow, there wasn't much she could do to stop him.

Tara marched across the lawn on the same path to Logan's house she'd taken countless times during her lifetime. She caught a glimpse of his truck in the drive, but turned toward the back and the kitchen door. She'd never gone in the front door and she didn't intend to start.

She reached for the doorknob, but hesitated, looking through the window first. Logan sat alone at the kitchen table, his long legs stretched out in front of him as he read the paper. His six-foot-two-inch frame had always made her feel small, even after she'd reached her full height. He looked just as she remembered him from all those years ago when he'd lived with his parents. He looked older, but the bigger difference was her pulse didn't speed up because she was in love with him and could hardly breathe in his presence. Instead, it pounded with anxiety and determination over what she was about to do.

Maybe she had moved on. That fact didn't help the knocking of her heart against her rib cage as she opened the door and forced a smile. "Hey."

"Tara, I didn't realize you were back from school." Logan's dark gaze looked past her. "Morning, Tyler."

Tyler followed Tara into the kitchen, not that there was any room for him to stand. She'd stopped right inside the doorway, unwilling or maybe unable to go in farther.

Time to get it over with. Logan's wary expression and Tyler's hand resting on her shoulder told Tara both men were braced for her to blow. "I just wanted to tell you—and Emma, too—congratulations on the baby. On the wedding, too, since I haven't seen you since."

Logan's brows rose. "I didn't realize you knew about us being pregnant."

Us. Logan was going to be one of those annoying husbands who used *we* when speaking about his wife's pregnancy. Tara had always thought that pretty ridiculous. The man wasn't the one getting huge, or with morning sickness, or pushing a bigheaded baby out of a very tiny space.

Thinking the word *ridiculous* in relation to Logan, who used to walk on water in her opinion, was a new concept to Tara.

Logan once again looked toward Tyler. Her brother shook his head. "I didn't know she knew, either, man. I didn't tell her."

She wasn't about to throw Jace under the bus and admit he'd slipped about the big secret. Stupid to keep Emma's pregnancy a secret, anyway. Not like people wouldn't be able to do the math. Count back nine months from the eventual birth of the baby and see it was conceived before the nuptials.

"Well, thank you, Tara. Em and I appreciate it. How are you doing? School good?"

"Yeah. Things are going good. So, I just wanted to stop by and say that. I'm gonna head home." Tara hooked a thumb toward the door. "I've got some stuff to do before I go back for the semester. Say hey to the wife and I, uh, guess I'll see you around sometime."

"All right." After Logan's nod, she turned and left the two men in the kitchen, most likely discussing her.

Fine. She didn't need an inquisition from her brother, anyway.

Tara was on the property line between the two yards when she saw a big ass truck that had become very familiar to her pull into her parents' driveway. Jace was there. They'd talked less than two hours ago. He'd said he had a session with Jacqueline. The thought had her stomach churning, and it wasn't because she'd never gotten around to eating breakfast.

Resigned that she might as well get all the bad stuff over with at once, Tara headed for the front of the house toward where she heard the sound of the truck's engine cut off. She braced herself for the inevitable—Jace telling her he and Jacqueline were back together. She'd get over this, just as she'd gotten over Logan. After that, there was nothing else that could get to her because really, what else could happen?

Even monumentally bad luck, such as the kind Tara seemed to have with the men in her life, had to run out eventually. Right? She could only hope. Her heart could only take so much.

Chapter Twenty-five

Tara came around the side of the house just as Jace was about to head for the back door. A frown marred her brow as she asked, "What are you doing here?"

"I wanted to make sure you were okay." He knew Tara well enough to figure out from the morning's phone call that she was upset.

"You drove two hours just to see if I was okay?" Her surprise was evident in the expression on her face. The face that had become so familiar to him, he'd started to see it in his dreams.

"Yup. It only took me about an hour and a half. I made good time." He was lucky he hadn't passed any cops on the way. He'd topped the speed limit by a good twenty miles per hour for most of the trip.

"You didn't have to do that."

"Yeah, I did." He'd upset Tara by telling her Logan and Emma were there. Upset her enough that she'd hung up on him. "You know what you said to me before on the phone about how I don't have to worry about you anymore. That's not true. You are still my concern and you always will be. Once travel-ing partners, always traveling partners."

Her expression softened. "How did you even know I'd still be around by the time you got here? I could have left for school by now."

"I texted Tyler from the road. Told him I was on my way to your place and he should keep you here no matter what."

"He didn't tell me that."

"I asked him not to tell you I was coming."

"Why?"

"Because you're contrary and do the opposite of what anyone tells you. I consider that one of your more endearing qualities. At least you're pre-dictable." He shrugged, wishing he could hold her. She looked like she needed it.

Tara wrapped her arms around herself even though the day was warm and she had on a long-sleeved shirt. "What about your couples counseling with Jacqueline? I thought you were busy this morn-ing with her."

Couples counseling?

"It's not couples—is that what you thought?" Things started to make more sense. "After I hung up with you, I told her I couldn't make it, but Tara, those sessions with the therapist aren't for us as a couple. They're for her alone."

"Then why do you go?"

"Turns out you were right about the bipolar thing. She needs medication and therapy. The first few sessions she refused to go unless I went with her. It's better now that she's over a week into it, but I was still going with her because I figured I needed to see it through. To make sure she can stand on her own two feet so I can make a clean break and get on with my life." Jace finished the explanation and waited for Tara's reaction.

She remained wary. "So you're not back together with her?"

"No, I'm not back with Jacqueline . . . and I wouldn't have gotten this done if I thought I ever would be." Jace pulled the neck of his T-shirt to one side.

Her attention snapped to his new tattoo. "Wow. You got the cover-up."

He smiled at her surprise. "I did."

"And the booty calls with her? They over, too?" Tara avoided making direct eye contact as she asked the question.

Jace took a step closer, into her line of vision so she had to look up and see him and the truth that he spoke. "No, there's been no sex with her or with anyone else. Booty or other."

"Good. I'm glad my orgasm therapy worked." She met his gaze and he saw her mood had lightened a bit. It made him feel lighter, as well.

"Yeah, it definitely did." Jace laughed but there were still serious issues to discuss. His relationship baggage had been laid out on the table, but Tara's hadn't yet. He wanted a clean slate and a fresh start on both their parts. "So, I hate to bring this up, but I told you mine, so you have to tell me yours. You go over and talk to them yet?" He tipped his head toward the house next door, where Logan's truck was parked in the drive.

"Yeah. Just left there."

"And?" Jace tried to gauge how it had gone. It didn't look as if she'd been crying, so that was a good sign. Of course, that didn't mean she hadn't yelled or thrown things. The girl had a temper on her.

"I didn't see Emma, but I talked to Logan and it wasn't so bad." Tara let out a short laugh. "I think I don't care all that much anymore."

Jace let himself breathe freely again. "Maybe that therapy of yours worked both ways."

"I think it definitely did." Her smile had his heart speeding.

Jace didn't know what to do with his hands. He wanted to reach out and pull her to him, but instead he pushed his fingers into the front pockets of his jeans. "Tara?"

"Yeah?"

"Don't faint or anything, but I think we—you and I—should go out on a date."

"A date? Like a dinner-and-a-movie kind of date?" She bit her lower lip to control the smile that started to bow her lips at his offer.

He didn't know if it was to stop from laughing at him because he was ridiculous, but he continued. "That's what I was thinking. Yeah." Damn, this was hard. He hadn't asked a woman out in so long, he might be the one to faint, not Tara.

"Dates are usually followed by sex." Her eyes, a deeper shade of blue than usual, sought his.

"Sometimes." Jace tipped his head in agreement.

"Real sex. You know, the full monty."

He laughed even as his pulse pounded in his ears. "I don't think that's what the expression means, but yeah, real sex could possibly follow a date."

"But you and I don't do that. Have real sex." Tara's hints were about as subtle as a sledgehammer—one of the things Jace was beginning to love about her.

"Well, I've been thinking about that arrangement and I'm open to revisiting the issue, given a change in our status from traveling partners with benefits to two people who are dating."

Jace wasn't prepared for catching a handful of woman as Tara leaped and wrapped her arms and legs around him. She was lucky she didn't knock him off his feet as her mouth crashed into his. The only thing to do seemed to be hold her tight and kiss her back.

They'd kissed plenty of times before, but not like this—as if a dam of pent-up emotions had burst. He needed to breathe and pulled back an inch. "Is this a yes to the date?"

"Yes."

"Good. But since we're in your parents' driveway, maybe we should wait on the sex part until we're someplace more private."

She released her hold on him and lowered her legs so he could set her on the ground. Her eyes narrowed as she met his gaze. "There's a cheap hotel in town."

Tara still stood close enough that he'd left his hands resting on her waist. The urge to pull her closer was strong. He resisted it, but the hotel idea was very tempting. "Maybe I don't want our first time together to be in a cheap hotel."

"I do. I grew very fond of those kinds of places after spending so much time in them with you."

"I'm not sure if I want that to be my legacy, but all right." He moved a bit closer, not caring so much anymore who saw them. "I really did miss you after I left."

"It's absolutely ridiculous, but I missed you, too."

He frowned at her vehemence. "It's not *that* ridiculous."

"You know what I mean. This is us. We used to get into it all the time. Nobody's going to believe we're dating . . . not to mention doing other things together."

That reminder about other people and those *other things* brought up a sore subject for Jace. "I guess we're gonna have to tell Tuck now."

Tara shook her head. "Jace, we can tell Tuck we decided to go out because we got to know each other better after traveling together. That's all. We don't have to tell him you gave me my first of many, many incredible orgasms while we were on the road."

"Hearing you put it that way, yeah, I guess we shouldn't tell him that last part." He felt his cheeks heat. Blood rushed to more than his face. Parts lower woke up in a big way after hearing her talk about orgasms. "How about we move our date from dinner to lunch?"

There was no way she could miss his arousal as she pressed her body closer against his. "How about we skip eating altogether and go right to the hotel?"

It was tempting, but Jace needed to say something first. "We're more than sex, you know. You and I."

"I know." Tara latched onto her lower lip with her teeth and drew in a breath. "We were both a little broken to start, and together, we healed."

Jace didn't consider himself a crier, but damned if he didn't feel the sting of tears behind his eyes at what she'd said.

"You're right." He swallowed away that emotion and felt it replaced with an overwhelming need to possess her. "To hell with it. Let's go to the hotel. We can eat after."

"Sounds good to me." Tara had to scramble to keep up with him as he pulled her to the truck.

He would take things slow once he got her into a big king-size hotel bed, but he didn't have any patience for the actual getting there. Looked like he'd be breaking the law and speeding one more time, but Tara was worth risking the ticket.

"You sure about this?"

Tara spun from the bed where she'd been pulling down the scratchy polyester comforter to turn and glare at him. "Dammit, Jace. Yes. I've waited too damn long for you already."

He smiled. "Okay, just making sure. I won't ask you again. Believe me."

As he drew a long strip of condoms out of his back pocket and tossed them on the nightstand next to the bed, she did believe him. The tip of his erection peeked out of the top of his underwear as he opened his jeans. He pushed them down his legs while kicking off one boot at the same time.

Reinforcing the fact that he was as enthusiastic as Tara, he beat her in the race to get undressed. She decided that wasn't a bad thing as he strode naked toward her, need showing in his eyes. He stood close as he put his hands around her waist. Jace's lean, hard body, which she'd never wanted to admit in the past was pretty nice, looked tempting enough to make her want to take a bite out of him. Maybe she would. They were dating, even if they'd yet to go on the actual date. Still, she could leave all the marks on him she wanted.

As Jace reached behind her back for the clasp on

the bra she hadn't gotten a chance to undo, she ran a finger over his new tattoo and then closed her mouth around his nipple.

He drew in a sharp breath, moaning when she scraped her teeth over his flesh. "Keep that up and I'll be done much too fast."

She eyed the half dozen condoms. "Then we'll have to do it again."

"Good plan." He grinned, before pressing a kiss to her lips.

Jace plunged his tongue against hers and the kiss intensified. He backed her up until they were falling onto the mattress. Kneeling over her, he pulled her panties down.

She'd been bare beneath him before, but this felt very different. She knew for sure they'd be as close as two people could get. As he looked down at her with desire etched on his face, Tara suspected he wouldn't fight her on it. When he reached for the condoms, she was positive.

He rolled the latex over his erection and glanced at her face. "You know I'm all about the foreplay, but I don't know if I can wait any longer for this."

"I know. I don't want to wait any longer, either."

Relief showed in his expression as he ran his hands up her legs and spread her thighs wider. "I'll make it up to you later."

"I know you will." Her answer sounded breathy in her own ears and her heart pounded.

Even after all they'd done, she was nervous, which was crazy since Jace was more familiar to her than any man had ever been. This one final act that he'd denied her for so long had taken on monumental meaning. Though maybe it *should* seem huge, because it was no small thing. It meant something. With him, it felt as if it meant everything.

Jace slid two fingers inside her. Tara knew what had his eyes growing dark and his mouth opening to draw in a shaky breath—she was already wet and so ready for him she might die if it didn't happen soon.

Braced above her, his eyes never leaving her face, Jace pushed inside, slow and steady. He filled her and she finally felt what she'd imagined so many times. He continued to watch her as he pulled out and slid deeper on the next stroke, ratcheting up the intensity of the moment.

Every stroke of his body into hers had Tara breathing harder and feeling more until she didn't think it could get any better. She squeezed her eyes shut and concentrated on the sensations assaulting her. The tingles spreading through her body. The muscles that clenched inside her. It was all too amazing.

She realized it could get much better as her orgasm built slowly and broke over her. It exploded within her and she came with him inside. Jace plunged deep and stilled above her, groaning as her cries filled the room. She felt him come right after her.

Panting, he braced his arms on either side of her, holding most of his weight off her even though he looked ready to collapse.

Tara wrapped her arms around his back and pulled him down on top of her, happy to be crushed beneath him. "That was worth waiting for. Thank you for making me wait until it was the right time."

His laugh vibrated through her. "You weren't

thanking me all those nights you cussed me out for that very thing. Making you wait."

"Eh, you know me. I like to be contrary."

"You certainly do." Jace pulled out and rolled to one side.

After tossing the condom in the trash, he rolled back to her and draped one arm across her stomach. He propped his head on his hand as he smiled down at her.

Tara took a closer look at his cover-up tattoo. Surprisingly, it was an old-fashioned insignia for the make of his truck. She traced the tip of one finger over the letters and felt how the ink made them feel slightly raised.

"I like the new tat. What made you choose this design?"

"Tyler came up with the idea. My first truck was a Chevy, so old it might have officially been an antique. Every vehicle I've had since has been one too, so it seemed like a good fit. That started me thinking about all the time you and I spent together in my truck." Jace went from peering down at his own chest, to staring into Tara's eyes. "You know, it was while Tyler was driving the truck that it hit me. I was going in the wrong direction. I didn't want to be heading away from you. I wanted to be where you were."

Jace shrugged, acting casual, but there was nothing casual about the emotions swirling through Tara at what he'd said. Since she'd been a child, that was the kind of thing she'd dreamed a man would say to her. She'd always imagined it coming from Logan, but Jace was the one saying the beautiful words.

It was strange and scary and had her insides fluttering as if a thousand butterflies had been set loose.

"So what's next?" Jace asked.

"Well, I was hoping we'd get to do it again before we eat. Or after. Or both." Tara had to joke or she might tear up.

He smiled. "I meant with school. You finished your internship with flying colors, I'm sure. What happens now?"

"I have to go back and finish the fall semester and then I'm done. I get my degree and get a job."

He didn't say anything, but there seemed to be an unspoken question hanging between them—where did this leave the two of them?

Tara continued. "Of course, I'll probably look for work somewhere close to family. You know, maybe around here to be near Tyler and my parents, or in Stillwater to be close to Tuck and Becca . . . and you."

A smile crossed Jace's lips. "Sounds like a very good idea—particularly that last part." He leaned over and took her mouth with a hard kiss that reinforced how much he liked her plan for the future.

Jace Mills—a part of her future and Tara was happy about it. Who'd have guessed it?

Her phone rang. Tara reached for it and read the display. "It's Tyler."

"Give me." Jace held out his hand.

"What are you going to say?"

"I'm going to get us over the next hurdle so I can get back to what we both would rather spend the day doing."

"Okay." Tara handed Jace the phone.

As she watched, he hit the button and pressed the phone to his ear. "Tyler. It's Jace. . . . Yeah, I've got your sister. She's fine. And actually, she and I are dating now—I wanted you to be the first to know. We

haven't told Tuck yet, so keep it under your hat."
Jace listened for a second, then frowned. "What do
you mean, about damn time?"

Tara felt like crawling out of her skin, waiting to
find out what Tyler was saying on the other end of
the line.

Finally, Jace laughed. "All right, man. I'll bring
her home in a bit and you can gloat more then.
See ya."

"What the hell?" Tara huffed out a breath. "What
did he say?"

Jace handed her back the phone. "That it was
about damn time we realized we liked each other,
because he's known for months."

She frowned. "He's crazy."

"Maybe. Maybe not." Jace let out a short laugh.
"Anyway, apparently your parents haven't seen you
yet since you've been home, which you neglected to
tell me when I whisked you away to have sex, thank-
you-very-much. They're asking Tyler where you are."

"Sorry. I wasn't exactly thinking about my parents
at the time."

"No kidding. Me, either. But now, we need to get
back there, I guess."

Tara ran a finger down his chest. "They can wait a
few more minutes."

As she moved her finger lower, Jace followed the
motion with his gaze. "I know I was a little quick on
the trigger just now, but believe me, you keep that
up, we're going to be here for a lot longer than just
a few minutes."

"I certainly hope so. You owe me some foreplay.
Remember?" Tara smiled.

"I remember." Jace's eyes narrowed while he ran

his palm over the bare skin of her stomach. "We're going to get to that date eventually."

"I know."

"And we have to tell Tuck as soon as possible."

"Yup. We will."

"And we do have to get you back to your parents soon."

"Okay." Tara wrapped her hand around his hardened length. "But not right now."

Jace moved over her. "No, not right now."

Read on for a sneak peek at Tyler's story, from the first book in Cat Johnson's new Midnight Cowboy series, *Midnight Ride*, available as a Zebra paperback next May.

There were times when a man should stick around and fight, and there were times when it was wiser to cut and run. It was clear to Tyler this was the latter.

Shoving the woman he'd been kissing just moments before out of the way, he clamped his hat lower on his head, and took off at a sprint as her bruiser of a fiancé followed him.

Cowboy boots weren't meant for running, but Tyler managed it. He sure had incentive. Avoiding being pummeled into the ground by a jealous fiancé served as fine inspiration. He knew the truck was unlocked but he didn't have the keys to start the engine. Colton had those with him inside the bar. He wasn't about to lock himself inside a truck he couldn't flee in, not with an angry lunatic hot on his tail, so he kept running.

The terrain worked in his favor, as did the darkness as Tyler crashed into the woods off the side of the parking lot. Branches whacked into him as he dodged between them. He twisted an ankle when one foot landed on a rock, but he kept going, limping in a half run. A pine bough caught him across the face, blinding him as he squeezed the injured eye tight and the tears began to flow. Still, he forged ahead. His life depended on it.

The woods broke into a clearing and he realized he was behind the lumberyard right off the main road in town.

Tyler slowed to a fast walk when he hit the concrete and glanced around him. He needed to get somewhere safe and tend to his eye, which hurt like hell and was still tearing up. He needed to zip his jeans and refasten the belt buckle the girl had undone, all while she'd kept to herself the one important detail that the fiancé she was mad at was just inside working the door of the bar. He also needed to make sure his cell phone hadn't fallen out of the back pocket of his jeans so he could call Colton to come and rescue him. But before any of that, he had to make sure the man in hot pursuit hadn't followed this far.

A crash in the woods behind him, followed by a loud cuss, told him the lunatic hadn't given up yet. Damn, but this guy was persistent.

Tyler took off running again, though at this point it was more of a fast hobble. He had to hide. A pickup truck parked in the lot in front of him provided his only hope. He should just take the truck and drive away. It wouldn't be stealing. He'd only be borrowing it. He could bring it back as soon as life and limb were no longer in jeopardy, but he didn't know if the owner had left the key inside and he couldn't waste precious seconds checking.

Maybe it was dark enough that if he lay flat and still in the back, he might not be seen. But if the guy looked closely enough and saw him hiding, he'd be a sitting duck. It was a chance he was going to have to take.

Running out of time, he sprinted to the back of the truck, planted both hands on the tailgate and vaulted into the bed. When he landed inside, Tyler knew his luck was holding. There was a big green tarp in the bottom of the truck bed. He flipped it over himself and held his breath, trying to move as little as possible. While he waited to be discovered, or not, he figured praying couldn't hurt. Silently, he vowed if he got out of this night unscathed, he'd never make out with a stranger in a bar again.

As his heart pounded, he heard heavy footsteps in the lot, and then a few more loud cusses and what sounded like a bear—or a really big man—crashing back through the trees. Seconds ticked by in silence, and the crazed fiancé didn't come back to whip the tarp off him and beat him to a pulp.

Against all odds, he might just be safe. Out of the woods, literally. In light of that, Tyler decided to add a small amendment to his deal with God. It would probably be all right to hook up with girls he met in a bar. However, he would be sure to ask them if they had a boyfriend, or any kind of significant other *before* he kissed them and let them unbuckle his pants.

Satisfied that was a promise he could live with, and hopeful that the guy had given up the chase, Tyler was about to take a peek to see if the coast was clear when he heard footsteps heading toward the truck.

It sounded like two people walking. They hadn't come from the direction of the woods, but rather from the building. He was most likely safe from being maimed by his pursuer, but he definitely was not in any position to be socializing with anyone.

His jeans still hung wide open, his eye remained squeezed shut, and he was hiding under a tarp in a stranger's truck bed.

It wasn't as if he could pop up and say *hey*, but he also couldn't stay hidden. If the owner of the truck drove away, who knew where he could end up.

Tyler was weighing his limited options when he heard a female voice say, "Hang on. Let me move this and then you can slide it right inside."

He lay helpless while the tarp was whipped to the side, exposing him to the beam of the parking lot light. At the sight of him, the woman screamed and jumped back.

Truth be told, he nearly screamed too. He scrambled to sit up, before he realized he might not want to be sitting up. He still wasn't positive where the scorned fiancé had gone.

"Hey, Tyler." There was amusement in the male voice that came from his left.

Still partially blinded, Tyler turned his head to the side to see a guy he'd gone to high school with standing next to the truck and grinning as he balanced a fence post on his shoulder.

Hell of a time for a high school reunion. Not having much choice, Tyler tipped his head in greeting. "Hey, Jed."

"You know him?" the woman asked.

"I do." Jed grinned wider. "Don't worry. He's harmless."

She let out a breath and held her hand to her chest. A fall of dark hair brushed her shoulders as her gaze swung from Jed to Tyler. "You scared the hell out of me. What were you doing under there?"

"Um, it's a long story." Sitting up, Tyler glanced at the woods and decided to take his chances with the crazed bouncer rather than look like more of a fool by continuing to lie in this woman's truck bed. He pulled himself upright and then went to work fastening the open fly of his jeans.

"Oh, don't worry, Ty. We have the time to hear your explanation. I'm sure it will be worth it." Jed grinned. He hadn't missed the fact Tyler's pants were hanging open enough to show his underwear.

Neither had the woman. Tyler saw her bite her lip to control a smile as she averted her eyes.

Books by Bestselling Author
Fern Michaels

___The Jury	0-8217-7878-1	$6.99US/$9.99CAN
___Sweet Revenge	0-8217-7879-X	$6.99US/$9.99CAN
___Lethal Justice	0-8217-7880-3	$6.99US/$9.99CAN
___Free Fall	0-8217-7881-1	$6.99US/$9.99CAN
___Fool Me Once	0-8217-8071-9	$7.99US/$10.99CAN
___Vegas Rich	0-8217-8112-X	$7.99US/$10.99CAN
___Hide and Seek	1-4201-0184-6	$6.99US/$9.99CAN
___Hokus Pokus	1-4201-0185-4	$6.99US/$9.99CAN
___Fast Track	1-4201-0186-2	$6.99US/$9.99CAN
___Collateral Damage	1-4201-0187-0	$6.99US/$9.99CAN
___Final Justice	1-4201-0188-9	$6.99US/$9.99CAN
___Up Close and Personal	0-8217-7956-7	$7.99US/$9.99CAN
___Under the Radar	1-4201-0683-X	$6.99US/$9.99CAN
___Razor Sharp	1-4201-0684-8	$7.99US/$10.99CAN
___Yesterday	1-4201-1494-8	$5.99US/$6.99CAN
___Vanishing Act	1-4201-0685-6	$7.99US/$10.99CAN
___Sara's Song	1-4201-1493-X	$5.99US/$6.99CAN
___Deadly Deals	1-4201-0686-4	$7.99US/$10.99CAN
___Game Over	1-4201-0687-2	$7.99US/$10.99CAN
___Sins of Omission	1-4201-1153-1	$7.99US/$10.99CAN
___Sins of the Flesh	1-4201-1154-X	$7.99US/$10.99CAN
___Cross Roads	1-4201-1192-2	$7.99US/$10.99CAN

Available Wherever Books Are Sold!
Check out our website at www.kensingtonbooks.com

Romantic Suspense from
Lisa Jackson

More from Bestselling Author
JANET DAILEY

Calder Storm	0-8217-7543-X	$7.99US/$10.99CAN
Close to You	1-4201-1714-9	$5.99US/$6.99CAN
Crazy in Love	1-4201-0303-2	$4.99US/$5.99CAN
Dance With Me	1-4201-2213-4	$5.99US/$6.99CAN
Everything	1-4201-2214-2	$5.99US/$6.99CAN
Forever	1-4201-2215-0	$5.99US/$6.99CAN
Green Calder Grass	0-8217-7222-8	$7.99US/$10.99CAN
Heiress	1-4201-0002-5	$6.99US/$7.99CAN
Lone Calder Star	0-8217-7542-1	$7.99US/$10.99CAN
Lover Man	1-4201-0666-X	$4.99US/$5.99CAN
Masquerade	1-4201-0005-X	$6.99US/$8.99CAN
Mistletoe and Molly	1-4201-0041-6	$6.99US/$9.99CAN
Rivals	1-4201-0003-3	$6.99US/$7.99CAN
Santa in a Stetson	1-4201-0664-3	$6.99US/$9.99CAN
Santa in Montana	1-4201-1474-3	$7.99US/$9.99CAN
Searching for Santa	1-4201-0306-7	$6.99US/$9.99CAN
Something More	0-8217-7544-8	$7.99US/$9.99CAN
Stealing Kisses	1-4201-0304-0	$4.99US/$5.99CAN
Tangled Vines	1-4201-0004-1	$6.99US/$8.99CAN
Texas Kiss	1-4201-0665-1	$4.99US/$5.99CAN
That Loving Feeling	1-4201-1713-0	$5.99US/$6.99CAN
To Santa With Love	1-4201-2073-5	$6.99US/$7.99CAN
When You Kiss Me	1-4201-0667-8	$4.99US/$5.99CAN
Yes, I Do	1-4201-0305-9	$4.99US/$5.99CAN

Available Wherever Books Are Sold!

Check out our website at www.kensingtonbooks.com.